DARK SEEKER

Taryn Browning

ISBN-10: 1466337524
ISBN-13: 9781466337527

DEDICATION

For my wonderful & supportive husband, two beautiful boys, and amazing family & friends.
Thank you for your ongoing support.
Without you, none of this would be possible.

ACKNOWLEDGMENTS

I am so happy to be able to share this story with you. I hope you enjoy it.

Thank you to my husband, Keith. You are my first editor and biggest supporter. Also, to my two precious boys. Huge thanks to my amazing agent, Christine Witthohn, for getting my stories out and believing in me. I'm so grateful to be part of the Book Cent's family. Thank you Brent Taylor, for making my books sparkle, and the YA blogging community for your reviews. Thanks to my friends and critique partners, Michelle Madow and Angie Baime. This book wouldn't be what it is today without your great critiques. Also, Catherine Van Herrin for your fantastic edits. None of this would be possible without the love and support of my parents, Ken & Sandie

Hackman and Sheryl Morgan. You've always encouraged me to follow my dreams. Huge thanks to my sisters, Lauren and Kim for always cheering me on. There are so many people who have influenced my writing. I am thankful for each and every one of you. And most of all, thanks to you for reading my book.

CHAPTER 1

Lesson three of Seeker Training—always be prepared.

Janie Grey kicked a crushed beer can across the litter-ridden alley. It was unusually quiet in the city; Baltimore normally roared with police sirens, especially this time of night. She perched on the lid of a trash can between two algae-stained brick walls. A liquor store bordered one side, and an abandoned row house was on the other. A graffiti-laden lamp post just outside the alley provided a patch of dim yellow light.

Janie tensed her muscles and willed something to appear in the darkness. Her adrenaline pumped. She needed to kick some ass. With the city's murder rate up, the silence certainly had nothing to do with the lack of undead.

A pulsating vibration quivered deep in her bones, indicating there was *one* nearby. *Finally.* She removed the silver-plated dagger from her boot and slowly crept quietly down the alley.

"Show yourself," Janie commanded.

She sensed at least one, maybe two. She could smell them. The smell of death and decay. She gripped the hilt of her dagger tightly. They were fast. She'd have to be ready. She deftly reached behind her to locate the other blade wedged in the waist of her jeans.

A large mass landed on top of her, knocking her to the ground. A male. She quickly twisted away from him and rolled onto one knee. He crouched in front of her, brandishing his fangs. She could tell by his wild, hungry eyes that he was newly born.

He looked so human, except for his fangs and soulless black eyes. His kind wasn't pale; they kept their human-like complexion. But just like a demon, they embodied an empty shell of what was once a living, breathing human being.

He swaggered forward, and she smiled. *This is exactly what I've been waiting for—a newbie. . .perfect.*

"Hey, girlie, what are you doing with that dagger? You could get yourself killed." He laughed.

She shook her head. "You're just a baby. You have no idea who I am, do you?"

"My first meal." A feral wildness danced through his eyes as he focused on the pulsating vein on the side of her neck.

"You want this?" Janie turned her head to expose her bare flesh—a perfect view of her jugular. She heard a click from behind. She turned, keeping the newbie in her peripheral vision. A silver trash can hit the concrete, spewing its contents across the alley floor. Two more appeared behind it, a blond woman and a large man.

Janie whirled back around. With a skipping side kick, she drove her foot into the newbie's chest, throwing him into the wall. She spun around and landed a punch to the woman's cheek, followed by a jab to her stomach with the other fist, causing the woman to double over and kiss her knees.

The man lunged at her, his large muscles bulging through his wife beater and jeans. He knocked Janie to the ground with his fist. She felt the side of her face. *Jerk, that's gonna leave a mark.*

She shot back to her feet and knocked him backward with the handle of her dagger. The woman lunged at her. Janie used the alley wall as a springboard, flying onto it and running up the brick. She flipped over the woman and plunged the dagger into her skull on the way down. Green blood oozed from the woman's head. Her entire body melted like hot candle wax and seeped into the black asphalt. All traces of her existence disappeared.

The newbie jumped onto Janie's back. She heaved forward, throwing him to the ground. But Mr. Muscles wrapped his arms around her. She wriggled in his hold. His grip was too strong to break. He clamped her arms to her sides so she couldn't use her dagger. The newbie crouched, facing her. He wore a wild stare, like a rabid animal ready to bite.

"Not so tough now, are you?" the newbie spat.

Janie's dark brown eyes narrowed into hateful slits. "I will kill you," she said.

In a flash, his teeth sank into her neck. Muscle man held her firmly as the newbie bit even deeper into her vein. She kicked the newbie, dislodging his fangs and sending him back crashing into the brick wall. They didn't have pure venom. There would be no lasting effects of his bite.

A blurry shadow streaked in front of her. *Crap, another one. And he's fast.* He materialized beside the newbie, taking the form of a golden-blond teenager with white highlights. The newbie scraped his body off the ground and propped himself up by his shoulder against the brick.

The blond, with medium-length wavy hair, stood about the same height as the newbie, but Janie couldn't detect any rancid odor around him, unlike the newbie, who smelled like rotten food mixed with sewer runoff. The blond teenager's eyes shot over to her. They were a deep green, the color of well-watered foliage. A green that could only be found in a rainforest. *I've seen those eyes before.*

He cocked his slender arm. She turned her head to avoid his strike, but his fist moved past her face and knocked Mr. Muscles to the ground, freeing her. Janie swung around and plunged the dagger into Mr. Muscle's head.

The blond drew a long knife from his waist. With its curving silver blade, it resembled a scythe used to cut grass. Janie's eyes widened. When he raised his arm, she noticed three jagged scars running down his forearm. The blade then circled in one rapid motion, beheading the newbie. Janie stepped back, dagger drawn and pointed at the blond.

"Watch where you point that thing. I'm not going to hurt you," he said. After the newbie disappeared into the asphalt, he holstered the scythe in his black leather belt. A hole had started to fray just above the knee in his faded dark jeans. The sleeves of his white tee had been torn off. Green goo was splayed across his chest, like he'd been slimed—demon blood.

"You're one of them," she said.

"And you're perceptive." He took a step closer to her. An aura of arrogance surrounded him. She gripped her blade even tighter.

"Don't come any closer, or I'll kill you."

"What, I don't get a thank-you?" He smiled smugly.

"For what? You're a monster."

"That's not a very nice thing to say to someone who just saved your life." A piece of golden hair fell into his eyes, a strip of white highlighting it. He brushed it back. Under his raised arm, Janie noticed he was slender, but fit.

"You didn't save my life. I was holding my own." *Lesson two, the most important—don't let them see your weaknesses.*

He laughed. "The newbie was about to have you for dinner."

"Think whatever you want. I'm still going to kill you."

"Okay, girlie," he replied, a shred of humor in his voice.

"Why is everyone calling me that tonight?" Janie glared at him.

"You're a girl, and you're young."

"I'm older than I look." She scowled. "Seventeen, as if I care what you think."

"You care." He bit his well-proportioned lip and glanced down at her from his long lashes. Ones boys don't appreciate and girls would die for.

"Am I boring you?" she said. It really bothered her that he didn't smell like the others. She could smell their blood, but he smelled more like lavender and sweat, human sweat. He was cleaner, more put together.

"No." He smirked. "You're actually rather amusing."

"I'm glad I amuse you. Now, can we get this over with? I've got a wrestling match to get to." Janie adjusted her stance. He didn't flinch. She seemed to be an annoying gnat to him. He didn't appear to be the least bit threatened, which infuriated her.

"What makes you think you can kill me tonight? You don't have your car to run me over." He placed his hand on his scythe again. His palm rested on the wooden hilt, but he didn't attempt to remove it from its harness.

She squinted. "That was you?"

Janie thought back to the previous night. After Seeking, she'd driven through the parking lot she frequently used while in that part of the city, preparing to head home for the evening. That's when he came out of nowhere. She tried to take him down with her car, at least until she could get her dagger, but she missed and slammed into a lamp post. By the time she regained her clarity, he'd gotten away. She'd gone over and over their encounter a hundred times since then. He *was* different.

She just didn't get the vibe. Usually she could feel when they were around, like that creepy *something's-not-right* feeling girls typically ignore, multiplied by about a thousand. But this time she got nothing. It was like he wasn't even there, until he was there...and then he was gone. And his eyes were so unusual. Not black, but vibrant green.

"Were you hurt?" he said, pulling her out of her reverie. "When your car struck that pole? Sorry I didn't stick around to find out." His hand left his scythe. He paused, assessing her hate-filled expression. After an awkward moment, he extended his arm. "I'm Kai."

"I'm not shaking your hand." Janie stepped beyond his reach. Something was off. He didn't smell or act like the rest of them, and she couldn't get over those eyes.. She glanced around the empty alley. "Why did you kill them, anyway?"

"They stink. There's enough trash on these streets. I'm just ridding the city of filth."

"And you don't stink?"

"Nope. Just took a shower, in fact." Kai glanced down at his shirt. "It was clean an hour ago, anyway, and I had sleeves."

"What *are* you?"

"You seem to have me figured out. I'm a monster."

"Is that supposed to scare me?" She raised her guard.

His voice softened. He forced the sharpness from his tone. "No, Janie. It's not."

Kai left his place next to the wall and approached her. Janie froze. The smell of lavender strengthened, filling her lungs. "How do you know my name?" she mustered.

"We all know your name."

"So you kill your own kind?" Her heart pounded against her rib cage.

"They are *not* my kind." She heard the disgust in his tone. She'd angered him.

"I know what you are. You're one of them. So, now tell me, how exactly are they *not* your kind?" she pushed, visibly stripping away his cockiness.

The muscles along his jaw line twitched. He glanced off to the side, shifting his stance, seemingly unsure of how to answer. "We're done here," he said.

She blinked and he disappeared in the same blur in which he'd appeared. Janie stood alone, still clutching her dagger. Sweat dripped from her palm. Her fingers ached from gripping the hilt so tightly.

CHAPTER 2

Janie returned home earlier than expected. Her unforeseen run-in with Kai had thrown her for a loop. She stepped into the outdated kitchen that she swore got uglier every day. They hadn't replaced the white cabinets, ivy wallpaper, and dark green countertops left over from the previous owners. Not that it mattered, as they only had one more year in the house—and the cycle would continue.

Janie's mother, Isabelle, stood over the stove making chicken soup. "You're home early."

Janie poked her head in the fridge. "I'm going to the wrestling match with Ava." She felt edgy and wanted to be anywhere out of the city, even if it meant attending a high school sports event. Plus, without her car, she was grateful that Ava, her best friend, offered to give her a ride.

After retrieving a Coke, she turned back around, noticing and half-expecting her mother's disappointed frown. *Here we go.*

"Janie—you have a job to do." She gave Janie a stern, straight-brow look—her way of issuing a gesture of warning before she handed out the punishment, like counting to three.

"I know." Janie frowned. "I Seek *every* night. High school sucks for me—for the second time."

Isabelle's voice softened. The lines across her forehead relaxed. "Janie, I know this is hard for you. Life won't always be this way. I did it, too. You were born a Seeker—try to embrace it."

Janie mouthed her mother's words—*yada yada.*

"And stop mimicking me. I'm serious." Isabelle placed the spoon on the counter and looped a sympathetic arm over Janie's shoulder.

"I know you're serious." *Same speech, different day.*

"I know it's difficult, but you're equipped to handle them. Abram trained you well." Isabelle pushed a strand of loose ponytail behind Janie's ear, her brown eyes sympathetic. "Go enjoy your match." She smiled, examining Janie as if staring at a younger version of herself. They looked strikingly similar with their long, straight black hair and tan, youthful Cherokee skin. Both were muscular, but petite in stature. "You've known your fate since you were a child."

Inwardly, Janie agreed. Growing up, her grandmother would tell her native Cherokee legends before bedtime. Her favorite story was about U`tlûñ'ta, a shape-shifter who could transfigure into anything she desired. She was said to be a "bloodthirsty" killer. The creature, which in true form resembled an old lady with tough, wrinkled, leather-like skin, used her long bony finger to stab people and take their livers. *Nothing like scaring the hell out of a six-year-old right before bed. It makes for great nightmares. Thanks, Gran.*

"How do you plan on getting to the match?" Isabelle said.

"Ava." Janie removed a piece of gum from her mother's purse. "When did Sal say my car would be fixed?"

"In a few days. Be safe tonight—and remember, you're special, and with your gifts come obligations." The stern look returned.

"You mean like the obligation of losing Dad?" Janie immediately regretted her words. Her father's death had been a closed subject for fifteen years. The crippling event had left her mother lifeless and empty for most of Janie's childhood. Under no circumstances was Connor Grey's name ever to be spoken, and her mother's flinch confirmed that.

"Sorry, Mom. I'm just tired. I'll see you tomorrow." Janie headed outside to wait for Ava.

Janie and Ava entered the humid gym. The room was filled with the smell of sweat. Ava sported a bright-white smile, hurrying across the wooden court with her auburn curls bouncing on her shoulders. As a pair, Janie and Ava straddled opposite sides of the spectrum. Ava favored vibrant corals and yellows, while Janie preferred muted blacks and grays. Janie wore a fitted black long-sleeve tee, a gray hoodie, jeans and her favorite black boots.

The wrestlers warmed up. Some jogged around a large, navy blue mat, and others rolled around on their heads, stretching their necks. Under their running pants, Janie noticed they wore their tight singlets, or whatever they were called. They resembled one-piece bodysuits with tight biker-short bottoms. She chuckled, glad most of them were still wearing their running pants. Singlets certainly didn't leave much to the imagination.

As they passed a group of cheerleaders bunched along the bottom bleacher, one sprang into a jump. She landed on her perfectly balanced feet and flitted back over to the group to chat with her leader, Molly Hall.

"Oh look, it's Ava, part of Janie's wannabe Goth nerd herd," Molly said. She looked them up and down, flipping her blond ponytail to the side of her heart-shaped face. The strap of her uniform arched around her thin, pale neck. Janie glanced at her black tee and dark, worn-in jeans. *Ah, simplicity makes life so much easier.*

Ava lowered her head and focused on the gym floor. Four years of Molly Hall, and Ava still couldn't look her in the eye.

"Give it a rest, Molly," Janie said, taking in the clique of on-looking cheerleaders.

Molly's flawless, rhinoplasty-perfect nose crinkled. "What's it to you, loser? You shouldn't even be here. You don't belong." Her lips curved into a half-smile. She turned to her entourage and started to laugh.

Janie took Ava's hand and led her up the bleachers. She could kick Molly's ass into next week, but she'd sworn to use her gifts for good. Sometimes it sucked having lessons. But the lessons kept her grounded. At times, they were all she had for guidance and structure. In a way, she guessed, it made her a better Seeker.

They chose a seat near the top of the bleachers. "Molly's so hateful. I wish I could stand up to her," Ava said, sporting a frustrated frown.

Janie waved her hand dismissively. "Don't worry about her. I've seen her kind so many times. She only picks on us because she needs to feel like she's important. Without her Junior Prom Queen status, she has nothing. Trust me. She's not worth it."

Ava drew a deep breath. "You're right." She smiled. "Anyway, this is exciting." Her positive energy must have been infectious. The smell of sweat and testosterone wasn't as nauseating to Janie now. And the guys didn't look *that* bad in their singlets. Not that she was interested.

In the first match, a Raider pinned his opponent in twenty seconds. The stands erupted in wild celebration. Two more Loch Raven Raiders wrestled opponents and won by considerable points. Janie joined in the school spirit, screaming, clapping and leaping out of her seat with the rest of the fans. Suddenly, she doubled over and started to wheeze.

"Are you okay, J?" Ava helped steady Janie.

"I'm fine. I just need my inhaler. I left it in your car." Janie drew a shaky breath. She held out her hand for the keys. "Watch the match. I'll be right back."

Janie couldn't believe she'd forgotten her inhaler. She wondered why the Apotheosis, a group of ancient Seekers who organized and ran the Seeker organization and set up chapters in each city to oversee problems, created a Seeker with asthma. It kind of sucked when she had to take a break from fighting evil to use her inhaler. Usually, if she used it before Seeking, she was okay. Tonight, obviously, that was not the case. *I knew I shouldn't have attended the wrestling match. It's apparently bad for my health. Lesson learned.*

Janie crossed the parking lot, found Ava's car, opened the passenger door, and reached into the console to retrieve her inhaler. The pleasant relief filtered into her lungs. She exhaled into the crisp autumn air, her warm breath expelling from her lips like a puff of smoke. The wind nipped through her dark gray hoodie, sending her into a whole-body shiver.

Stars sparkled in the cloudless night sky. Each star seemed spaced perfectly to create a twinkling picture in the sky. It reminded her of her old Lite-Brite, a toy with multicolored lights that her mother had passed down to her from her childhood. Janie lost herself in the shimmery scene, forgetting about the chilly fall air and her bizarre encounter with Kai. After a few more moments of star-gazing, she decided to head back to the sweaty gym, a sharp contrast to the dry air she currently breathed.

As she cut through the rows of cars, her skin started to crawl and a deep gnawing sensation grew in her stomach. Janie slowed her pace, striding cautiously down the line of cars. As she stalked forward, her body pulsated and her heart rate quickened. He was close, very close. She knew it without a doubt—it was a Daychild.

One advantage Seekers had over their prey was their ability to eliminate the element of surprise. It was impossible for a vampire or a Daychild to sneak up on a Seeker, or even stay off a Seeker's radar. All Seekers could feel the undead's proximity through waves of tell-tale goose bumps. Janie referred to it as her sixth sense, or Seeker sense—where her hair stands up on her arms and the back of her neck. How to detect the presence of vampires or Daychildren was one of the first skills she learned during training. Honing in on the ingrained feeling to hunt and survive served as an imperative strategy for saving lives, including hers.

She heard a shout—a deep voice—followed by a loud crunch of metal. Janie ran in the direction of the commotion, about one row from where she stood. Overhead lights illuminated part of the parking lot. Other areas were only lit by the stars and a crescent white moon. Still focusing on the struggle, she retrieved her silver dagger from her boot.

A passage from her mentor's teachings cycled through her head. *"Things are much different now. A demon is a human who has been taken over by a fallen angel. One night the vampire king drained the blood of a demon, creating a hybrid vampire. Daychildren—vampires that can walk in the sunlight and possess demonic abilities."*

Janie spotted the Daychild and his victim. She agreed with Abram. Things were much different than they used to be.

The Daychild had a student pinned to the hood of a red Ford pickup. The guy squirmed, doing his best to fend the monster off with his muscular arms, but his attacker had the upper hand. The Daychild forced his head down to the guy's neck. *Lesson four—save innocents, but minimize exposure.* She didn't see how this was possible, but despite herself, she heard herself speak up.

"Hey! If you want to mess with someone, mess with me." She planted her boots firmly on the ground and gripped her dagger. She never had to kill one of them on school grounds before. They usually stayed in the Baltimore city limits, where they could blend into society. With Baltimore's murder rate continuously on the rise, many of the deaths weren't fully investigated, and were considered gang activity. This Daychild was brave, coming all the way out to the suburbs—*her* turf.

The Daychild raised his head from his victim and cocked it, appraising Janie. He was in his thirties, unattractively balding, chunky and short. Releasing the boy from his grasp, Pudgy jumped off the hood of the car and strode over to Janie. His deep black holes studied her. He licked his lips and balled his hands into fists.

"Hey, pretty girl. How would you like some of this?" He laughed, and the rolls of his stomach jiggled, giving the phrase 'bowl full of Jell-O' new meaning. Janie swallowed the bile rising in her throat and pressed forward.

"I'd love some," she taunted. She rotated to the side, taking a fighting stance with her fists covering her face for protection.

He leapt forward. She spun into roundhouse kick to the gut, forcing him backward into the pickup's fender. He stumbled awkwardly onto his feet, his cocky smile replaced with a hateful scowl. "You'll pay for that," he hissed.

"Let me have it," she said teasingly. With her free hand, she made a come-to-me gesture.

He lunged at her, fast and clumsy. She lifted her leg into an outside-inside kick and caught the side of his head with the insole of her boot, knocking him to the ground. He caught his fall with his hands and looked up, glaring at her with his hateful black eyes.

It was time. She plunged her silver dagger through his skull. He let out a horrifying growl. His body shook, and green blood oozed from his head. His fleshy mass disappeared, sucked into the earth—or, for him, Hell.

Janie scooped her dagger off the ground and still fueled with adrenaline, marched over to the curb. She drew the blade across the cold, stiff grass to remove any traces of blood and shoved her favorite Cherokee dagger back into her boot.

Remembering the guy on the pickup, she flicked her eyes over to the hood. The guy sat, legs tucked into his chest, with his arms wrapped around his knees.

Janie assessed the situation; it wasn't good. She'd definitely failed lesson four—*minimize exposure*. The guy had seen her kill the Daychild, and even worse, she suddenly recognized him—the Junior Prom King.

Matt Baker jumped off the hood of the pickup, staring at her wide-eyed. Tall and strong, with eyes the color of autumn leaves turning from sage to chestnut, the girls flipped out over his dark brown, tousled thirty-second hairdo and killer dimples. "W—What w—was that?"

"You tell me. He was attacking you," Janie said.

"But—you killed him." Matt blinked hard.

"Don't worry, he wasn't human, and if it wasn't for me you'd be a corpse without blood." She bent over and pushed her dagger deeper into her boot. If she were caught with a weapon on school property, she'd be expelled.

"The d—dude tried to b-b-bite my neck." He clutched his throat.

"He's part vamp, they do that. Are you okay?"

He moved his hands up and down his body. "Yeah, um, I'm cool, thanks."

Janie felt uncomfortable. He hadn't taken his eyes off her since she had saved him from a very painful death. "What are you doing out here anyway? Aren't you supposed to be wrestling?"

"I left my headgear in Pete's truck." He rubbed his forehead.

She nodded. "Look—you're fine, so let's just forget this happened and all is good." Janie knew she'd be ridiculed at school tomorrow. As soon as he told Molly about what happened, she would make sure Janie was ostracized even more than usual. She'd have to leave high school early for the first time, not that it sounded like a bad idea. She just didn't know how the Apotheosis would handle her exposure.

"You saved my life," he said.

Janie broke his unflinching gaze. "You'd better get back in there before you miss your match. I'd hate for you to mess up your perfect 'pin-everyone-in-ten-seconds' record."

"You know about my record?" he said, grinning at last.

"It was just a guess." She turned in the direction of school. "I've got to go. Be careful."

"Wait!" He jogged up beside her and kept pace.

"There's nothing left to talk about." She pressed on, hoping he would take the hint and go away. He didn't.

"I'm not gonna say anything. Anyway, everyone will think I've lost it." He half-laughed.

"Uh-huh." She tried to limit their communication as much as she could, but he wasn't having it.

"It was really cool what you did. How did you learn all those moves?" His confused stuttering had turned into excited curiosity. "You were like a tiny Bruce Lee." Out of her peripheral vision, he made a karate-chop gesture.

Her straight lips parted into an unintentional smirk, and she let out a quick chuckle at his lame imitation. *Five minutes ago, this guy was practically in a fetal position, and now he's making jokes.*

"Are you laughing?"

"No, I think you're ridiculous," she said, still stifling a smile.

"Janie Grey, you think I'm funny."

"I don't think you're funny."

"So tell me, really—how did you learn to take down dudes?" His karate chop hand gestures returned.

Now only feet from the door, she wanted to run to the entrance. She felt uncomfortable and completely enraged by her abnormal, jittery "boy feelings." She stopped mid-step and turned to face him. "Look, I don't want to talk about it. You're fine. Please go away and forget this ever happened."

"Why are you so mad at me?" His once-prominent dimples disappeared.

"I'm sure you're an okay guy and all, but I really can't discuss this with you." She dipped her head and returned his gaze. "There's nothing left to say."

His hazel eyes bore into her. "Yeah. I have a match to win." He pushed his shoulders back, re-aligning his spine, and strode into school.

Good. That's where you belong—in school, with the rest of them, not with me.

The next morning, Janie walked into first period, fidgeting with the string edging of her gray scarf. She knew it; she was going to be exiled to Siberia. People were going to look at her, and people never looked at her.

A thin girl with frizzy hair peered up from her backpack as she loaded her locker with books. The girl quickly broke her stare and placed a textbook on the shelf. Janie recognized her from English class. An Asian couple holding hands passed by, but unlike the girl, they ignored her. *Maybe Matt didn't say anything.*

To Jane's relief, it was turning out to be an uneventful day, but she hadn't had History with the cheerleaders yet.

She noticed Molly standing outside the classroom in her uniform. Her loyal posse swarmed around her like bees to a hive. Janie slid by undetected. Molly didn't even glance in her direction. *She doesn't know.*

After class, she met Ava and her only other friend, Luke, by her locker. Luke rewrapped his stylish scarf around his thin neck over a fitted cream sweater, tapered dress pants and tan loafers. Luke Turner was a good-looking kid in a dorky, boyish kind of way. He was of average height, somewhat nerdy, but always fashion-conscious. He wore thinly rimmed glasses after getting an eye infection from wearing contact lenses. He had assured Ava and Janie that he would switch back to blue contacts within the month; brown eyes were evidently not "posh." Plus, blue apparently proved a good contrast to his dark brown hair. He followed the latest fashion trends, even if they only belonged on a runway. His tight, tapered jeans looked great on the members of Fall Out Boy, but on Luke, they made his legs appear even more pencil-thin.

"What's for lunch?" he said. "No fast food. I'm watching my figure."

"Are we going off campus?" Ava asked Luke, but his eyes were locked on something else.

Janie followed Luke's stare, then wished for a large rock to materialize and block her from *his* view.

"Hi, Janie," Matt said.

Janie lined up Ava's textbooks along her shelf, ignoring Matt and still waiting for the large rock to appear.

"Janie, Matt's talking to you. Aren't you going to answer?" Luke's voice fluttered like he had a butterfly lodged in his throat.

Janie turned to face Matt. "Hi."

"You look good, considering—" Matt made a see-saw motion with his eyes.

"I already know," Ava said.

"Know what?" Luke eyed them.

"Nothing," Janie and Ava said.

"Why do I feel like I'm missing something?" Luke cocked his head, giving Matt the once-over. "And why are you here?" He cleared his throat. "Sorry to be rude, what I meant to say was—"

"Why are you here?" Janie finished.

"Janie, can I talk with you?" Matt said. "Alone?"

She rolled her eyes. "Whatever will get you to go away faster."

"We'll meet you outside at the car," Ava said, shutting her locker and starting for the door. Luke didn't budge. "Luke, now." Ava snapped her fingers.

"Okay, fine, harsh much," Luke said. Ava dragged him down the hallway by his scarf. Janie spotted them arguing in the distance. One of Luke's hands rested on his hip while the other made figure-eights in the air.

"So, you're going off campus for lunch?" Matt said.

"You're asking me about lunch?" Janie noticed Molly glaring at her from across the hall.

"I guess that's pretty lame." He followed her gaze. "Forget about Molly."

"Easy for you to say." She left Molly's I'd-like-to-kill-you expression and focused back on Matt's gorgeous hazel stare.

"Are you okay?" He brushed his fingers along the side of her eye. "Did that happen last night?"

Janie touched her eye. She'd tried to cover the mark with her dark eye shadow and heavy studio foundation. She found it covered the lingering bruises better than regular cover-up. Fortunately, Seekers healed faster than the average human.

"Yes, but not with you—" Janie caught herself. "I mean, I'm fine. Is there something you need, or can we end this conversation?"

He fidgeted with something in his jacket pocket and focused on the floor, surprising even himself. He was usually so confident when it came to girls. "Uh—I just wanted to thank you again for last night."

Her voice softened. "No problem. I guess I should thank you for not saying anything."

His eyes returned to hers. He paused, looking for the right words. "You're different, you know, than other girls."

"Wow—thanks for pointing out the obvious."

He stepped closer, moving into her personal space. "No, I don't mean that in a bad way." His smile was comforting. A feeling she didn't feel "comfortable" having.

"Look, I've got to meet my friends. Don't sweat last night. It's over. You can go back to doing whatever wrestlers do." She bit her tongue. She sounded like an idiot.

"I'll see you around, Janie." He touched her arm.

"Sure." She squirmed out of his reach. "See ya."

Janie sat on the cold sidewalk staring at the large neon "Power Plant Live!" sign. It towered over a semi-circle of linked buildings, housing bars and restaurants, and lined an expansive courtyard. During the summer, the courtyard was a popular venue for concerts, but too cold for outdoor concerts in November. Janie checked her cell—college night in downtown Baltimore. Drunken students would spill out of the bars after last call, perfect prey for the undead.

There had been a rash of unexplained deaths in the area. Janie figured the murders had to do with the growing population of Daychildren. Ever since she reached the age to Seek, more and more had been born. True vamps were usually not a problem anymore. They seemed to be evolving, wanting to live among the human world without issue. They looked down upon demons. Most vampires had no interest in drinking a demon's filthy blood, let alone changing a demon into a vampire, creating the vampire/demon half-breed known as Daychildren.

"Find any?" Kai said. Janie jumped off the curb, tripping on a crack in the asphalt. She righted herself. He started to laugh. "It just kills you that you can't feel me coming."

"What do you want?" Letting her heart return to its proper place outside of her throat, Janie reached for her dagger.

"Whoa, you don't need that. I'm not going to hurt you. I could've already killed you." Kai put his hands out. "You're still alive, aren't you?"

"Is this fun for you? Some kind of game?" Janie retrieved the blade from her boot. She didn't trust him.

"Your eye looks awful." He pointed to her bruised face.

Janie stared at the three jagged scars lining his forearm. White lines appeared where new tissue had formed. Judging by their location, they appeared to be defensive wounds, as if he were protecting his face from something or someone. She thought it odd. Vampires, or Daychildren, in Kai's case, didn't scar. Their bodies healed quickly without leaving a mark. She guessed the scars had formed during his human days.

She ignored his comment about her eye. "You know I have to kill you. It's my job." Her eyes flicked to his waist. His scythe glistened under the light of an overhead lamp post. Thirty degrees outside, and he wore a T-shirt. Lucky for him, Daychildren didn't feel temperature. Janie, on the other hand, could feel every bit of the biting cold, and she shivered.

Kai nodded, ignoring her. He looked in the direction of the parking garage. "Did you hear that?"

"What?" Janie clenched her jaw. He distracted her. She couldn't do her job with him around. "If you'd stop talking to me, I could listen." She held her breath and focused into the distance. A girl screamed.

"The parking garage." Kai jumped off the curb and took off in a blur.

"Uh—he's too fast." Janie shoved her dagger back into her boot and raced into a full sprint toward the garage. She ducked under the arm gate and curved up the ramp. She arrived at the first floor and stood in between the rows of cars, listening for any sound. The screaming had stopped, but Janie's skin still crawled.

She swerved around the maze of cars, scanning the garage. The door to the staircase slammed shut. She ran down the middle row and jumped up onto the walkway. She flung the metal door open. The metal slammed against the concrete wall, creating a shower of rusty paint around her. The top of the door fell off its hinge, causing the metal door to crash to the ground.

She retrieved her dagger from her boot and started up the empty stairwell, skipping steps in her ascent. She reached the second floor and opened the door to the garage level, her dagger ready to strike. She smelled decay and maggots.

Out of the corner of her eye, she caught a flicker of something large. She flung her dagger in the direction of the movement. The blade sliced through flesh and bone. The Daychild slumped over and landed on his knees, clutching the dagger between his hands. The potbelly with a mullet staggered back to his feet. His hollow black eyes focused on Janie. With one forceful tug, he dislodged the dagger from his chest.

"Where's the girl?" Janie said, breathing heavily after hurtling the staircase.

"Around," the man said. "You forgot to shut the door."

I closed it. Crap! The door swung open and a rush of stale city air blew by her. Janie sprang onto the hood of a car; the heavy metal door came only inches from striking her. The Daychild had an ability—telekinesis.

He released the sticky green-encrusted dagger. Instead of clanging to the ground, it floated in mid-air, slowly rotating until the tip of the blade faced Janie. "You're a fast little Seeker. Do you think you're fast enough to move before I drive this dagger through your head?"

"Are you fast enough?"

"For what?" He laughed.

Janie reached behind her and removed the second dagger from her waistband. She flicked her wrist and wound the dagger into the air as if it were a football spiraling toward a receiver. The blade punctured his temple, knocking him down to all fours. His fleshy mass dissolved and both daggers clattered to the concrete floor.

Someone clapped. "Nice."

"You're back, great." She retrieved her daggers from the ground, both covered in green goo.

Kai peeled what was left of his T-shirt over his head and threw it at her. She caught it with one hand. "Wipe them off. I'd hate to see you ruin those boots with demon blood," he said.

She wiped both daggers, careful not to touch the demon blood; it burned human flesh like acid.

"Do you want your shirt back?" She held out the wad of shredded cotton. "How did it get so ripped up?"

"There was a group of them on the sixth floor. You must have found the one that got away, Mr. Telekinesis with a kick-ass mullet," he said.

"And the girl?" Janie placed one dagger in her waistband and the other in her boot.

"She's fine, back with her drunk friends. Other than a killer hangover, she shouldn't remember anything tomorrow."

"Thanks," Janie said. She looked down at the tattered charcoal-colored T-shirt in her hand. A clean lavender smell mixed with rotten vegetation filled her nose. "I'll find a dumpster to throw it in. Once the blood dries, it won't harm anyone."

They coiled the ramp to the garage exit. Under the garage lights, Janie noticed two five-inch scars formed an X over his left pectoral muscle, where his heart used to beat, before he became a member of the undead. He wasn't tan or porcelain white; there was a slight beige tint to his skin. Hers was darker. She tanned well in the summer, and kept a summer hue for most of the winter. Another perk of having a Native American heritage.

She eyed his naked chest. He wasn't a large guy, but fit with sculpted, lean muscles and chiseled abs. She figured the fighting kept him in good shape. She still wondered why he killed his own kind, and why he'd just rescued a human. Her biggest question, though, was why he hadn't attempted to fight her, let alone kill her. *He can't be trusted*, she reminded herself.

He caught her staring. "Is something wrong?" They cornered the exit wall and headed down the sidewalk in the direction of the Orioles Stadium.

She looked away. "No, I just noticed your scar."

Kai turned, making the scar less visible. "It's nothing." His words were sharp.

"You asked."

"Forget I asked." He pointed. "There's a dumpster. Throw my shirt in there."

Janie forced the heavy metal lid open and tossed the shirt into the rancid-smelling container.

They passed a homeless man who had found a place to sleep next to the heat of an old stone building. Everything he owned fit into an army-green canvas bag.

"I've got to catch the bus. You don't have to walk with me. I can take care of myself." He was too close for her comfort, and she widened her strides away from him

"Your car is still in the shop?" He pulled a strange metal disk from his waistline and spit on the glossy material, shining it with his fingers.

"Yup, thanks to you."

"I didn't tell you to try to run me over with your car. You've had enough training to know you can't kill me with a Honda Civic. Anyway, I'm too fast."

Janie drew in an annoyed breath and spun around to confront him. "Speaking of training, lesson one of Seeker Training—never trust the undead."

Kai laughed. "Interesting."

She bit her tongue, upset she'd shared Seeker information with one of *them*. She couldn't get too comfortable with him. "Look, if I'm not going to kill you, can you at least leave me alone?"

"I could drive you home," he said.

"Even if I considered it, and I'm not considering it, do you even drive? What are you, like sixteen?"

"Eighteen, and I do drive." He flipped the metal disk between two fingers. "Like any of that matters. I don't follow human law anymore."

"What is that?" She pointed to the disk.

"Something a friend gave me."

Janie waited for him to elaborate, but he just flipped the disk in the air like a coin. She stifled the urge to yell *tails*. "Then where's your car?"

The disk shot upward, past the tip of a Mini Mart sign, to the crest of a three-story row home. On its slow decent, the metal disk spun, growing larger and larger. Janie squinted. She swore she saw two tires form, and handlebars, then a tailpipe and a long seat. Her eyes widened. The vehicle levitated for a moment, and the Harley Davidson bounced to the ground.

"Are you just going to stand there? Get on." Kai threw her a helmet.

She laughed, noticing the strip of flames across the side of the helmet. "Flames?"

"It's fire, fire's cool. Put it on." He threw his leg over the seat and gripped the handlebars.

Janie clutched the helmet, hesitant. Was she really going to get on his motorcycle? She glanced down at the hilt peeking out of the top of her boot. *I should be driving my blade into his skull. Why haven't I killed him yet?*

Kai revved the engine. “Hello, earth to Janie. Let’s go. I don’t have all night.”

“Do you have somewhere you’ve got to be?” She glared at him.

He smirked. “Unless you want to confront the gang of Daychildren who are seconds from opening that door and sucking you into their lair, I’d get on.”

CHAPTER 3

The old stone building, with its rounded façade and barred first floor windows, appeared desolate. A row home turned office building, closed for the evening with a brass plate fastened to the gray stone that read *Bower, Reed & Associates.*

Then the wooden door creaked open, releasing the sound of hissing demons. An arm reached through a crack in the door. Janie knocked the arm away, but another took its place. The hand grasped the front of her hoodie and banged her head roughly into the wooden door. The arm retracted again, smacking the side of her head into the unforgiving wooden frame. Janie stumbled to find her feet, but everything spun into blurred, dark shapes, and all she could taste was metal. She spit out blood, her tongue following the grove of her split top lip.

She collapsed. A strong arm wrapped around her waist and hoisted her onto a moving vehicle. Wind whisked through her hair. Her ponytail whipped around behind her head as the cold air froze her face. They moved at a brisk pace, snaking in and out, as if winding through an obstacle course. They lurched to one side and back in hard, jerky movements. She kept her eyes closed, too disoriented to open them. She was faintly aware of a pair of legs, and the scent of clean lavender and denim invaded her nose—*Kai.*

Slowly, she realized he had removed her from the Daychild's lair. She hadn't come prepared to take on an army of them. She realized that this time, Kai may have really saved her life. This didn't change how she felt about him. He was one of them. He couldn't be trusted.

The bike skidded to a stop. Janie opened her eyes, staring down at the asphalt and a black Sketcher. "You wear Sketchers?" she asked, still feeling a bit lightheaded. Kai lifted her upright so she straddled his lap.

"You're asking me about my shoes?" He shook his head. "You've got serious issues. You almost got yourself killed, and you want to know what kind of shoes I wear." He flipped her off him.

Janie stumbled to her feet, attempting to assess her surroundings. "I mean, thanks for getting me out of there. I didn't realize—" *Aww,* her head hurt. She reached up to touch the searing pain. Her hair was wet, sticky and matted to her head. It felt as if there were an open gap in her head and her brains were sliding out. "Ouch."

"You hit your head pretty hard. I'd watch those wooden door frames next time."

It was too difficult to speak through the pain. “Where are we? Can you just take me home? I’ve had enough of you for one evening,” she managed to say.

“We’re at my place. I want to check out your head.” He booted the kick stand and dismounted from his bike. They stood in front of a red brick row home—concrete steps led to a house-length porch with green carpet resembling Astroturf. In front, the address was displayed in a multicolored stained glass window hanging directly above an oak front door. A three-window bay jutted out on the second level.

“I’m not going in there.” Janie crossed her arms stubbornly.

“Are you prejudiced?”

“Look, I don’t want to enter the home of a Daychild. One I should have killed days ago.” Janie turned her back to him, staring at a row of similar homes across the street. There were only slight differences. Some homes were missing the bay window and others were surrounded with chain-link fences. She winced, clenching her teeth too tightly; her head really hurt.

“Suit yourself. The bus stop’s down the block.” Kai started up the walk to his porch.

She spun back around. “You’re just going to leave me here, bleeding?”

“I told you to come in. What else do you want me to do? I don’t have to beg to get a girl.” He glanced down at his bare chest and smirked. “They come willingly.”

She ignored him. “Tell me one thing.”

“Go ahead.” He removed a key from his pocket and slid it into the deadbolt.

"How did you get that scar across you chest?"

Janie rested on one of two black leather couches. She scanned the stark white wall next to her for a mark or a ding, anything to indicate the house was inhabited. Not even one picture hung on the walls of the very simple room.

"You promised you'd tell me about your scar if I came in," she said.

"I lied." He disappeared up the steps and returned minutes later wearing a clean navy blue T-shirt.

"You can't lie. It's not right."

"I'm undead, what do I care what's right?" He sat down across from her on a dark rectangular coffee table. One lonely coaster sat upon it. *I guess he doesn't have many guests. Shocking!*

Janie remembered the disk he had retrieved from his belt. Her eyes shot to his waistline. "Well, then, at least tell me how a small metal disk turned into a motorcycle."

"I told you. I got it from a friend."

"What kind of friend?" She leaned forward, somewhat interested.

"A witch," he dismissed. Kai grasped her hand and guided her to the edge of the cushion. "Now, no more questions. Let me see your head." He twisted her head to examine the injured area. He fumbled through her hair, tugging at her sore scalp.

"What do you mean no more questions—and, *ouch*—that hurt." She drew back from him. "Can't you be gentle?"

"You need stitches." He reached for her head again.

She swatted him away. "If I didn't before, I certainly do now."

"Then have someone else look at it," he said.

"I'm not going to the hospital, if that's what you're suggesting."

Kai stood and walked toward what appeared to be the hallway entrance to the kitchen.

"Where are you going?" she said.

"To get a needle and thread."

"You *are* not." She shot to her feet and followed him down the hallway.

"Chill out. I'm just kidding. I'm calling my friend."

"The witch," she said.

He stopped and pivoted to face her. She ran right into his chest.

"I do have more than one friend, you know." He reached around her and grabbed his cell off the circular kitchen table. The metal table only provided seating for two. Not that Janie knew anyone who would want to keep him company there.

"Then who are you calling?" she said.

"The witch."

"I thought you said you have more than one friend."

"I do."

Janie shook her head. "Never mind. You're so frustrating."

"Right back at you. Why do you look so nervous? You're supposed to be tough; thicken up." He pinched her arm.

She stepped back. Her back hit the wall. "I've never met a witch. Is she green with a pointed hat and—"

"...a broomstick?" he mocked and flashed an arrogant grin.

"Don't make fun of me." She put her hands on her hips. She wanted to pull out her dagger and end her misery. This was why she had only two friends. She didn't get along with people, and she definitely did *not* get along with the undead.

Seconds later, Kai ended the phone call. "She's on her way. Why don't you go make yourself comfortable...if that's possible?" He reached into a small stainless-steel mini-fridge. It rested on his black, polished-stone countertop. Like the rest of the first floor, the walls were hospital white, but everything else—the furniture, drapes and cabinets—were either metallic or dark and solid. She examined the hardwood floor, the mahogany-stained flooring so dark it blended with her black boots.

"Do you want some water?" He offered her a bottle of water from the fridge.

"No. I mean, yes." She snatched it from his hand. In the open fridge, he had leftovers wrapped in foil. A clear bowl of washed red grapes sat in a pool of water on the top shelf. "So you don't live off of human blood."

"I kept my old demon diet of eating anything I want, which includes blood, if I choose." He popped a grape in his mouth. She tried to picture demons eating grapes. *Not likely.*

"So you don't want me?"

Kai's face paled, like someone had punched him in the stomach. For the first time, he looked uncomfortable. She thought he might choke on his grape. This humored her.

"Hmmm, a Seeker's blood is tempting," he mused, becoming sardonic again.

"So why don't you," she hesitated, "try?" She brushed her hand over the dagger in her waistband.

"You really do want to kill me. You're a persistent little thing." He smiled.

"I don't understand you. I've been killing your kind for over seven years, and I've never met one like you." She stared into his green eyes. Daychildren had soulless, hollow eyes—not green and full of life. "How long have you been a Daychild?" she said.

He eyed her waist. "I'll answer you when you take your hand off your blade."

Janie removed her hand from the hilt and placed it by her side. Feeling nauseous again from her head wound, she supported her weight against the bare kitchen wall.

"It's been at least eighteen years. I was one of the first demons to be 'Turned.'" He removed another grape from the bowl and threw it in the air, catching it in his mouth.

"But you killed humans. You still may, for all I know." She wanted to reach for her dagger again. Her Seeker instinct screamed to take him out. She needed to look past his beautiful exterior at the monster inside. She'd learned how to see through a vampire's glamour. She just wondered why it was so hard for her to do the same with him.

"Think what you want," he dismissed. His features hardened, leaving him once again cold and unreadable.

A knock at the door broke their conversation. Instinctively, Janie tried to spread her feet apart in a protective stance, but she couldn't find her equilibrium. She swayed back into the wall.

"It must be Albania." Kai slung Janie's arm over his shoulder and slid her across the floor. "I'll help you to the couch."

"Is that what you're doing?" she said. "It feels more like you're dragging me."

They reached the sofa. Janie unhitched her arm from his broad shoulders. "I can do it, thanks." She shook herself free of him. "You'll probably just drop me anyway."

"It's your call." He let her go. She collapsed on the leather cushion.

Albania stepped into the house, lighting up the entrance. Bright red, green, blue and yellow jewels sparkled from her ears and neck. They trickled down to her wrists and snaked around her ankles and toes. Her fire-red hair spiraled clear down her back. She was dressed in a knee-length body-conforming black dress. It dipped in the front, exposing her cleavage.

Janie checked out her own chest, covered by her T-shirt and zippered hoodie. Not that there was much to look at anyway.

Albania placed a kiss on Kai's cheek. He held her hand gently, as if not to break her. A quiet intimacy lingered between them. They regarded each other in a different manner than Kai regarded her—not abrasive, direct and clumsy, but kind. Janie wondered if Kai and Albania were a couple.

"You must be Janie?" Albania left Kai's gaze and extended her long thin arm. Gold bracelets jangled around her wrist. "Please don't stand. You're injured. I will come to you." Her light green eyes smiled.

"You're so young and pretty." Janie sucked in a breath, realizing the words had left her mouth involuntarily.

"She was expecting green skin, warts and a pointed hat—" Kai broke off with a laugh.

"You forgot the broom," Janie jeered. She looked past Kai, too irritated to meet his sarcastic expression.

"She's feisty. I like her," Albania said. "And my broom's outside. How else would I have gotten here?"

Janie laughed, not sure if Albania was joking. Vampires and Daychildren, she could do. Witches were a whole new territory.

"Now let me see your head." Albania skirted the table and gently placed herself next to Janie on the couch. She smelled of citrus, as if she'd just rolled around in a barrel of oranges. "This might hurt a bit."

Albania gently separated the hair along her scalp. Janie winced.

"Sorry, dear," Albania said.

"What do you think?" Kai peered over Albania.

"I can get that out," Albania assured him.

Janie moved from Albania's grasp and glared at Kai. "Get what out? I thought you said I needed stitches."

"You will, as soon as she gets the demon splint out of your skull," he said.

"The what?" Janie's eyes rolled into the back of her head. She imagined a stake sticking out of her skull. *I surely would feel that.* "I have wood sticking out of my head?" she said, on the cusp of passing out.

"It's worse than that," Kai said. "I would have just taken you to the hospital for a stake in your head." He winked at Albania. "And let Albania sleep."

"Worse?" Janie swallowed repeatedly to moisten her dry throat. "My fingers feel numb."

"It's an effect of the poison," Albania said. She rolled a leaf into a ball and dipped it into some kind of citrus-scented oil. "This may sting for a second, but this should soak up the poison after I've removed the splint."

Janie bit down and tasted the blood from her split lip. Kai held her head tightly while Albania dug around in her skull. Janie's dinner rose into her throat. She was a Seeker—tough. But this was different. The poison burned, and her insides felt as if they were on fire. She heard a rip and a tug, and then everything went black.

Janie woke in a strange bed. She lay under black satin sheets on top of fluffy pillows. The sheets were warm and soft. Her legs slid across them, as slick as an ice-skating rink. *Legs!* She sprung upright and immediately remembered the splint. She grabbed her head, spreading her fingers out in her hairline, but there was nothing there, not even a bump to indicate a scar. And the searing pain was gone. Her nausea and numbness had also dissipated.

Remembering her bare legs, she lifted the sheet and peered down. *Where are my jeans?* She felt slightly panicked. She was clothed in a deep maroon tee. The color of dried human blood. It smelled like clean lavender.

"You're up." Kai poked his head in the door of the white bedroom with bare walls. There was a black dresser across the room. A flat screen hung on the wall over a stack of DVDs. "I thought I heard you."

"Where am I?" She gripped the satin in her fists. "And where are my clothes?"

"Let's start with question number one." He strode over to the closet wearing only a towel. "You're in my room." He put his hand in the air. "Before you get your panties in a bunch, I didn't undress you. Albania did. She thought you'd be more comfortable that way."

"That was nice of her. Please thank her for healing me." Janie flipped her legs over the side of the bed, so they dangled in the air. "Where did you sleep?" His eyes stayed on her bare legs longer than she would have liked. She felt uncomfortable.

"Downstairs, on the couch." He retrieved a fresh T-shirt from his closet and slid it over his head. "I'll put my jeans on in the bathroom."

"Thanks." She tried to look away, but his towel dipped below his abs, exposing the V-shape swimmers have. She redirected her attention. "S—so what's a demon splint, other than a thin piece of wood?"

"It's something demons use to inject poison into their victims." He placed a black leather band around his wrist.

"Humans?"

"Usually."

"Why do Daychildren have them? I've never seen one. They usually just fight me with their speed, strength, and in some cases, abilities. I rarely see them with tangible weapons," she said.

"A demon brought them up from the demon community. They're made of wood. Since Daychildren can't touch silver without getting burned, they took a liking to this kind of weapon. Unfortunately, now the Daychildren know how to make their own poison. It's lethal to humans. You would have been dead within hours."

Janie straightened her spine, wide-eyed and outraged. "And you were just going to let me ride the bus home with a poisonous demon splint in my head?"

"You came in, so I didn't have to consider it," he said.

Janie sank into thought. "What is your last name?"

"Why?" He stood in front of the mirrored closet doors and ran his hands through his wet, highlighted hair, placing each platinum strip in its proper location.

"I'm just curious."

"Sterdam."

"Kai Sterdam," she repeated.

Janie checked her watch. "Crap—it's three—in the afternoon." She jumped to the floor.

"You were tired, effects of the poison."

"I missed a whole day of school, and my mom, she's got to be worried sick." She fumbled around, looking for her things.

"Just think about how she's going to feel when you tell her you stayed with a Daychild," he said.

She rolled her eyes. "Where are my clothes? Can you drive me home?"

He pointed. "Albania folded them on the dresser." Kai removed a pair of jeans from a drawer and exited the room. "I'll meet you downstairs."

Janie retrieved her phone from the nightstand and called her mom.

When she opened the front door, the sun battered her in the face. It felt as if she'd been asleep for days. It was chilly, but the blue sky helped soften the bite. In the daylight, Kai's neighborhood seemed friendly enough. Kids rode their bikes up and down the sidewalks, and teenagers and adults sat on their porches and lined the entrance steps to their homes.

"Are you ready?" Kai appeared at the base of the staircase.

"Where's your bike?" she said.

"Out back." He waved for her to follow.

They exited through an unfinished basement. Nothing but concrete, wooden beams and exposed wires. She did notice a washing machine and dryer. Kai opened the sliding glass door for her. She stepped onto a compact paver patio. It extended into a small patch of grass. A tall wooden privacy fence outlined the small yard.

Not even a bush or a potted plant surrounded the patio. "I still don't see your bike."

Kai removed the metal disk from his pocket and threw it back into the air. Like before, a motorcycle formed and glided toward the ground. The rubber tires bounced onto the stone pavers.

"Why didn't you just leave it parked on the street like everyone else?"

"Not in this neighborhood." He lifted the kickstand and hopped on.

"If I didn't need to get home, I would ask you again how a thin metal disk turns into a Harley."

"I'll be anticipating that question, then." He threw her a helmet.

She caught it and held it between her palms. "Pink? This helmet's different from last night's."

"I had to get another. You dropped the other one in the city." He didn't seem as annoyed as she had expected.

"Why pink?"

"Don't human girls like pink?" Janie stared at him. "Okay, next time, I'll go with black."

She nodded. *There won't be a next time.*

She placed the helmet on her head and threw a leg over the side of the bike. She wrapped her arms around his waist and leaned forward, hugging his back and interlocking her fingers. "Ready," she said. "One question—how are we going to get out of your yard with the fence?"

Kai removed a small knife from a hidden compartment on the bike. He raised his arm and flung the knife forward with full force in the direction of a double gate. It lodged in the lock, flipping the metal latch open. The double doors swung out. The engine roared to life and the bike lurched forward. They slipped out of the gate, veering left into an alley, and exited on to the street.

Janie's house was located in a quiet suburban neighborhood in Towson, only a few streets away from school. They drove down her cul-de-sac. She pointed to her driveway. A white two-story Colonial with black shutters and a red door sat squarely on about a quarter acre. Its wraparound porch made the three-bedroom home appear larger. She smiled. Her dark blue Honda Civic waited for her in the driveway.

"Who's that?" Kai said.

"That's my car. The one I tried to hit you with. It had to be fixed." A familiar silver Acura sat across the street, parked in front of Ava's car.

"No, not what's that, who's that?" Kai said, louder this time.

Janie's eyes slid over to her porch. Then she realized. It *was* his Acura across the street. "Oh—that's Matt," she said. *What's he doing here?*

"Is he your boyfriend?"

"No!"

"Then why is he holding that?"

She had no idea why he'd shown up at her house, and certainly couldn't imagine why he'd be holding a rose. Janie dipped her head into Kai's back. "I don't know."

CHAPTER 4

The motorcycle's engine roared to life. Kai sped down her street and disappeared around a turn. Janie breathed in a sigh of relief. She wondered if Matt would disappear too if she walked slowly enough up her front walk. Nope, still there. *Damn!*

She searched the porch for Ava, but didn't see her. *Did she really have to be alone with him?*

"Hey, Janie." Matt greeted her a few feet from the steps, wearing his varsity wrestling jacket, a lightweight sweater and jeans.

"What is that?"

"A rose." He smiled.

"I mean, why?" She focused on the single yellow rose; the petals had just started to unfold. From what she remembered, yellow only meant friendship. It was red she had to fear.

"You saved my life. It's the least I can do. Besides, I was worried about you when you didn't show up at school today." He handed her the rose.

"Thanks." She half-smiled. "I was sick today."

"Who was that guy on the bike? Your boyfriend?" he said.

She blinked and replayed his question in her mind. It sounded ridiculous.

Janie coughed, stifling a laugh. "Who, Kai? Hardly."

"Yeah, who was that?" Ava appeared in her doorway. Luke followed behind her, wearing plaid pants and a solid gray sweater. A white scarf hung meticulously around his neck.

"When did you two get here?" Janie said.

"A few minutes ago," Ava said. "We stopped by to check on you. Your mom let us in. I noticed your Honda in the driveway this morning. When you didn't answer the door, I figured you got to school some other way."

"Where were you, and who was the hottie on the Harley?" Luke added. He gazed off into the distance, no doubt picturing Kai riding off into the sunset.

"Nowhere, and nobody important." She brushed by Matt and climbed the porch steps.

"So, Janie, there's this bonfire tonight, at Pete's. His parents own like acres of land. Are you interested in going?" Matt said.

Janie swung back around. "Um, what?"

Luke hung over the porch rail, entranced by every word that rolled off of Matt's tongue. "Sounds fun." His scarf acted as a good bib to catch his drool.

"Um—" Janie glared at Luke. "I'm busy."

"Come on, Janie, it does sound fun." Ava shot her an *are-you-crazy* look. "Live a little."

She didn't participate in lame school activities, but Janie knew she wasn't going to win this argument. Anyway, Luke had probably already mentally picked out his outfit. "Fine, I'll think about it," she said.

Isabelle rested the phone between her ear and her shoulder. She waved her hand for Janie to sit. Janie plopped down into the leather armchair and propped her feet up on the ottoman. She massaged her calves. It was nice to finally take her boots off. Her dagger had been digging into her leg half the night, well before she ended up in a T-shirt asleep in a very odd Daychild's bed.

Her living room was large enough for a sofa, chair and ottoman. A flat screen hung above the brick fireplace. The walls were still a light sage green from when they moved in. Isabelle never put any effort into painting since they moved every four years. One large scenic picture of a barn blanketed in snow hung above the sofa. A picture of Janie's dad perched on the side table next to a bulbous lamp. Janie sighed. The ache in her heart twitched. *Dad, I miss you.*

"Sorry, that was Abram." Isabelle entered the living room, her dark brown eyes serious under knitted brows. "Did you come home last night?"

Isabelle had seemed too preoccupied with her conversation with Abram to be that angry. "The city was crazy last night. You know how it is. Some nights are worse than others."

From Isabelle's blank expression, Janie wondered if she'd even heard her explanation. "Is everything okay, Mom?"

Isabelle sighed. "The Apotheosis had a meeting last night, over at the old Baptist church on Dulaney Valley Road." Pieces of her straight black hair had fallen out of her loose bun. They wisped around her forehead as she spoke.

"What did Abram say?" Janie knew whatever it was, it wasn't good. The Baltimore-based Apotheosis Chapter only met under troublesome circumstances. The Chapter consisted of three men—all former Seekers, Abram included. He'd been her mentor for as long as she could remember. Janie regarded him as a second father.

"Apparently there's been some sort of uprising in the city. It seems as though the Daychildren have upset the vampire community."

"But why would they do that? Vampires created them," Janie said.

"Somehow, Daychildren have figured out how to 'Turn' humans. They no longer need vampires or demons to create more of their kind." Isabelle paced the floor, mulling over the ramifications of the new information. "Fortunately, humans who are Turned are not as powerful as demons that are Turned, since they don't possess a demonic ability, but we still need to consider them a threat." She turned to Janie. "They are still Daychildren, ability or no ability. You will have to treat them the same."

Janie thought back to the Daychildren she'd fought over the last week. Mr. Muscles didn't appear to have an ability, but Mr. Telekinesis with the mullet did. Even though only one of them possessed an ability, they were both equally as dangerous to human society. "Mom, not all Daychildren have abilities. In fact, more and more I come across don't possess an ability, but that's not the issue right now. . .we can't allow humans to be Turned. We've got to put a stop to this. It's hard enough to keep humans from dying, but now I have to keep humans from Turning?" Janie exhaled in frustration. "It's going to be twice as much work."

"According to Abram, they are forming gangs to support their cause," Isabelle said.

"That explains why there was a gang of them in a law office downtown. I ran into them last night." Janie touched her head, remembering the demon splint.

"Were you prepared?" Isabelle examined Janie for cuts or bruises.

Janie brushed it off. "It was fine. I got away. But at least I know where they are now." She sank back into the chair and clutched a green throw pillow to her chest. She wasn't ready to tell her mother about Kai. Isabelle would be furious to hear she'd spent the night with a Daychild, even if he had saved her life. "So what's the plan? How do we stop them?"

"The Chapter is meeting again tonight to discuss action. Abram will come by tomorrow morning. Hopefully they'll have a plan by then." Isabelle aligned the magazines on the coffee table into a fan pattern. "I wouldn't confront them again until we hear from Abram. Maybe you should lay low tonight."

"You mean take a night off?" Janie leaned forward and rested her palm on her mother's forehead. "Are you feeling okay?"

In the background, she heard a news anchor reporting on a high school kid's disappearance. Janie and her mother turned their attention to the TV. *". . .his parents reported the Towson High School student missing after he went out to play basketball and never returned home. If you know anything about the student's disappearance, please call the Baltimore County Police Department."*

Isabelle shut off the TV. "I hope they find him. I can't begin to imagine what his parents are going through right now." She placed the remote in line with the magazines. "What are your plans for this evening? I noticed you had quite the entourage on the front porch."

"It was just Ava and Luke."

Isabelle directed her attention to the rose Janie had placed on the side table. "Who gave you the rose? I doubt it was Luke. You don't seem like his type," she said, smiling despite herself.

"Matt Baker. Now can we drop it?" Janie escaped her mother's stare.

"This is the first boy you've spoken about, and you want me to drop it." Isabelle slid Janie's feet over to sit on the ottoman.

"How many more years do I have to repeat high school? I'm feeling intellectually stunted. Normal humans don't have to repeat their teenage years over and over again. When do I actually get to *turn* eighteen?"

Isabelle smiled. "I did, and I turned out okay. I even got to go to nursing school and become a nurse." She settled in, ready to gossip about a subject Janie knew little about—boys. "Does he go to Loch Raven?"

"He's the wrestling captain," Janie said.

"Is there a problem with a jock taking an interest in you? I don't understand your reluctance." She traced the imprint of the dagger on Janie's calf. "Ouch, how long did you wear that thing in your boot?"

"Practically all night." Janie shook her head, indicating she didn't want to discuss it.

Isabelle thankfully took the hint. "So, are you seeing Matt tonight? What's he like?"

"Uh, Mom, slow down." Janie bit her lip and winced, remembering she had a split lip. She didn't taste any blood. It had already started to heal. "Matt should have no interest in me. He's only speaking to me because I saved his life."

"You did what?" Isabelle's interested gaze flipped to a disappointed frown. "Janie, that's dangerous. You could have been exposed, and Matt—" Isabelle rose to her feet. "What were you thinking?"

"What was I supposed to do—let the Daychild kill him?"

Isabelle began to pace again. "I'll have to speak to Abram about this. This is *not* good."

"Matt said he wouldn't say anything."

"That's not what I'm worried about. The Chapter can deal with the secrecy issue. Your father—" her words broke off. "Never mind."

"Why, what's wrong?" Janie stood to confront her mother. "What does this have to do with Dad?"

"Just trust me." Isabelle turned and left the room. "I've got to call Abram back."

Luke picked Ava and Janie up in his classic red Mustang. Ava arranged her cotton turtleneck collar, while Luke patted his well-fitted, and even tighter, cashmere turtleneck. He'd paired it with straight-legged dress pants. They wound around one of the only roads still considered "country" in Towson.

"Aren't dice rear-view mirror decorations from the fifties?" Janie said, playing with the stuffed cubes dangling from the mirror.

Luke rolled his eyes. "The fifties was a classic era. You gals don't appreciate the quintessential."

"What does that even mean?" Ava said. "For being such a hick, you sure do sound a lot like Webster's dictionary."

"I'm a refined, well-dressed hick," he said, straightening his spine.

"Is that the house?" Janie pointed to a large country home. It reminded her of Tara, the mansion in *Gone with the Wind.*

"Either that, or there's another party we didn't know about. Check out all the cars," Luke said. "I think the whole senior class is here."

"I recognize Pete's red pick-up. We're at the right house." Janie buttoned the last two buttons of her black, fitted waist-length Pea coat. She'd donned her usual skinny jeans and black boots. The boots hid her dagger, and the jeans made the dagger more readily accessible, not that she expected any action tonight. But she couldn't be too careful after she'd caught a Daychild on school grounds.

Bright red and orange flames illuminated the forest backdrop. Piles of wood, rubble, even an old La-Z-Boy lay in a heap in the middle of the field. Hot embers crackled off the gigantic fire, whistling around in the dry air and flickering out. Seniors encircled the blaze—laughing, dancing and hanging out.

"Janie—" Matt directed her over. He stood with two other wrestlers, Billy Reynolds and Chandler Baime. Matt still wore his varsity jacket, but he'd changed into a navy and white striped sweater. Partial horizontal lines were exposed under his open jacket. "You made it. Come join us." Matt closed the distance between them.

"Go ahead," Luke said. "We're going to find something to drink."

"Do you think they have Sprite?" Ava said.

"Doubtful." Luke shook his head, wrapped his arm around her waist and shuffled her forward.

"Did you find the place okay?" Matt said. The fire's refection flickered in his hazel irises, making them eerily pretty, like cat's eyes.

"There aren't many other houses around, so we figured Pete's was the house with all the cars." Janie scanned the area. "Are Pete's parents home? That's pretty cool of them to let him set fire to their La-Z-Boy."

"His parents went away for the weekend. They have no idea." He smiled.

"Who invited you?" Molly appeared around a group of cheerleaders, her angry gaze set on Janie. She strode over to Matt and looped her arm through his. She'd cut her Loch Raven Wrestling sweatshirt around the neck so it slid off one shoulder. She eyed Janie's footwear, raising one perfectly waxed brow. "Nice boots."

Janie threw her palms out. "Look, I'm outta here. Matt, have a good night." She whirled around and set off to find Ava and Luke. Molly was right. They should've never been at the party in the first place.

"Janie, wait!" Matt shook Molly off his arm and headed after her.

"Matt, it's no big deal." Janie waved him away. "Go be with your friends." This was why she didn't want a boyfriend. Things got too complicated, and she didn't need any more tricky situations in her life.

He reached for her arm. "Will you at least stay? Don't let Molly dictate whether you have a good time or not."

Good time—huh. "I'll think about it." She removed her arm from his grasp and strode away.

Janie searched through the smoke for Ava and Luke. Seniors threw beer cans into the fire and girls danced to music flowing from an iPod plugged into someone's car stereo. Teenagers lay across the hoods of cars, laughing and talking. A couple made out on the grass next to the fire. A twinge of envy ran through her.

She forced her thoughts back to her friends. *Where are they?*

Her skin started to prickle and a tingle inched up her spine. *They are getting bold. Why are they suddenly leaving the city?* Janie focused on the woods. A subtle movement behind a tree caught her eye. Instinctively, she touched her boot, but she wouldn't remove her dagger until she got closer to the woods.

The canopy of dormant branches muffled the sound of teenagers yelling and laughing, and lessoned the thudding vibration of the car stereo's bass. She listened for any crackle of a tree branch or the crunch of dead leaves. Footfalls gave way to someone's approach.

"What are you doing in the woods?" Matt appeared next to a tree.

She swallowed the lump in her throat. "Matt. You need to get out of here. It's not safe."

He puffed up, aligning his shoulders to make his six-foot stature appear even taller. He was a wrestler; he didn't need to appear any more muscular. "Is it a vampire?" he said.

"You need to leave."

"I'm not leaving you alone in the woods." He stepped closer to her. "You saved my life, remember. I owe you."

"Is that why you're talking to me, because you owe me?" She'd figured it out. The yellow rose, his interest in her, was all out of obligation.

"Don't be ridiculous." His jaw tightened. He broke a thin branch off a nearby tree.

"Get down!" Janie suddenly threw Matt to the ground and spun into a roundhouse kick, planting the bridge of her foot into a Daychild's side.

The redhead lunged at Janie. She slid to the right, spun around and slammed him into a tree trunk. Janie reached into her boot and brandished her dagger.

"Watch out!" someone said.

The newly Turned demon, otherwise known as a newbie, stared at Janie with bloodshot, wild black eyes; he kicked her in the stomach, knocking her to the ground. Matt jumped on the newbie's back. He threw him off with one shake and Matt landed at the base of a tree.

"Matt, are you okay?" She scrambled across the forest floor.

"I don't think my arm's broken, but my shoulder's definitely dislocated," he said, holding his arm tightly against his chest.

Janie flipped onto both feet and drove her fist into the stomach of the approaching newbie. He doubled over. The redhead went for Matt. Janie sliced the dagger through the air. It pierced through the redhead's skull, spraying green goo like an April shower. *Oh no! Matt, the demon's blood!* Janie hurdled the newbie. When she landed, Matt was gone.

She followed a dirt trail and discovered Kai crouched over Matt, gripping the collar of his varsity jacket. She sighed in relief. With his extraordinary speed, Kai had dragged Matt to safety.

"Are you trying to burn a hole in your boyfriend?" Kai said. "You can thank me later for saving him from a fountain of acidic blood."

Kai let go of Matt's jacket. Matt fell forward, catching himself with his hands.

Kai retrieved his scythe from its holster. With his arms above his head, Kai lunged forward and spun in a circle, in the direction of the newbie.

Janie extended her arm, looking past the dead eyes at his curly mop-top hair. . .she knew him. "Wait, Kai, no—"

Kai finished his swing, beheading the newbie.

Janie stared in horror.

Matt appeared just as shocked. "Was that Billy Reynolds?" He scrambled backward in a crabwalk until his back hit a tree.

"Who the hell's Billy Reynolds?" Kai wiped his blade with a pile of dead leaves and reholstered it.

"He's a wrestler." Janie stared at the empty spot where Billy's body had just lain. She could hardly process what had happened. How could she expect Matt to understand?

"You were talking to Billy when I arrived tonight. Did he seem alright to you?" Janie asked Matt.

Matt gripped his shoulder. Sweat trickled down his forehead. "He wasn't scary and psycho like he was just now." Matt's eyes were wide and his chest rose and fell in rapid, shallow spasms.

"Are you saying the newbie was alive earlier this evening?" Kai asked Janie.

“Less than an hour ago.” Janie leaned down and placed her palm on Matt’s forehead. “You’re burning up.” Although breathing, air didn’t appear to be reaching his lungs.

“They’re making their own now. Vampires are no longer needed,” Kai said, ignoring Matt’s condition.

“I know. The Chapter is aware of this. They’re meeting tonight to discuss options.” Janie knelt down next to Matt. “Are you sure it’s just your shoulder? Your forehead’s really hot.”

“The Chapter, as in former Seekers?” Kai’s harsh tone redirected her attention.

“Is that a problem?” she said. Kai ignored her. She glared at him. “Help me relocate Matt’s shoulder.”

“What’s he to me?” Kai plucked a fresh leaf blade off of a branch just above him and cleaned it off on a tree trunk.

“Then I’ll do it.” Janie placed one hand around Matt’s bicep and one around his forearm. “This is going to hurt.”

“I know. Just do it.” Matt flashed Janie a pain-filled smile. “Thanks.”

“Don’t thank me yet. On the count of three—”

Janie’s boots slipped. She did her best to find her footing on the dry leaves. “One—two—” She jerked his arm forward on three. With a load crack, she snapped his shoulder back into its socket. He collapsed, writhing in pain on the forest floor.

“Sorry,” she whispered.

“I—I’m o—okay.” Matt rolled over, doing his best to mask the pain. His facial muscles constricted and he appeared to be holding his breath. “What happened to Billy? He tried to kill you,” Matt said through a strained voice.

“That’s what newbies do, they’re babies,” Kai interjected, as if Matt should already know the answer.

Janie glared at Kai. “Stop being a jerk.” She helped Matt to a seated position. “A newbie is a newly created Daychild.” she answered. “They’re part vampire and part demon.” Confusion danced across Matt’s face.

“Does he have to know the details?” Kai said. “You’ve already disclosed too much.”

She stood to confront Kai. “His friend was just beheaded in front of him. I think he deserves some answers.”

Kai didn’t back down. “Your boyfriend’s friend was dead when he was Turned.” He squinted his green eyes and his jaw tightened. His hair appeared darker in the forest, with no light to accentuate his highlights.

“Stop calling him my boyfriend. And anyway, where did you come from? Did you follow me?” Janie remembered her dagger. She left Kai’s angry stance to retrieve it.

“Why would I follow you? I couldn’t care less what you do on a Friday night.”

“Then why are you here?” She searched the dead leaves. “Where’s my dagger?”

“Looking for this?” Kai flipped her dagger up so the hilt faced out.

She snatched it back, noticing it had already been cleaned. “Thanks.”

A commotion of angry voices echoed from across the lawn, just outside the trees. Janie ducked, spotting the uninvited guests. There were two groups, but they weren't seniors, and the dark made it hard to see them clearly. Her heart rate accelerated, heightening her Seeker sense—her skin crawled. *Oh, no. Not again!*

Someone grabbed her arm. She spun around and slammed him to the ground, pinning him to the forest floor.

"It's only me," Kai said, his palms raised. Blond waves of hair fell into his eyes. She exhaled in relief and released him. Her hand slid across his chest. She gasped.

"What's wrong?" he said.

"Your heart. It's beating. How is that possible?"

He sloughed her off him and rose to a seated position. "Now's not the time."

Her mouth hung open. *He's undead, so how does he have a beating heart?*

"Janie—drop it!"

She did her best to hide her shock. "How's Matt?"

"He's safe, for the moment. Did you see them?" He used his chin to signal in the direction of the visitors.

"Are they Daychildren?"

"One group. The other is made up of vamps." He brushed the dead leaves off his jeans. "You sure can pack a punch."

"Let's get a better look." Janie pushed off the ground. Her hand crossed over his. His skin felt oddly neutral in temperature.

Kai focused on his hand under hers. He didn't attempt to remove it. Instead, he followed the curves of her arm with his eyes.

Janie cleared her throat. "What are we going to do?"

"About?" His green eyes stayed on hers.

She shuddered at his touch, and removed her hand. "Them. We can't just leave them here with the seniors."

Kai blinked and glanced back at the circus of wild teenagers. "Some of the seniors need to be put out of their misery."

Janie thought of a few cheerleaders who could certainly use a good scare. "Seriously, what's the plan?"

"You're the Seeker." He crouched closer to the forest's edge for a better look.

"We need to get Matt out of here. But we also need to do something about the 'undead,' no offense."

"None taken."

"I'll confront them while you get Matt to safety," she suggested.

"That's suicide. Forget it." The muscle in his jaw tightened.

She stood. "I'm a Seeker. It's my job." He caught her leg. "Let me go."

He administered a light karate chop to the back of the knee. She collapsed and landed in his lap, her face only inches from his. He grasped her arm, holding her in place. "You have only two daggers, and there are about ten of them."

She caught his breath and shivered. Being so close to Kai scared her. She shrugged him off and squatted next to him. "Yeah, but five are vamps. They're easy to kill. It's the ones with demonic abilities that are sometimes a challenge."

His eyes tightened. "We'll both get rid of them; *then* we'll get Matt out of here."

"Does he have the time?" she argued.

"He'll have to."

"Why do you suppose they're here, in the suburbs, at a bonfire for high school kids? This isn't the first time I've caught them in Towson. One attacked Matt at school the other night."

"Who gets attacked that many times?"

"I do."

"*You* go out looking for it." Kai shook his head. "I'm pretty sure it has something to do with the shift of power. The vamps have it and the Daychildren want it." He glanced back at a group of jocks chugging beer and pounding their chests like gorillas. "As for why they're targeting Loch Raven Raiders, you've got me, other than they're annoying and the world would be better without a few of them." Kai flipped a stake out of his belt and handed it to her. "You'll need this for the vamps."

"It's like the Bloods and the Crips, demon-style." Janie cocked her head and contorted her fingers into gang signs.

"You're a mess. I don't know why I hang out with you."

"You call this hanging out?"

"Whatever." He shot to his feet and held his hand out for her. "Can we kick some vampire ass already?"

"I'm right with you." She ignored his gesture and jumped to his side.

Janie and Kai approached the rival gangs. Her hand rested on her dagger. She eyed Kai. He appeared confident with a cool, tough-guy arrogance. The kind of tenacity someone developed when they'd persevered. Kai signaled for her to move ahead of him. Janie guessed it had to do with the element of surprise or something. Whatever. These vamps were hers.

A vampire caught a whiff of Janie and cleared his throat. "Mmm, I smell Seeker blood." The vamp was tall and skinny, dark-skinned and in his early twenties. He wore a red bandana around his head. Janie chuckled, recalling her Bloods and Crips joke.

Gold chains hung from the vamp's neck, layered over a white tank. His jeans hung off his butt, exposing a pair of striped boxer shorts. Janie wondered what Luke would think about the vamp's choice of attire—*Ghetto style.*

"Fresh Seeker meat. This one's all mine," the vampire said. He turned into the faint light of the distant bonfire, exposing an arm-length tattoo of a dagger entangled in vines.

"I suggest you and your boys return to the city. I'll only warn you once," Janie said. She removed the dagger from her waist, ready to remove the stake just as quickly. She bore into the vampire, refusing to show an ounce of weakness.

"There's one of you and ten of us." He laughed, his teeth sparkling gold. Janie wondered whether his fangs were gold-plated. She'd stake him before she'd have to find out.

"I thought the vamps where changing. Why are you hanging out with filthy Daychildren?" Janie said.

"Who are you calling filthy?" A Daychild shot to the front of the pack, a white boy with tanned skin. He reminded her of a mobster from *The Sopranos*.

"Step off," the vampire said. He stuck his tattooed arm out and held the mobster back.

"You're not the boss of me." The Daychild pushed up on the vamp, his face in his. The vamp may have been slightly taller, but the mobster was definitely chubbier. Four more vamps surrounded the feuding leaders. Getting the hint, the Daychild took a step back. "You'll see. The vamps aren't in charge anymore. There's a new leader in town. We don't need you anymore."

The vampire pounded his chest with his fist. "I *am* the den leader—Jerome. You got that, half-breed?" He beat his chest again and pointed. "Jerome—the den leader. Either get down or lay down, Antony."

Jerome addressed Janie. "Seeker—I'm out, for now." He kissed two fingers and spread them in the air. He switched his focus to Antony and the Daychild gangsters who'd taken a protective stance around their leader. "You won't be getting what you came for tonight. So roll."

Antony nodded. His face became twisted with anger; lines sliced across his bad skin. He ran his hand through his wiry short brown hair and glared at Janie. "Antony will be back." He referred to himself in third person, which she recognized as a common theme within this group of undead. Antony placed his hand on his chest. "This isn't the last you've seen of me, Seeker."

The gangs dispersed. Neither turned their backs on the other. Jerome snapped his fingers and they took off in the direction of the city.

"Well played." Kai appeared at her side.

"I told you to go. I can handle them." She let out a relieved laugh.

"You did," Kai agreed. "You knew I was here if you needed me."

"Huh—thanks." She placed her weapon in her waistband. An image of Matt, sweaty and lethargic, flashed before her eyes.

"Uh—guys," Matt said from just a short distance, where Kai had secured him, behind the base of a huge tree. "There's something sticking out of my shoulder, a stick or something. It's wedged in my bone."

Janie and Kai shot each other the same look. "Demon splint," Janie said.

"Sounds like it," Kai agreed, the urgency less apparent in his tone.

"A what splint?" Matt said. "I'm feeling a little weak."

Janie hurried to Matt's side. "Let me see." A thin piece of wood resembling a long needle stuck out of his varsity jacket. She spoke to Kai. "Is that what the splint looks like?"

Kai hovered over them. "I can smell the poison. He's not as strong as you. He doesn't have much time."

"We can't just let him die. Can't we take him to Albania?"

"My bike only holds two."

She glared at Kai. “Then you take him. I’ll stay here.”

“I have my car,” Matt said, falling in and out of consciousness.

“Check his jacket pocket for the keys,” Kai ordered.

Janie slipped her hand into his pocket. “Found them.” She jingled them in the air.

Kai bent over and hoisted Matt over his shoulder.

“Meet me around the front of the house,” Janie said. “I need to talk to my friends. Matt drives a silver Acura. It’s—”

Kai nodded and disappeared.

CHAPTER 5

Janie found Ava and Luke roasting marshmallows. "Ava, I need to talk to you."

"What's up? You look terrible. Did you forget your inhaler again?" Ava handed her poker to Luke and followed Janie, out of Luke's earshot.

"No, it's in my pocket." Janie searched her pocket. No inhaler. She realized she must have lost it in the woods. No time to go back. "I've got to go. Take Luke and get out of here. A Daychild has attacked Billy and Matt."

"What?" Panic stretched across Ava's face.

Luke got up and started over.

"Shhh—" Janie said. "I need you to act like everything's okay." Ava started to shake. Janie clutched her arms. "Now, listen to me. Billy is dead, but Matt is still alive. He needs help. I'm leaving with Kai."

"Who's Kai?"

"The guy from earlier. On the motorcycle."

Ava stared at her blankly.

"I'll tell you tomorrow. Just get Luke and leave."

"What should I tell him?" Ava said.

"Tell him you feel sick or something, but go."

Luke moved up next to them. "Is everything okay? Ava—you look like you're gonna hurl." He looped a worried arm around her waist.

"Can you take her home? I think she's got the flu. She has a fever." Janie patted Ava's face.

"She was fine just a second ago." He appraised Ava's ghost-white complexion. "Sure, but what about you? Are you coming?" he asked Janie.

"I think I'll stay with Matt." Janie flashed him a fake smile. Inside, she felt terrified, and she never felt terrified. She'd been around death too much for it to affect her. *Why is this time any different?*

"You like him, J." Luke nudged her with his shoulder and waggled his brows. "Have fun. I'll get Ava home. Don't do anything I wouldn't do."

"Thanks, Luke." She touched Ava's forearm. "You feel better. I'll call you tomorrow."

Kai carried Matt up two flights of steps. The three scars were visible along Kai's forearm as he braced Matt's body with his hand, balancing the wrestler over one shoulder.

Albania's apartment, located within the upscale yuppie area of Federal Hill, looked out over Baltimore's Inner Harbor. The expansive, multilayered skyscrapers were backlit by an orange moon. Its reflection cast rippling highlights across the water. Red, white and yellow lights roped the masts of a pirate ship, stretching out along the water below a triangular, iridescent peek of the aquarium. From Albania's apartment, the city nightlife flickered like multicolored fireworks on the Fourth of July. Janie shuddered, thinking about the evil plotting within the city's limits.

Janie peeled herself away from the panoramic view of the harbor and returned to the couch to wait for Matt to regain consciousness. His body stretched the length of the couch, so she sat on the floor by the cushion's edge. She didn't know him well, but she felt obligated to stay by his side. She nodded off a few times throughout the night, catching herself when her head slid from her palm to the cushion. Kai had tried to convince her to rest in Albania's room, but she'd refused. The sun would soon be rising. She wished she could relish in the security of knowing the undead would go to bed and leave the unsuspecting public alone. But they had evolved. No one was safe, anytime.

"Albania made coffee. Do you want some?" Kai entered the living room and took a seat in the chair next to her on the floor, holding a steamy mug in his hand. "Cream and sugar," he enticed.

"Thanks." She accepted the mug. The hot liquid coated her sore throat. During the ride to Albania's apartment, she had fought through a wheezing spell. She was grateful it was mild, since she'd lost her inhaler in the woods. "I didn't know witches and Daychildren drank coffee," she said.

"I don't. It'll turn your teeth yellow. I tend to like my smile white." He flashed his braces-perfect teeth. "Albania keeps it around for her human clients." Janie's brow dipped. "You know. . .gypsy stuff, like fortune telling and palm reading," he said.

"Oh." Janie set her mug on a small coffee table. Kai slid a coaster over to her. "Thanks." They waited in silence. It had been that way for much of the night, uncomfortable silence, and waiting.

"Where's Albania?" Janie asked.

"I think she's taking a nap. She's tired after healing Matt."

Janie fidgeted with the mug. "Are you two—?"

He smirked. "What, a thing?"

"You just seem—close." She let her dark hair fall into her face to hide her embarrassment.

"We're close. We've been through a lot together." A reminiscent gaze tainted with a twinge of pain crossed his eyes.

Janie rose from the area rug and moved back over to the window. The sun had started to rise, casting a fiery glow over the city. "She's very pretty."

"Yes, she is." He joined her at the window, causing her pulse to quicken. It was different than her Seeker sense, a feeling she didn't quite understand. She focused on a large yacht leaving the dock and wondered who had enough money to afford such an elegant boat.

Kai placed both hands in his jeans pockets and stared out into the city. "It looks like your boyfriend's going to pull through."

"He's not my boyfriend," Janie insisted, feeling as if she might start wheezing again.

"Could've fooled me. You're with him every day." She felt his stare on her cheek.

"Every day. As in three days?" Janie drew in a rough breath and exhaled. "He doesn't like me that way. He just feels indebted to me since I saved his life."

"I see the way he looks at you. It's more than that." Kai's voice deepened. He seemed almost nervous. He cleared his throat. "Not that I care."

The energy between them had become frenetic, crazy and mixed with discordant emotions. She realized that just the day before, she had wanted to kill him. Her extremities started to tingle and her heart felt as if it could pound out of her chest. She wondered if her reaction had everything to do with being born and trained to kill him. Any emotion other than loathing and hate felt unnatural.

"You don't have to try to make me feel better. I haven't thought about Matt for three years. I'm not going to start now." Janie folded her arms in front of her chest.

"Do what you want with your life." Kai turned and left the room, exhibiting another one of his unexpected attitudes.

She blinked at his directness. She'd assumed they were having a heart-to-heart. "Okay, then."

Matt stirred. His muscular legs stretched over the sofa's arm.

He moaned. "Where am I? It looks like my great-aunt's house. And what's with all the bright colors, and the beads?" he said, attempting to lift his head off the pillow.

Janie whirled over to his side. "You're okay." He looked pale, but otherwise healthy. She helped him to a seated position.

"What happened?" He grabbed his forehead. "Aw, my head. How long have I been asleep?"

Janie decided to blurt out everything at once, which she quickly regretted. "You're at Albania's, downtown. She's a witch. She healed you after you were punctured by a poisonous demon splint, and you've been asleep for about eight hours, if you count the time you passed out due to the poison."

Matt sprung up off the couch. "What? You're crazy. This is all crazy. I've totally gone insane." He pointed to Janie. "*You're* insane."

"Okay, maybe not the reaction I was going for, but we'll go with it," she said. *How do I explain this in human terms? I can't. Uh—* She smacked her forehead with her palm.

"There's no need to hit yourself," Kai said, returning from the kitchen clutching a powdered doughnut.

Matt pointed to him. "What's he doing here? He killed Billy." Matt fell back on to the sofa. His head slid into his hands. "I mean, the totally mental Billy with black eyes, and fangs."

"I think your boyfriend's losing it." Kai moved back to the chair, not the least bit fazed by the commotion.

A stream of long, wavy flame-red hair flew by Janie's peripheral vision. "Is everything okay out here?" Albania said, dressed in light green silk pajamas with spaghetti straps. Albania's vibrant red hair swam around her body and her celery-colored pajamas accentuated the green of her eyes. *And she doesn't need anything else accentuated.*

"Janie's boyfriend's lost his mind." Kai popped the last piece of doughnut into his mouth and brushed the loose powder off his lap.

Janie glared at Kai. She spun around and addressed Albania. "Do you have anything to calm Matt down? Valium or tranquilizers, or. . .something. He's not taking all of this very well," Janie said, waving her hands around in the air, signaling the "magic atmosphere."

"I'm fine. Just give me a second to process everything," Matt said through his hands. He massaged his forehead.

"Oh, sorry—" Janie wheezed and dropped to her knees. Unable to breathe, she tottered on the rug like a Weeble Wobble.

"Janie, are you okay?" Kai knelt down beside her.

She shook her head. Speaking required air, and at the moment she couldn't find any.

"She needs her inhaler. She lost it last night." Kai anchored his arm around her back. "You're going to be okay." He looked up at Albania. "Can you do anything?"

"Sorry, Kai, I can handle demon poison, but asthma is out of my area of expertise. She needs a medical doctor."

"See that Matt gets home," he instructed Albania.

Kai flipped Janie into his arms. Her head slipped back onto his bicep, her dark hair spilling over his arm. "I'm taking her home. During the car ride here she said she had another inhaler."

Matt stood. “Towson is at least fifteen minutes away without traffic.” His anger switched to genuine concern. “You need to get her to a hospital. There are plenty of well-respected hospitals in the city. Why risk taking her all the way home? Hopkins is right down the road.”

“No one asked you,” Kai growled. He scowled at Matt, stifling an unexplainable hunger. Fortunately, he seemed to find the will not to drain the human of his blood. Janie whimpered in his arms. “It *won’t* take me fifteen minutes.”

CHAPTER 6

Kai felt Janie's chest rise and fall in erratic jerks against his back. Her shallow exhales resembled the sound of a honking goose. Still conscious enough to put her arms around him, he held her wrists together to keep her secure on the seat behind him.

He slid off the bike, careful not let her fall on to the driveway. *And she said I wasn't gentle.* He swung her into a cradle hold and crossed the front walk. He regarded her weak state, limp and breathless in his arms. She was always so tough, never wanting to accept his help, but she was human. A sudden fear he couldn't understand gripped him. It shouldn't matter to him if she died. They only shared one commonality; they both killed his kind. It sounded demented, *killing his kind.* He wondered what she must really think of him. He shook his head. She didn't ever have to know what had happened to make him this way. He'd sworn to never talk about it again, the memory too painful to expose.

Kai glanced up at the single second-floor window—Janie's bedroom. The night she tried to run him over with her car, he had followed her home, pathetically concerned that she'd been injured in the accident. He shouldn't have cared, yet now he found himself in the very same spot, looking up at her window.

Kai placed his foot on the porch step, formulating alternatives to going in through the front door. Janie sucked in a shallow breath and erupted into a coughing fit. The honking became deeper, more intense. She didn't have much longer. He could use his ability, but he had no idea where to find her inhaler. With no other option, he had to confront her mother. A former Seeker, she'd know what he was immediately. With all the commotion of Matt's injury and Janie's asthma attack, he hadn't thought about the ramifications of bringing her home. Only part vampire, he didn't need permission to enter, and he could walk through sunlight without bursting into a pile of ashes. He hoped Janie's mother would be more focused on helping Janie than killing him.

His hand shook as he reached for the doorbell. Janie's home reminded him of his childhood home, only greener—he grew up in the Southwestern desert before losing so many years of his life. He often thought about his parents. He knew he could never return home, even if they still lived there. As Janie had said when she first met him, he was a "monster." He let out a deep sigh. At least when he really was a monster, he couldn't feel. He didn't have a conscience that weighed on him every day, threatening to rip the beating heart from his chest. Being a part of three worlds was the greatest curse a man could be given, and at eighteen he was just barely a man.

The knob clicked and the door swung open. The woman who answered could have been Janie, only twenty years older. Her tanned skin had aged well, revealing barely any wrinkles on her flawless face. Her near-black hair framed her angular face. She gasped and her beautiful brown eyes squinted in horror.

"What happened!" Isabelle said.

"She's having an asthma attack. She needs her inhaler." Kai stepped through the doorway into the foyer.

Her eyes appraised him. She hesitated. *She knows what I am.*

Her voice shook. "I'll get it. Stay here." He wondered if she'd also retrieve a silver blade. A feeling of panic washed over him, and he never panicked. He'd been through too much to panic over anything. Then he realized why he had the overwhelming urge to drop Janie and run.

A man emerged from the living room. "Is everything okay, Isabelle? Is Janie home?"

Their eyes locked. The man's blue eyes had aged fifteen years, now fully edged by crow's feet, the markings of a stressful life. Kai knew all too well how stressful the man's life had been. A fulminate rage swirled within his irises, deepening the light blue to indigo. His black hair was now sprinkled with flecks of white, and lines creased his once-smooth forehead. Kai's scars started to burn; a searing pain sliced down his forearm and fire burst through his chest. He gripped Janie tighter, afraid he might drop her. The man's eyes were as hate-filled as he remembered. It was *him*; Kai had no doubt. He'd remember that face for eternity—Abram.

Isabelle appeared at the base of the steps, clutching Janie's inhaler. "Give her to me," Janie heard a familiar man speak.

"Abram," Janie wheezed. He removed her from Kai's arms and rushed her into the living room. He placed her on the sofa, propping her up with pillows on the couch.

"You're going to be okay," Abram said, stroking her hair.

"She needs her inhaler." Isabelle hurried to Janie's side. "Here, use this."

Janie pressed the plastic tube to her lips, breathed out a small puff of air, and sucked the medication into her lungs. Within seconds, she felt better. Her lungs reopened. A flood of air expanded into her chest like a balloon. Only something else weighed on her now. The atmosphere was even heavier than the feeling of not being able to breathe.

"Where's Kai?" Janie tried to sit up, but she was still slightly dizzy and fell back on the couch.

"I'm right here," Kai said with forced calmness. He stood across the room, looking sick. Abram glared at him.

"How did this happen?" Isabelle knelt down next to Janie, concern etched across her forehead.

"I lost my inhaler last night, during a fight." Janie left her mother's worried eyes to search for Kai again. She found him, still on the opposite side of the room, stiff and restrained.

"A fight? I thought you went to a bonfire," Isabelle asked, rising.

Janie finally lifted herself to a seated position. "Abram, did you speak to the Chapter? What's going on? Last night we ran into a gang of vamps and Daychildren. They were in Towson, at a student's home."

The tension hung suspended in the air. No one answered her. Her mother conversed with Abram in hushed tones. Kai appeared to have one foot out the door. With one flinch, she feared he would disappear. It was the most on edge she'd ever seen him. His confident arrogance had disappeared, or more apparently, been taken from him. Then, she realized. How could she have been so stupid? She'd spent so much time with Kai over the last few days that she'd forgotten. The three of them were Seekers, and *he* was a Daychild.

A bouncing fleck of light caught Janie's attention. She traced it along the ceiling. She searched the immediate area for the object creating the bright fragment. The spectrum of light moved whenever her mother did. Something sparkled at her mother's waist. Then Janie saw the light source—a silver blade wedged in Isabelle's pants, slightly hidden under her shirt. Janie's eyes shot over to Abram. He nodded to Isabelle, signaling her to move forward.

Janie leapt off the couch and sprinted over to Kai, barreling into his chest. He didn't move. Hitting Kai was like smacking into a brick wall. She spun around and faced her mother and mentor. Both of them had taken fighting stances and were brandishing silver blades.

"Don't touch him!" Janie yelled.

"Janie, I need you to move away slowly," Abram instructed, his eyes fixed on Kai. A shiny silver blade glistened in his fist. Janie's eyes grew to the size of saucers, horrified at the thought of Abram plunging a dagger through Kai's skull.

"He's not going to hurt me," she said. She extended her arms as if her little body could block the dagger from impaling Kai. She flicked her eyes back and forth between Abram and Isabelle, but neither stood down.

"Janie, listen to me." Isabelle inched forward. "He's not human."

"Don't you think I know that?" She put her hand on her waist, searching for her dagger, but it was gone. She realized she had taken it out at Albania's apartment and set it on the side table next to the couch. Not that it mattered. She wasn't going to use it against anyone in the room. Going for her weapon was only a reflex. "Put your blades away. He's my friend."

Abram lifted his blade, aiming for Kai's skull. "If you want any chance of leaving this house, you'll remove your weapon and slide it over to me."

Kai removed the scythe from his belt. He bent forward and slid the large curved blade across the hardwood floor to Abram. Janie wondered why Kai wasn't speaking or defending himself. She hadn't known him for long, but one thing she did know—he didn't keep his thoughts to himself. She wanted to tell him to run. He was faster than any vamp or demon she'd ever come across, so she couldn't figure out why he'd stayed to face death at the hands of a Seeker. Janie studied the lines on Kai's face—empathy mixed with rage and fear.

"Now explain yourself. What are you doing with Janie?" Abram said. He kicked Kai's scythe behind him. It hit the wall with a thud.

"It's like Janie said," Kai explained. "There were two gangs of them at the bonfire. I helped her friend Matt when he was punctured by a poisonous demon splint. We sat with him all night until he recovered. Then, this morning Janie had an asthma attack, so I brought her home to retrieve her inhaler. She lost the other one last night." His voice sounded deep, vulnerable. "I don't want any trouble." He flashed his palms.

Abram assessed Kai. The wheels in his head visibly spun as he contemplated Kai's fate.

"But you're one of them. Why would you help a human?" Isabelle said. Her worry lines had aged her at least ten years. Janie caught a glimpse of what she'd look like when she was *much* older.

"I'm different," Kai said. "I'm not like the others." His voice lowered. "At least not anymore."

"Mom, he's different. Trust me," Janie said. "That night in the city, when I came upon a Daychild lair, Kai saved my life. I didn't have enough weaponry to defeat that many of them. One of them poisoned me with a splint. Kai got me the help I needed." She willed Isabelle and Abram to believe her. "You should be thanking him, not pointing daggers at him. I am alive right now, standing in front of you, because of him." Janie's hands balled into fists. Her teeth locked together. She couldn't remember the last time she felt so angry—maybe when her father died and her mother refused to discuss it.

Janie stared at Abram. He glared at Kai as if he knew him from somewhere. He really wanted to kill him, and not just because he was a Daychild. It was something else entirely. "Abram, is there something you're not telling me?" Janie said.

Abram didn't speak. Flashes of pain and fear lit up his face. Janie realized his expression was oddly similar to Kai's. He hesitated. "N—no. No I don't." Janie knew he'd lied, like when she used to ask him the specifics about her father's death. He'd get anxious and sweaty, and his eyes would fall anywhere but on hers.

Janie pushed her feelings back. "Then can you put away your weapons so we can talk? We have to discuss what is happening with the undead." Janie rethought her choice in words. "Other than Kai, of course. Like I said, he's different from them."

"Abram, lower the dagger," Isabelle said. Her tan face had paled. After a hesitant second, Abram did as she asked. Isabelle's eyes met Kai's. "You should leave." She let out a sigh of defeat.

"Mom—"

Isabelle cut her off. "Janie, we will discuss this later."

Janie reached behind her, searching for Kai. The roar of his motorcycle swept through the room. He'd already left. She didn't even hear the door slam behind him.

Janie spent the rest of the day in her room, too angry to face Isabelle or Abram. She didn't know whether she was angry at herself for feeling anything but hatred for a Daychild, or at her mother for not understanding her feelings. Maybe a little of both.

The sun had set. She lay on her bed staring at the plastic glow-in-the-dark stars on her ceiling. She contemplated whether to go into the city. Abram thought she should hold off until the Chapter knew more.

She looked down at her cell phone with worry. She hadn't heard from Matt since that morning. She wondered if he'd ever want to speak to her again. After everything he'd witnessed, she doubted it. Not that she ever really had a chance with the most popular guy in school. She wasn't even sure if she liked him that way. She gripped her pillow tightly, too frustrated to think about it anymore.

"You still look pissed." Janie sprang upright. Kai stood inside her window. The curtains blew around his body, surrounding him in a cloud of cream-colored silk. Only the breeze didn't come from outside her window; the window was still closed and locked. The silk material settled to the floor. Kai was dressed in the same gray T-shirt and dark jeans, his golden hair windswept around his head. He shook it back into place.

"Please tell me this is the first time you've done that." Janie clutched her heart. It about jumped out of her chest. She wondered how he'd gotten in, if not through the window.

“What, snuck into your room?” He smirked. She eyed him accusingly. He caught her look. “It’s the first time,” he said.

“Why are you here anyway? If my mother catches you, she will surely plunge a dagger through your skull. This time I don’t know if I can stop her.” Janie checked her cell again, even though she knew she hadn’t missed any calls.

“Matt hasn’t called?” he said, not really seeming to care either way.

“I called him after you left. He hasn’t returned my call. I just wanted to make sure he made it home okay.” She placed it back on her nightstand.

“He did. I spoke to Albania.” Kai coughed, not so subtly changing the subject. “So, does the Chapter know why the ‘undead,’ as you call them, have taken an interest in the suburbs?”

“No, but there’s been a rise in the disappearances of high school kids. A junior from Towson High disappeared from his neighborhood just this afternoon. He went out to play basketball and never returned home.”

“From what I’ve heard downtown, vampires are pissed,” he said. “They’ve been able to fly under the radar lately. Some have even started to blend into the human world unnoticed, even accepted, but not for long. Daychildren are creating a mess that vampires have to keep cleaning up. I think that’s why Jerome and his crew were at the party. They knew what Antony’s gang was up to.”

"It's just going to keep happening." Janie let her bare feet fall over her bed and jumped to the floor. "That lair downtown, in the old law firm, I want to go back."

"We don't know how many live there. Even with me by your side, there could be a fight." He displayed a cocky smirk. "Not that I can lose." He placed his hand on his waistline. Kai had at least two blades pushed into his belt. There was a hole where his scythe usually hung.

Janie lifted her comforter off the floor. She retrieved his scythe from under her bed. "Here. I thought you might want this back. I got it after Abram left."

He grasped the hilt. Their fingers brushed together. He retracted his hand and placed it into his belt. He removed a dagger from a holster strapped to his ankle. "And you left this at Albania's."

"My dagger, thanks." She regarded the wooden hilt. "It was my mom's. Her mentor gave it to her."

Kai fingered the carved inscription. "What does it mean?"

"*U-le-tsu-ya-s-ti.* It means 'brave' in Cherokee."

"*U-le-tsu-ya-s-ti.* Very cool. It's too bad you're not brave."

"I'm brave."

"No, you're reckless; there's a difference." He combed his fingers through his hair. Janie stared at the long scars along his forearm. She wanted so badly to ask him what had happened. "Speaking of reckless, why do you want to go back to the law firm?" he said. "Are you asking to have another splint shoved into your skull?"

"Not so much, but it's the only place I know to start my investigation, and the Chapter hasn't been any help."

"Ah, the Chapter. . .you know they aren't going to want you to associate with me anymore. They may even be angry that you haven't attempted to kill me yet."

"Attempted," she said, astonished. "I have. Remember my Honda and the pole that jumped out in front of it? I attempted."

Kai smiled. "You'd never succeed. I'm too strong and fast for you."

"Is that a challenge?" She angled her body.

"If you make it one. I'm just stating the obvious." He smirked, biting his lower lip.

Janie jumped into a sidekick. Kai caught her leg and flipped her onto the floor. She shot back to her feet, hands fisted and blocking her face. She kneed him in the groin followed by a quick uppercut to the jaw. Hardly fazed, Kai took hold of her hips and spun her onto her back. She lay on the floor, out of breath and staring up as he hovered over her.

"Done yet?" He smiled victoriously.

"Nope." Janie rolled out from under him, scrambling back to her feet.

She squatted into a sweeping circular kick along the floor, taking his feet out from under him. He landed on his backside. She slid over to him and raised her arm, pretending to plunge a dagger into his skull. Kai swiped her knee out from under her and she landed directly on top of him.

"How about now?" he said, their faces only inches apart. Not a puff of air touched her skin.

It wasn't like being face to face with a human. He didn't need air to breathe. She noticed sometimes he did, an instinct left over from his human years. Janie paused to feel his heartbeat under her chest. It sped quickly, in equal rhythm with hers. She counted the beats to make certain his heart really beat. It did.

"Pink," he said. He looked past her.

"What are you talking about?" She pushed back from him.

"The walls, your room is pink. I thought you didn't like pink. That's why I got you a black helmet." Kai rolled her onto her side so they were facing each other.

Janie propped her head up with her hand. Her elbow rested on the floor. "I don't. We move every four years, so my mom doesn't paint. A ten-year-old girl had this room before me." She pointed up. "Hence the glow-in-dark-stars. I'd prefer a much darker color. I'm hoping the next house we move to has a boy's room, much better color selection." They lay on the floor for few long seconds of silence. "Why does your heart beat?" she said.

Kai rolled his eyes in annoyance. He sat up and propped himself up against her closet door, resting his arms over his knees. "I already told you I don't want to discuss it."

She moved to her knees to meet his eye level. "That's because the Bloods and the Crips were about to brawl last time." Janie made fabricated gang signs with her fingers again.

“The who?” He squinted, confused.

“You live in the city. You really should know who the gangs are.” He didn’t seem to care. She glanced down at his chest, letting her playful demeanor mellow. “Will you ever tell me why your heart beats?”

“No—” His green eyes turned steely.

“You know I’m going to ask you again,” she pushed.

“I know, you’re annoyingly persistent. My answer’s going to be the same.” His voice deepened, making it obvious he wasn’t playing around.

She continued anyway. “One day you’ll tell me.”

Kai’s face tightened. “We won’t ever be that close.”

CHAPTER 7

Maybe this wasn't the best idea. It was too late to rethink her not-so-brilliant, spontaneous plan. Her bruised ego had gotten the best of her, and now she was surrounded by a gang of Daychildren. She quickly learned the law firm of *Bower, Reed & Associates* no longer existed, and if it did, they no longer practiced law on Eastern Avenue.

She'd filled her school backpack with stakes, not knowing what to expect in the city. She didn't anticipate running into any vamps, but since she'd thought her plan out *so* well, she figured she'd bring some along. Her first mistake, making the trip to the city. Her second, knocking on the large wooden door packing only three silver-coated daggers.

She swore under her breath. How could she let a Daychild get to her like that? If she made it out alive, she was done with Kai Sterdam.

Janie scanned the inside of the abandoned row home. She stood on a 17th century Persian rug. It's once-vibrant colors were now dull and covered with dirt. The paisley wallpaper hung torn from the ten-foot-high walls, under thick wooden crown molding. The office smelled like a rat-infested sewer combined with the rotting stench of an unkempt morgue, minus the formaldehyde. At least ten Daychildren surrounded her, males and females of all ages. She could see the hunger in their black, hollow eyes. But not one of them made a move toward her. Something held them back. She wondered if they were waiting for her to make the first move. A familiar voice broke through the circle.

"Well, well, if it isn't the Seeker, back for more. I told you we'd meet again," Antony said. He knocked a bald guy with a goatee to the side with his pudgy body. He stood at least four inches taller than the rest, the alpha male of the pack.

"Why were you in the suburbs last night?" Janie said. She'd removed two blades and adjusted the backpack across her back. With this bunch she wouldn't need stakes.

"You think you can come up in my place asking questions?" Antony crossed his arms over his chest.

"Then tell me why the vamps stopped you," she said.

"No one stopped us. We don't listen to vamps. We got what we came for." He scowled at the mention of vampires. Sweat seeped from his brow.

"It didn't look that way to me," Janie pushed.

"Then you don't know anything, little girl. You're grasping for straws." A cocky smirk formed on his face.

"Did you Turn that missing teenager?"

"What, the little punk in Towson? Take a look for yourself." He glanced to the side.

A skinny teenager with pimply skin stepped forward. Janie recognized his face from his photo on the news. His eyes were no longer blue, but she recognized his buzz cut. He wore a pair of athletic pants and a long-sleeved tee, matching his parents' description. She remembered he'd disappeared after he went out to play basketball.

"Can we eat her yet? Just a nibble?" a round woman growled. Drool dripped from her fangs.

"Go ahead," Antony said. "But her blood is mine."

The circle closed around her. Janie slashed the two blades out in front of her, causing a few to step back. She nailed one in the ribs with a side kick. A thin arm swung at her. She ducked and swept the legs out from under the scrawny woman, taking the opportunity to plunge a dagger into her head. The man with the goatee jumped on her back. Janie shot up, launching him back into a tall guy with glasses and a woman with short spiky hair. All three tumbled to the ground.

The "missing" teenager caught Janie's lip with a right hook, splitting it open again. Blood flowed on to her tongue. She wiped her mouth with the sleeve of her navy hoodie. The teenager then kicked her in the ribs, causing her to drop her dagger. She reached into her boot for her other, favorite one. Blindsided again, she landed squarely on her shoulder, the bald guy with the goatee on top of her. He held her against the floor by her throat, squeezing her neck so tightly she couldn't breathe. Janie clutched at the hand on her throat. Her slippery fingers gripped the dagger in her other hand. The spiky haired woman held Janie's arm down so she couldn't strike the bald guy with her dagger. Her lungs burned. She could feel the tiny air pockets caving in.

Suddenly, the bald guy collapsed on her chest, releasing his grip around her neck, viciously forcing the trapped air out of her lungs. Janie sucked in large gulps of air, coughing uncontrollably. She glanced down at his massive, limp body covering hers. The guy lay on top of her with a scythe lodged in his skull, covering her in green goo. She sloughed him off her.

A black Sketcher cracked the spiky haired woman's sternum. She flew into the wall. Janie stumbled to her feet. She lost her balance and landed in Kai's strong arms.

"What were you thinking?" he said. He dragged Janie upright and removed a smaller blade from his belt. He propelled it forward, into the skull of the missing teenager.

Janie drew in the clean smell of lavender and sweat. She tried to speak. Kai placed his finger over her lips. "Don't answer. We've got to get out of here." He scooped his scythe off the ground.

Pounding erupted at the door. "Stop," Antony said. "We have more guests."

Surrounded by the last of the gang, Antony stood with his arm extended, blocking another newly Turned teenager from attacking.

"Who do you think it is?" Janie whispered. She raised her dagger and fist, her feet planted firmly in a side stance, preparing for the new visitors.

Kai removed the metal disk from his jeans pocket. He caught her glance. His mouth twisted into an arrogant smile, making her feel more confident they'd make it out alive.

"Antony," an angry voice called. "Move out of my way. Where's Antony?"

Jerome entered the main office area of the row home. Janie pictured the room once being filled with mahogany desks, expensive leather chairs and shelves lined with thick law books. A painted portrait of a man in his sixties or seventies dressed in a dark suit and a crisp white shirt and tie hung crookedly behind Jerome, taking up a large portion of the wall. The gold frame had chipped and split in two, spilling the portrait on the floor. Janie wondered if the old guy was Bower, Reed or an "Associate."

Four gold chains looped loosely around Jerome's neck over an oversized red T-shirt, hiding his tall, lanky body. The largest chain read *Jerome* in cursive. A red bandana was tied around his shaved head, just like Janie remembered him at the bonfire. His jeans hung low around his butt, exposing his white boxers.

He glanced past Janie and Kai, to Antony. "I warned you." Jerome removed a silver-plated dagger from his waist and plunged it into the skull of a young Hispanic girl with plump red lips, towering legs and long, curly black hair. She had been the unfortunate Daychild to answer the door. She'd invited Jerome in. Her skull burst open, discharging a faucet of green. Her body dropped to the ground. "One for one. Like I told you before, you take one of mine, I take one of yours," Jerome said to Antony.

"Veronica, you killed her." Sadness and rage exploded in Antony's deep voice. He moved around Janie and Kai, his black eyes fixed on Jerome. "Don't come into *my* place killing *my* crew and making threats."

The Daychildren left their circular formation around Janie and Kai to stand behind their leader.

Jerome scanned the room. "Your place? These streets belong to the vamps. You half-breeds are on our turf." Jerome glanced behind him. A handful of vampires filtered in through the doorway.

"These streets don't belong to you," Antony spat. "They belong to the humans. You've become passive. Do you even kill anymore, or do you just drink their blood and let them go on their merry way? You're pitiful." He hocked a gooey ball of spit onto Jerome's pristine white sneakers.

Jerome stepped nose to nose with Antony. "I'll let that go, for now, but your pudgy ass will pay. You're done. Do you hear me? No more vamps."

"You won't stand in the way of Tavares's work," Antony said. "He'll drive a stake through your dead heart."

Kai stiffened. He grabbed Janie's shoulder. "It's time to go."

She shook her head to argue. "No, finally the truth is coming out. They'd never tell us all of this to our faces. Jerome's too angry to even notice we're here."

Kai's hand slid down to her bicep. He forced her closer to him and whispered in her ear. "Trust me, Jerome knows we're here. We've got to go—now."

"But who's Tavares?"

Anger and hatred creased Kai's hard features. His dark green eyes sharpened into black narrow points. "Not now!"

He launched the thin metal disk into the air. Kai's Harley landed in the middle of the room, splintering the hardwood and knocking an Asian Daychild backward. Kai threw Janie on the bike. The two gangs dispersed faster than Janie could focus, but they were too slow to catch them. They barreled toward the large wooden door. Janie slammed her eyes shut. Her elbows dug into Kai's ribs and she interlaced her fingers around his abs. She clenched her jaw, waiting for the impact of the motorcycle smashing into the wooden door.

Then, cold air pelted her face. She drew in a long, icy breath. Her eyes flew open. They were shooting down Eastern Avenue at mock speed. *How did we get through the door and on the road—and how are we moving so fast?*

The lines of row homes and parked cars smeared into blurs. The forceful blast of air dried out her tear ducts. She closed her eyes again. Rippled waves of flesh threatened to detach from her bones. Janie's skin felt as if it were peeling away from her skeletal structure. Just when she couldn't take the scoring of air slicing her lungs, Kai slid to a stop.

She'd clasped her hands together so tightly, her hands had molded into an inflexible weave. Janie unbraided her sore, stiff fingers. The blood from her split lip had dried, tacking her mouth together. Janie tried to open her mouth and groaned. Her lips tugged at the torn flesh as they separated.

She attempted to slide off the bike, but her stiff bones held her in place. Kai dismounted and turned to face her. With an uncharacteristic look of sympathy, he placed his hands under her arms and gently lifted her off the seat. He held her steady until she found her footing. She forced a thankful smile, her throat too dry to speak.

Inside his house, Kai retrieved a bottle of water from his mini-fridge and joined Janie on his leather couch. "You look at little less green." He unscrewed the cap and handed her the bottle. "Drink this."

Janie took small careful sips. Her insides felt like a dried-out, cracked desert floor. Kai dabbed a wet washcloth on her lip. "You're being gentle," Janie whispered. Even her hushed tone echoed loudly between her ears.

"Don't get used to it." The cotton material caught a piece of loose skin. She drew back from the washcloth. "You look like you've been in a bar fight," he said.

Despite herself, Janie let out a laugh. The expulsion of air shot splinters of pain through her ribcage. She recoiled and turned away from Kai. She peeled up her tank and hoodie to check out the bruise the teenager had left along her ribcage when he'd kicked her. As she suspected, her skin was decorated with swirls of red, indicating she'd have a colorful bruise the next day. Over the redness she noticed tiny white dots bubbling up on her skin, resembling tiny fluid-filled blisters. "Kai—" she gasped.

"What's wrong?" He spun her around. Her eyes widened. She realized her bra was exposed. "It's the demon blood. It seeped through your clothing. You've got to get your clothes off."

"I *am* not," she protested. She yanked her top down.

"It's burning your skin."

"Then I'll remove my jacket." Janie unzipped her hoodie and slid it off, feeling not quite as vulnerable as before, but still vulnerable enough in her black tank. She squirmed. Her flesh burned under her shirt.

Kai looked at her in annoyance from under his blond lashes. "Your skin is burning and you're being modest right now?" He took the hoodie from her hand and wadded it into a ball. "This is trash." He lifted her off the couch and placed her feet on the floor.

"What are you doing with me?" She pushed on his chest.

He held her tighter. "I'm helping you up the steps to the bathroom. You need to take a shower and get that demon blood off your skin."

"I can make it to the bathroom myself." He loosened his hold and she spun away from him. She hadn't forgotten what he'd said to her. *We'll never be that close.* It's not like she had any expectations about their relationship, but hearing him tell her they'd never be friends after all they'd been through over the last few days was hurtful.

He stepped away from her. "As you wish. Towels and soap are in the bathroom."

Janie examined her chest in the bathroom mirror. The tiny white bubbles had turned into oozing blisters. She looked like she'd been attacked by a flesh-eating bacteria. She raised her eyes to examine her face. Her eyeliner and black mascara had bled, deepening her already dark purple eye. Kai was right. She did look like she'd been in a bar fight.

Her bottom lip was swollen and split. She popped it out to assess the injury. It wasn't that bad. She'd had worse. Janie reached up and disentangled the clear plastic band from her hair. Her hair spilled out of the ponytail and streamed down her back. She attempted to comb it with her fingers. Knots stopped the fluid motion of her fingers and jerked at the sensitive hair along her scalp. "Ugh—" she groaned.

In the shower, Janie squeezed Kai's lavender body wash on to a washcloth and gently removed any traces of demon blood. As she drew Kai's clean scent into her lungs, a pleasant ripple coursed through her. *He's one of them.* He was right; they would never be close, at least not as close as she ached for him to be at the present moment, surrounded by his smell and personal products.

After her shower, she wrapped a towel around herself and left the bathroom. She noticed a sweatshirt lying on the floor outside the bathroom door. Janie picked it up and slipped back into the bathroom. She slid her jeans over her legs; they had luckily been spared.

She held her breath and lowered Kai's sweatshirt over her head. She already smelled enough like him after using his body wash. The scent of Kai's clean cotton surrounding her face battered her senses. She searched under his sink for anything to brush her hair. Beside a stack of magazines, she found a long comb. She used it to separate the knots in her hair. She spun around and examined her hair in the mirror. It looked even longer, straighter and darker when wet, splaying out over the hood. Kai's hood—Kai's sweatshirt. *What am I doing?*

Janie found Kai in the kitchen, microwaving a burrito. She could smell the spicy cooked-bean concoction upstairs. As she entered the kitchen, his back faced her. Under the recessed lighting, his white highlights streaked through his golden blond waves. "You know, girls pay good money to have hair like yours," she said.

Kai peered over his shoulder. He already knew she was there. "I can't help it that I'm so pretty." He turned back to the microwave to retrieve his burrito. "You look better, well, minus the eye and your lip."

"Is that supposed to be a compliment?" Janie pulled out one of the two chairs and took a seat at the round table. "How did you get us out of the lair?"

"My motorcycle."

Janie inhaled and exhaled loudly. "Really. Do we have to? I'm tired and sore. Spare me your ambiguous responses, at least for tonight."

"Fine." He joined her at the table. "You'll just ask me again if I don't tell you now." He smirked, a pleasant surprise. She expected more resistance. "I used to be a demon and I was created by a very powerful vampire, so

I have an ability." He extended the burrito to her. She put her hand up, wincing at the thought of any food sliding down her scratchy throat. "I think you know how we got out. What are your thoughts?"

Janie leaned back in the chair. "You're fast, extremely fast. Even your motorcycle is extraordinarily fast. But that doesn't explain how we went through the door without taking it off its hinges, busting it or ourselves into pieces."

"What is a door made of?

"Wood, or metal," she said, wondering where he was going with his questioning. Couldn't he just tell her?

"I mean other than the visible materials that are used to make doors. You've been in high school twice. Didn't you take Chemistry?"

"I've only actually taken one semester of Chemistry, three years ago. I don't have it again until next semester." Janie stared past Kai as if the answer was written on the wall. Her face lit up. She remembered. "Matter."

"Very good," he said. "I can use my speed to manipulate the molecules of an object. Therefore, anything that has mass and volume, or otherwise takes up space, such as the door, I can pass through." Kai rocked back and forth in his chair. "I can break down the electromagnetic force of matter, or something like that," he dismissed.

Janie stared at him blankly.

"The force that holds objects together." He waved a dismissive hand. "Nah, I just sound smart. I'm not one hundred percent sure how my ability works. I just know I can do it."

"So you're saying we literally drove through the door."

"Yup."

"Cool," Janie said. "So how did you first learn you could do that?"

"I assume I could do it as a demon, even though I can't remember any of my truly demonic days. Although I don't think I was a demon for very long." He sighed. "Not remembering my demonic days is probably not a bad thing. Living with what I did as a Daychild is hard enough."

Janie realized this was the most vulnerable she'd ever seen Kai. He'd lowered the wall he'd put up to hide his secrets. And he had a lot of secrets. "Earlier, I wondered how you got into my room. The window was closed," she said.

"I went through your window, just not the way you'd think." His thin lips curled into a sneaky smile.

"How about your life as a human? Do you remember anything?" Janie focused on Kai's eyes, waiting for the twitch, indicating he wasn't going to answer. His green eyes stayed steady and locked on hers.

"Yes. Some of it's hazy, but for the most part I remember my life as a human."

"So you've been eighteen for awhile."

He shrugged. "I'm assuming for at least twenty years."

"We're kind of alike in that way. I've been fourteen, fifteen, sixteen and seventeen twice. I'm still waiting to turn eighteen. I get so close and then, bam—I'm fourteen again. It sucks having a late June birthday and always being the youngest in my class." She scowled. "Senior year, school's out and then we move and start all over again." Janie leaned closer to Kai. "The only good thing is I don't really age until I leave the Seeker life. It buys me more time on earth. . .if I live that long." His stare fell heavily on her. She changed the subject. "Finish your story about your ability."

"When I was Turned," he continued, happier not discussing her death, "I had no idea what I was; let alone what I could do. For the most part I didn't care. The only thing I thought about was where, or from whom, I would get my next meal." He smirked, more out of disbelief than humor. "One day I got in an argument with another one of my kind. He'd taken my kill." Kai paused to explain. "Daychildren frown upon drinking the blood of another's kill." Janie nodded in understanding. "The jerk launched me into a wall without even touching me. He was telekinetic." He placed his finger on his chin. "Bruno, I think that was his name."

Kai rolled his eyes to the ceiling and placed his hands behind his head, rocking back in his chair. "Anyway," he said. "I didn't hit the wall. I went through it and landed in someone's family room. That's when I knew I could use my speed to move through things."

"Have you tried to move through people?"

He grimaced. “No, I’m not a ghost. I mean, I guess I could if I tried, but that’s just creepy.”

Janie covered her nose. “Are you almost done with that burrito? It stinks.”

“Royal Farms—best burritos ever.” He shoveled the remaining portion into his mouth. At least he chewed with his mouth closed. *A Daychild with manners, who knew?*

“You’re not that bad to hang out with when you’re not being all sarcastic and cryptic,” she said.

He placed his hands over his chest as if to say, *“Who me?”*

“You always seem to avoid my questions.” Janie looked off to the side, focusing on the blank white wall. “Oh, yeah, that’s because ‘we’ll never be that close.’ Isn’t that what you said?”

He let out a stunned puff of air. “So that’s why you decided to commit suicide—death by a lair of Daychildren. You really aren’t that smart, are you?”

“If you’re only going to be rude, I’ll leave.” She removed her phone from his sweatshirt pocket to check the time. “It’s getting late anyway. My mom’s going to worry if she notices I’m not in my room.”

Janie stood up. Kai landed in front of her, blocking her path. She stumbled back. “Stop doing that,” she said. “Just because you’re fast doesn’t mean you can jump in front of unsuspecting people.”

“Don’t leave,” he said. She couldn’t read his straight face. He stood so close, unnervingly close, his eyes locked on hers.

"Look, its fine. I'm not mad. I know the limits of our relationship. I didn't expect us to become friends." She moved her gaze to the dark hardwood floor, afraid to meet his intense green eyes. There was something different about the way he regarded her. She wasn't the most intuitive when it came to the opposite sex, let alone the opposite species, but something had changed.

"Friends—" His words seemed to trickle down her skin, causing goose bumps to form along her arms. Her heart raced. She swore she heard his heart beat just as fast. "So that's where this is going, friends?"

She lifted her head. "I know it's never happened before. A Daychild and a Seeker not trying to kill each other, but I'd say we've already broken most of the rules."

"Most," he agreed. He seemed satisfied, an underlying sadness in his tone.

Her breathing quivered. "So, then, it's settled. We're friends."

Kai's focus fell to her mouth, his gaze emitting a longing she couldn't begin to understand. He hesitated. "My heart beats because I'm partly human."

CHAPTER 8

"What?" Janie stepped back from Kai. Her mouth fell open. She quickly closed it. A police siren blared outside his house, first faint, then so loud it could have passed through the kitchen. It faded, leaving the room filled with uncomfortable silence.

"I'm part-human," Kai said again. "You asked me why my heart beats." He fidgeted with the edge of his T-shirt. "You asked. I'm answering your question!"

"I remember," she said softly in an attempt to calm him down. "You said we'd never be close enough for you to tell me."

"I'm telling you now," he snapped. He shook his head. "I'm sorry."

Janie let it go. He'd already said so much. She didn't want to push him. "And your scars?" she asked.

"Human." He traced the scars on his forearm with his forefinger. "When I stopped being a monster and was granted the capacity to feel again."

"And your blood?" she said.

"Red."

They stood in place, staring at each other. Her cell phone rang. Startled back to reality, she pulled it out of her pocket. "It's my mom. I'm sorry. I've got to answer it. She's going to be so pissed that I went into the city."

Kai stepped away from her and headed into the living room without another word.

The ride home was silent. Neither seemed to know what to say. Kai parked in front of Janie's house. She climbed off his bike, still stunned by his confession. Janie removed the helmet from her head and tousled her matted hair with her fingers. "I never thanked you." She handed him the helmet.

"For what?" He placed it on the back of his bike.

"Following me to the lair." She smiled.

He gripped the handlebars tightly. "I didn't follow you."

Her brows rose. She didn't believe him.

"Okay, fine. I followed you," he said. "But only because I knew you'd go looking for trouble. You're reckless. You have a habit of jumping in over your head."

"True," she agreed.

He reached into a hidden compartment, retrieved her dagger and handed it to her. "You might need this."

She placed it in her boot. "So, I'll see you later?" He didn't say anything. She ran her fingers along the edge of his bike. The black and chrome shone under a single lamp post. "It's been interesting." Janie pushed her hands into the sweatshirt's pockets. It was cold, but that wasn't the reason she shivered.

"Janie—with you, life is always interesting," he said. "I never know what you're going to do next." He balanced on his bike and drifted backward. He smiled. "You keep me on my toes, Janie Grey." The bike's engine roared to life. "Later." He nodded and took off in a flash.

Janie sat with her back against the sofa cushion, clutching a throw pillow in her arms. Isabelle glared at her. She couldn't seem to do anything right lately. "Does it really matter why Kai was with me at the lair tonight? If you'd just listen to me instead of yelling at me, I could tell you what we learned," Janie said.

Isabelle paced the living room. Abram sat in the armchair wearing his usual attire, a tan suit. With his hands clasped together, he tapped one brown dress shoe on the floor. Creases lined his forehead. He refused to look at her.

"I see we're getting nowhere with this conversation," Isabelle said. "It's now midnight. I can't discuss *him* anymore. Just tell us what you learned tonight." She marched back and forth. Her hair flopped around on top of her head. Dark circles framed her eyes and her face was gaunt.

"Finally we can discuss something of meaning." Janie huffed. "Apparently, Daychildren are killing vampires, and the vampires aren't happy about it." She played with the fringe along the edge of the pillow, focusing on the small pieces of string and not her angry mother's stare. Her face flushed. They trusted her to do her job, but didn't trust her to follow her instincts—about fighting, or Kai.

"What would be the purpose of killing vampires?" Isabelle said, slicing through Janie's thoughts.

Unusually silent, Abram spoke for the first time since they started the conversation. Her father figure since her father's death, he wasn't usually so passive. When she was seven and wanted to play in the street, he'd swept her off the ground and moved her to the grass, lecturing her about getting hit by a car. In junior high, the beginning of Seeker training, she wanted to go out on her own and test out a new kick she'd learned. Isabelle caught her climbing out of her second-floor bedroom window, so Abram refused to train her for a week.

He'd taught her everything she knew about Seeking. He had taught her every lesson she had learned. Only none of the lessons seemed to apply to Kai. He was the exception to every rule. It frustrated her that everything she'd learned about the "undead" wasn't necessarily true; there were gray areas. It also frustrated her that she was relieved Kai wasn't like the rest of them. She enjoyed having him around. He definitely made life interesting. And as much as she tried to deny her feelings, they were there.

"According to the Chapter, Daychildren need a vampire's pure venom to create their own," Abram said. "Their venom isn't pure enough since they're half-breeds. That's why they're killing vampires. They need the venom from their fangs." He kept tapping his shoe on the floor. "They need something else as well, something from the demonic world. We aren't sure what it is yet. Leo is looking into it."

Isabelle twisted her ponytail around her fingers. "So you're saying Daychildren need vampires in order to create more of their own kind, but the vampire community isn't willing to just hand them their venom." She finally stopped pacing and took a seat at the coffee table.

Janie held up her hand. "Don't get mad at me for using *his* name again, but Kai said the vamps have had to clean up after the Daychildren because they are wild and uncontrollable. The vampires are trying to blend into human society, even become accepted, but they can't while Daychildren are killing everyone they come across." She looked over to Abram, who looked distracted, and continued. "Abram's right. It seems as though Daychildren are killing vampires in order to obtain their pure venom. The vamp gang leader told the lair leader to stop killing vamps. There is a definite turf war going on. The gangs don't see eye to eye."

"Although I despise the source," Abram said through gritted teeth. "He's right, Isabelle. The vampires we used to kill are changing, evolving in some way, and Daychildren are the new babies, a youthful demonic species who only live to kill. They have no intention of blending into the human world. It's not like when we were Seeking. There were few of them then. Now that they don't need actual demons, their race is multiplying quickly."

"Antony threatened Jerome with a name—Tavares," Janie said. She turned to Abram. "Do you know who he is?"

Abram met her stare. She could see the disappointment in his eyes. It stung. "Unfortunately." He stroked his brow with his fingertips. "The Chapter wasn't aware he was still in charge. He's been quiet for years. He was the vampire king when your mother and I were active Seekers; the leader of the head vampires, or den leaders, as they call themselves." Abram's fingertips lowered to his eyes. He rubbed them in silence. The stress of the recent events had clearly gotten to him, although Janie still felt it was something more. "He's pure evil. It wouldn't surprise me if he's behind all of this," he continued. "There were rumors that Tavares was relieved of his throne, but who knows. The vampire community isn't exactly predictable."

Janie leaned forward. "What can I do? I can't just sit around and let Antony get away with this. The missing teenager from Towson High—" Janie turned to her mother. "Remember the student we saw on the news? I saw him tonight. They Turned him." She raised her shirt to expose the bruise on her ribcage. "He did this to me. Antony is targeting high school kids. That's why they showed up at the bonfire. They Turned one of Matt's friends, too, a wrestler. Unfortunately, Kai and I had to kill him. I've got to do something to stop this. I refuse to let Antony get away with this."

Abram lurched forward. Hate fumed from his blue eyes, making them appear an ashen gray. "Janie

Marissa Grey—never speak *his* name again. You heard your mother. You are *not* to see *him* again!"

"Abram—" Isabelle gasped.

He stood, smoothed his dress pants and took in a few meditative breaths. "I've got to report to the Chapter. See if Leo's found out anything. I'll come by tomorrow," he said more calmly. Abram kissed Isabelle on the forehead. He glanced over at Janie, disappointment on his brow. "Stay away from the city. There is nothing you can do right now. Wait for my instructions. And for God's sake, stay away from *him*."

After Abram left, Janie excused herself from the living room. She stomped up the steps to her room and threw her bedroom door open, striking Kai. He blocked the door with his forearm.

"Ah!" Her voice lowered to a whisper. "What are you doing here? You scared me." She hurried into her room and closed the door behind her.

"You're a Seeker, you don't get scared," he said. He walked farther into her bedroom and pivoted around on one foot to face her. "I don't understand you. You'll go into the city and knock on the door of a known Daychild lair the night after you were poisoned by a demon splint, but you freak out when I show up in your room."

She squinted. "Usually when I enter my room I don't open the door into guys who can run through bedroom walls, or windows, or however you got in here." Out of breath, she stopped waving her hands in the air. "I don't usually have to wonder if something undead is creeping around my room, so I'm not on guard."

"Undead," he said with a scowl.

Janie realized her words had come out sharper than intended. "Sorry. I didn't mean that. I'm just upset with my Mom and Abram. They're being so closed-minded." Janie shook her head and set her stare back on Kai. "Is there a reason you're here? Did something happen?"

"You said you'd see me later; it's later." He smiled, immediately making Janie forgive him for lurking like a stalker in her bedroom.

"We must be friends. Otherwise, you wouldn't hang around so much," Janie said. She brushed past him.

"Are we still friends?" He turned in her direction, leaning up against the wall with his hand in his pocket. His blond hair fell into his eyes.

"Why would you ask me that?" She plopped down on her bed.

Kai moved his shoulders around uneasily against the wall. "Your conversation downstairs. I was included in over seventy-five percent of it, and most of what was said about me," he paused, removing his hand from his pocket to raise his finger, "no, let me correct—*all* of it, wasn't good."

"They don't know you like I do. All they see is a Daychild. They don't see your human side."

Kai leaned forward, meeting Janie's eyes. His straight, even features could have been etched from stone. "Have you ever thought that it could be more complicated than that?" he said sharply. "That their hatred for me is ingrained in them? That they could have a good reason for despising me?" He crossed the room and clutched her arms. "Have you?" His voice deepened. She didn't back down.

Janie straightened her spine, squaring her shoulders to meet his intensity. “Why would they? They don’t even know you. All they know is what I knew the first time I saw you—you’re a Daychild, but you’re different from the others. Otherwise, we wouldn’t be having this conversation. You’d be dead. I usually kill, then analyze later.”

“I wouldn’t be so sure about that.” His smile returned, but a foreboding energy still loomed. He released his grip.

Janie’s phone rang. Kai rolled his shoulder, settling into an annoyed stance. He focused on the ceiling. “Does it ever stop ringing?”

She held her phone out. “It’s Matt. I should take this.”

“Go ahead.” He slid his hand back into his pocket and stared out the window.

“Hey, you made it home,” she said to Matt.

“Yeah, sorry I didn’t call you today. I didn’t really know what to say after my behavior this morning.” Kai rolled his eyes, apparently listening in on the conversation with his heightened sense of hearing. He still hadn’t turned to look at her, but she could see the side of his tight jaw.

“You know it’s one in the morning?” Janie said.

Janie heard a pause on the other end of the phone. “Did I wake you?” Matt said. “I couldn’t sleep. Albania said it might be a side effect of the poison.”

Kai had fully turned his back on her. She decided to hurry along the conversation. “No, I’m awake. It’s cool.

Well, I'm glad you made it home okay. Try to get some sleep. I'll see you on Monday."

"Hey, Janie," Matt said, catching her before she hung up. "Would you mind if I came by tomorrow? There's something I want to ask you in person."

Kai spun around and shot Janie another look. He scanned the walls of her room. Not that there was much to look at—a 1980s *The Lost Boys* movie poster and a sketch of James Dean she'd bought in Manhattan during a Seeker convention.

She stuttered, "S—sure. I'll be home most of the day. I'm going over to Ava's to study for an Algebra test, but other than that I'll be here."

"I'll come by around noon, if that's okay?"

"Yeah, it's good. See you then. Bye." She hung up quickly.

Kai didn't move from the window. "So he's coming by to ask you something. Do you know what it is?" he said flatly, eyeing her.

"How would I know?" She folded her arms in front of her.

"He's *your* boyfriend."

"He's *not* my boyfriend. Can we please *not* discuss Matt? You get all weird."

"Weird?" He spun around to face her again.

Janie stood to confront him. "Yes, weird. You look at me in this strange way. I can't tell what you're thinking, but I don't think it's good."

"It's not your business what I'm thinking." He took a step closer to her.

"You get angry with me. Like now."

"Can't you see, Janie, I'm not angry with you. It has nothing to do with anger." He stared down at the carpet. She crossed the distance and lifted his chin with her finger, forcing him to look at her.

"Then what does it have to do with?"

"Your mom's coming. I'll be back." Janie blinked and he disappeared.

Isabelle knocked on the door. "Janie, can I come in?" Her voice sounded calmer.

Janie scrambled onto her bed and grabbed her book from her nightstand, flipping it open to the bookmarked page. She scanned the page. "Come in."

The lines across Isabelle's forehead had smoothed and Janie noticed she'd neatly placed her hair into a loose bun. "I'd like to talk with you without Abram around."

"Sure." Janie crossed her legs and set her book beside her. "Have a seat. But I don't want to discuss Kai anymore."

Isabelle gave her a dubious look. "We'll see." She lovingly placed her hand on Janie's leg. "I'm just worried about you. It's a mother's job."

Janie sighed. "I don't get it. There's a species of vampire out there using high school kids to multiply their demonic race, and you're concerned about a friend of mine." She folded her arms in front of her, legs crisscrossed. "It sucks."

"Janie, I've been where you are. It wasn't that long ago that I had to deal with the same issues you're dealing with, but everything isn't black and white."

I'm realizing that.

"Kai and I are just friends. He's helping me investigate what's happening among the undead community. That's it," she snapped. She realized her blood pressure had risen to an unhealthy level. She drew in a breath to calm herself.

"As much as Abram might think it's possible, I know I can't keep you from seeing Kai while you're in the city." Isabella's eyes tightened. "This doesn't mean I condone your relationship."

Janie interrupted. "I told you. We don't have a relationship—we are *just* friends."

Isabelle held up her hand, squelching Janie's words. "Okay. Your friendship, whatever you are calling it. Just be careful. He's not like you. As much as he may profess to be, he's not," she told Janie, her tone sharp.

"Fine, Mom, I'll be careful. Just don't tell Abram. He seems really angry. I've never seen him this way."

"He has his reasons. Abram will share them when he's ready. He doesn't deal with things the same way you and I do." Isabelle hung her head. She paused, reluctant to finish her thoughts. After a few moments of silence, she returned to Janie's eyes, a mirror of her own. "Abram didn't like your father at first. I suppose he had his own reasons for those feelings as well. But he grew to love your father. They became very close friends."

Janie sat in silence, staring at her mother, shocked by this new information. Isabelle never wanted to talk about Connor. The only tangible memory of him she'd taken with her during every move was the picture in the living room. All Janie had to remember her father by was a single picture in a plain wooden frame and distant childhood memories that faded as the years passed.

Isabelle continued, her words and tone more severe. “I’m not comparing Connor to Kai. Connor was a human, and Kai is something entirely different. Remember—he is part demon, which means he is also partly evil.”

“He’s not evil.” Janie sat up straight.

“Janie, I already told you. I’m not going to tie you to your bed so that you can never see him again. I’m just warning you to be careful. I’m still your mother.” She pointed a long slender finger at Janie.

“Fine.” Janie sank into a slouch. “I’ll be careful.”

Isabelle stood to leave.

“Mom—wait. I have something else to ask you. I’m afraid this thing with Matt has gotten worse.” Janie exhaled loudly. “He seems a little, for lack of a better word, ‘into’ me.”

Isabelle shrugged. “He’s a high school boy, why shouldn’t he like you?”

“Do you remember what you told me a few days ago? You said Matt was a problem, other than the problem of him possibly outing me to the whole school. You even brought up Dad.”

She waved her hand dismissively. “I talked to Abram. I’m sure everything’s fine.”

“Mom—” Janie knew she was hiding something. “Tell me what you know.”

Isabelle’s hands found her hips. “It rarely happens anymore. Humans are more aware than they used to be. It’s not needed.” Janie waited impatiently for her to continue. Isabelle let out a puff of air. “Okay, I feared Matt may have been Imprinted.”

“What does that mean?” Janie clutched her comforter in her fists. Whatever “Imprinted” was, it didn’t sound good. She suddenly pictured Matt as a baby duckling, a disturbing image she quickly dismissed.

“It’s when a human falls in love with a Seeker because she has saved his life. It was meant to ensure secrecy back when no one knew vampires existed. If a human were in love with the Seeker, he would never tell anyone about the Seeker’s gift or about the vampire that attacked him. He forms an unwavering loyalty to the Seeker who saved him. Often, this comes out as a form of love.”

“Are you saying Matt’s in love with me?” Janie’s mouth hung open. She didn’t even know what to say. *The Junior Prom King, the star wrestler, the most popular guy in school—he’s in love with me.*

Isabelle sounded upset. “That’s exactly why I didn’t want to tell you. I’m not saying that at all. He probably just likes you. It’s a normal teenage crush. Teenage love can be intense.” Isabelle moved over to Janie and retrieved her inhaler out of her nightstand drawer. “You look like you might need this. Breathe, will you?”

“I’m okay.” Janie flung her hand in the air, signaling she didn’t need her inhaler and stared at Jason Patric on her *The Lost Boys* poster. “Let’s just say you’re wrong. How do I stop it?” Janie returned to her mother’s warm brown eyes, hoping desperately for an antidote.

Isabelle frowned. “You can’t. He’ll love you forever, or at least until he can find someone else to settle for, unless you fall in love with him, too.”

Janie choked. “I’m not in love with Matt Baker. Besides, I’d have to kill a human if that happened.” Isabelle stared at Janie, clearly expecting an explanation.

“Molly Hall. She’d never let it happen, and I’d be forced to kill her.”

“Janie.” Isabelle furrowed her brow. “That’s not how you should be using your strength. I didn’t raise you that way.”

“I’m just kidding, Mom. I’d only hurt her.” Isabelle’s brow didn’t straighten. “A little.”

“Whatever you do, be nice to that boy. Imprinted or not, the poor thing was attacked by the undead twice.”

“How will I know if he just likes me or *really* likes me?”

Isabelle let out a reminiscent laugh. “You’ll know. He won’t leave you alone. And he may profess his love.” Isabelle’s features straightened. “I’m not trying to make light of this. It can have serious consequences on the human Imprint. Seekers can destroy Imprints without lifting a finger.” She paused. “But as I said before, it’s most likely just a teenage crush.”

Great! Janie shook her head. *What have I done?* Most girls would dream of Imprinting the most popular boy in school. Janie just wanted to bury her head in the sand.

Isabelle gave Janie a reassuring tap on the knee. "You'll figure it out. Get some sleep," she said. "It's late." She smiled and shut the door behind her.

"You imprinted him!" The deep boom of Kai's voice made Janie jump off her mattress.

"Kai," she said. "Stop doing that. Can't you knock or something?"

Kai whirled over to the side of her bed. "Answer my question. Did. You. Imprint. Matt?" He spoke slowly, enunciating every word.

"No, I don't know, maybe." She shook her head, confused by his sudden anger and feeling slightly frightened by his temper.

"That's just great." He removed a small blade from his belt and flung it to the opposite side of the room. The blade's tip lodged in her closet door.

Janie pulled her down pillow in front of her as if a pile of feathers could protect her from an enraged Daychild. "What do you care? You didn't Imprint him!" *How dare he?*

"That's a good thing, since I'm not into dudes."

"Only witches," she mumbled.

His head shot up. "Are you jealous?" he said.

"No." She leaned back against her headboard and swallowed deeply. His outburst felt like an interrogation. All they were missing was the metal desk, solitary room and harsh bright lights.

"I'm not with Albania. At least not anymore," he said more calmly.

"So you were?" Janie pushed, then realized maybe she didn't want to know the answer.

"Briefly. We realized we were better as friends." He seemed slightly calmer since they weren't discussing Matt.

"Did you sleep with her?" she said. He didn't answer. Janie wanted to take her question back. "You're right; it's none of my business."

Kai flopped down on to her bed. He hunched over his legs with his elbows resting on his knees. A chunk of white highlight fell into his face, obstructing his profile.

Janie checked her clock. She was tired. It had been an exhausting day. "It's late. You should go."

He lifted his head. The hard lines around his face had dissipated. "Or, I could stay?"

CHAPTER 9

Janie reminded herself to blink. *He wants to stay over?*

"I'm not going to try anything," he said. "Besides, you're already spoken for."

"Shut up. I am not." She smacked him in the arm with her pillow. "Where are you going to sleep?"

"You have a queen-size bed." He glanced over at the empty spot next to her.

"You want to sleep *with* me?" She stifled the urge to hit him again with her pillow. *Was he serious?*

His sarcastic guard lifted. His features appeared softer, unprotected, exposing the innately human side of himself. "Is it a problem?"

"No." She tried to seem indifferent. She had every reason to feel nervous, frightened in a way. Their relationship had changed. Her feelings for him were evolving into something completely foreign to her. "I have to get changed for bed." As Janie slid off the bed to retrieve a T-shirt and flannel pajama bottoms from her dresser, her eyes caught his. She quickly looked away, embarrassed.

"Go ahead—change." His sarcastic smile returned.

"Not right here—in the bathroom." Her cheeks flushed. She wanted to cower behind a very tall object.

"I'll be right here when you get back," he told her, masking a smile. She stepped into the hallway and peered around the door. Unsteadily, she stumbled and closed the door behind her.

When Janie returned to her room, Kai lay on her spare pillow with his arm propped behind his head. A lump formed at the base of her throat. *It's simple, just go lie down on your side of the bed like you usually do.* She closed her bedroom door, swallowed and took hesitant steps toward the bed. His fitted tee exposed every hard line on his muscular chest. His legs were crossed and he'd removed his shoes. He looked so comfortable. She wished she felt the same.

"Nice PJ's," he said.

"What were you expecting, Victoria's Secret?" She peered down at her cotton and flannel ensemble.

"Maybe a little lace, but I guess the flannel will do." He laughed.

"I thought this sleeping situation was platonic. Anyway, I don't do lace." She slid under her covers. He lay on top of them, pulling the comforter tight against one side of her body. She squirmed to loosen the bedding.

"Even black lace?" he said after a quiet pause.

"Even black lace," she repeated.

Janie extended her arms over the top of her comforter so they weren't constricted under the covers. She supported her head on her thick down pillow and peeked out of the corner of her eye. Kai lay about a foot away. Nothing on him moved. Not even the rise and fall of his chest. He didn't need air to live.

"Are you still awake?" she said.

"Yes, your ceiling is glowing. It's kind of distracting."

Janie focused on the collage of plastic glow-in-the-dark stars spaced sporadically over her ceiling, ranging from tiny to large yellowish-green glowing shapes. "Then close your eyes," she said flatly.

"I guess it's better than focusing on your corny poster. That movie was lame."

"*The Lost Boys* is an eighties classic." Nobody messed with her 80s movies.

"You're a Seeker. What are you doing hanging vampire movie posters on your wall?"

"Coming from someone who has nothing on his walls." She became serious. "Tell me about your family." Janie rolled over to her side. Kai peered down at her.

"Years ago, I'm not quite sure how long, at least twenty, I lived in Tucson with my parents and golden retriever, Max. The last time I saw them was my senior year in high school. I went into downtown Tucson with a few of my friends, and none of us made it home that day—" his voice trailed. Her night light created an eerie shadow around his face. His eyes appeared darker.

"Do you miss your parents?" she said.

"Of course, but I know I can never go back. I'm not the son they loved anymore. I've spent the last fifteen years thinking about what I would say to them if I ever got the opportunity to see them again. They are much older now, retired I'm sure. It doesn't matter. I can't even remember the exact year I became a demon."

"There are ways of finding out. Have you thought about looking into your high school records, or old newspaper articles about your disappearance? You can get just about anything online now. I could help you." Janie reached out to touch his arm. He flinched, then relaxed. A warm smile crossed his face.

"Fifteen years ago I made the conscious choice to never go back, that my life would start over fresh from that point on. It was the only way I could make peace with what I'd done."

"What exactly happened fifteen years ago?" Janie traced the scars on his forearm with her fingers. His face tightened. She wondered how long it had been since someone had really cared about him, and showed it. He started to speak, but only a breath squeaked out before his voice broke.

"It's okay," she whispered. "You're safe with me."

He nodded. His features relaxed. "I was very close to death. Albania took pity on me. She always says she saw something special in me, that I wasn't like the others." His lips formed a soft smile. "She brought me back to her apartment and healed me. After an agonizing twenty-four hours, I was no longer a monster." He touched his heart, where the crisscross scar hid under his shirt. "She gave me a new human heart that beat human blood through my veins. I kept my ability, but that was all that was left of the demon inside of me. She removed the fallen angel who had taken over my soul so many years earlier." He stroked the hand Janie had rested on his scarred forearm. "She couldn't do anything about the vampire part of me. I still have fangs full of venom, and I only breathe out of habit."

"Can I see your fangs?" Janie removed her hand from his and touched his mouth. His lips parted. She ran her finger over his teeth. They were smooth, like hers.

"They only come out when I'm angry or hungry."

"Is it hard. . .being different?"

He paused. Janie waited patiently. "I've lived in this new body for fifteen years with the knowledge of everything I'd done as a Daychild."

Fear returned to his voice; it shook as he spoke, frightening Janie. He reached over and gripped her hand. His eyes appeared black in the darkness and pierced straight through her. "Trust me, if you knew what I've done, you wouldn't be next to me right now. You wouldn't be friends with me. You would've made sure you killed me the first time we met."

Kai shot up in bed, listening for something Janie's human ears couldn't hear. Her Seeker sense set in and Janie felt the vampire's presence.

There was a rap at her window.

"Stay here," Kai said. He extended his arm over Janie so she couldn't move. "Don't worry, he can't come in uninvited."

"Jerome, I'll stake you faster than you can blink," Kai said sharply, glaring at the ghetto vamp.

Janie hurried to her feet and sprinted over to the window. "I thought I told you I'd handle this." Kai glared at her.

"It's my window." She drew the curtain back.

"Janie, invite me in," Jerome said.

"Forget it. What do you want?" Kai said, pulling the curtain out of Janie's hands and blocking her view of Jerome. "Go back over to the bed. I'll deal with him."

"I can answer him myself." Janie yanked the curtain back and unlocked the window to open it. Jerome stood on the shingled roof below her window, sporting the usual red bandana, tank top and gold chains.

"Janie, invite me in," he said again.

She cast him an icy stare. How dare he come to her window in the wee hours of the morning? Then she remembered—he's a vampire. When else would he visit? He slept during the day and would burst into a pile of ashes in the sunlight. She answered him. "Forget it. What do you want, Jerome?"

"That's what *he* said." Jerome eyed Kai.

Kai smirked.

"I agree with him. I'm not inviting you in," Janie said. "Have you forgotten? I'm a Seeker. Why would I invite a vampire into my home?"

"Seriously, do you think I'd travel all the way to the 'burbs to stand outside your window all night if it weren't important?"

Janie turned to Kai. He shook his head vehemently, indicating the answer was still "no." He'd never let Jerome have access to her home.

She grumbled to Kai, "Why don't we go outside, then. I've got stakes."

He didn't even have to contemplate his answer. "No!"

Jerome rustled outside the window. "You don't need stakes. I just wanna talk."

Janie's eyes swung back over to Jerome. "Okay, Jerome. We'll be out in a sec." Janie let the curtain fall, obstructing her view of the ghetto vamp leader.

Kai spun her around to face him. "I'll go," he said. He moved over to her bed and slipped on his shoes.

"So will I." Janie stomped over to her closet.

Kai moved next to her and hovered over her as she laced her shoes. "We don't know how many are out there. It could be an ambush," he argued.

"So I'm going to let you walk into a possible ambush, alone." She finished tying her laces and rose to meet his indignant stance. Without leaving his eyes, she unhinged her backpack from a hook in her closet and slung the strap over her shoulder.

The veins in his neck throbbed and he forced himself to speak calmly. "We need to rethink this."

Janie spoke through tight lips, afraid if she opened her mouth any wider her mom would here her yelling at Kai. "I'm a Seeker. I don't back down. What's your excuse for being so scared?" Janie pushed by him and marched to her bedroom door. He didn't attempt to restrain her or follow. She spun around. "Well, are you coming?"

He didn't move from his place in front of the closet. "Don't you see, this isn't about me? I don't care what happens to me."

"We're in this together, as a team," Janie said. "I don't need a protector." She reached for the doorknob, sick of arguing. He was being ridiculous. *And what's with the sudden act of chivalry?*

Kai rolled his eyes. "Fine, we'll both go, but we're not going out the door. I don't need to take the chance of your mother catching me in your house."

Janie paused. Was she really going to? *Yes, I am.* She hurried over to him. Scared excitement coursed through her.

"Are you ready?" He flipped her up into his arms. "You might want to close your eyes."

She clasped her arms around his neck. Her heart rate pedaled toward an alarming level. She dipped her head into his chest. "Wait—"

He huffed. "What? It's not like we haven't done it before."

"But I didn't know. This is different. I'm fully aware of what we're about to do. Sorry if running through walls isn't exactly standard for me. I'm fully human, remember?"

He stared at her. "Are you finished rambling?"

She tightened her grip. "Okay, go—"

He took three steps back and sprinted forward. Like on the motorcycle, she felt cold air prickle her face in their descent. When his boots hit the earth, she opened her eyes. He placed her in the grass and she righted herself, like it was no big thing. *Cool.*

Kai unzipped the backpack and removed four stakes. He handed two to Janie. "Just in case."

Jerome emerged from the side of the house with the clatter of gold chains and a gangsta swagger. His jeans rode low as he boosted his ego with an urban strut, an attempt to hide his vulnerability through a homeboy façade. He seemed to be the only gang banger around. Janie eased her fighting stance, dropping the stakes to her side.

"We're here. Now tell us why you came," Kai said. He stepped closer to Jerome.

"How about we first lose the stakes? I'm rollin' solo tonight." He raised his arms. "Like I said, I just wanna talk."

Janie slid her backpack off her shoulder. She shoved the stakes through an opening. Kai hesitated, but handed his to Janie. She noticed he still had one shoved in his waistband. She dropped the bag on the grass and displayed her palms. "No weapons. Let's hear it."

"I'm here to offer help. We want the same thing—to stop Antony," Jerome said.

"Go on," Kai said.

"They're killing vamps and jacking up our lifestyle." He cocked his head. "And I hate that tubby bitch. If you want help taking Antony out, we're your vamps."

"So we can count on you to help us when the time comes?" Janie said.

Kai leaned into Janie and whispered in her ear. "There will be a price."

Jerome flashed a smile. "He's right, Seeker. We do have a few minor requests before we agree to help."

"I thought you wanted Antony dead and Daychildren to stop killing vamps," Janie said.

Jerome brought his hand to his chin. "Well, Miss Seeker, you know, it sounds all fair when you say it like that, but I know you need us more than we need you. You aren't gonna take 'em down without my crew. They have the big dog behind them."

"Tavares—" The name sounded like acid rolling off Kai's tongue. His shoulders squared and he swallowed back a repugnant lump in his throat.

"You're right, my man. Tavares isn't gonna be happy if we wipe out his Baltimore crew."

"What do you want in return for your help?" Kai said.

"Her." He pointed to Janie.

Kai flew across the patch of grass, stake in hand, ready to take out Jerome. "No deal!" His hand shook. He pressed the stake against Jerome's chest.

"What do you need from me?" Janie said.

Kai shot her a rage-filled look. "No, Janie. You can't trust him." Janie tensed. It was the first time she'd seen Kai's fangs.

Jerome focused on the stake crushing into his chest. "Man, back off. I didn't threaten your girlfriend. I just need her to do somethin' for me." Jerome barred his fangs. A low growl emerged from his chest. "If you kill me, no one's gonna help you. Those teenagers are gonna keep gettin' Turned."

"Kai, get off him. He has a point. This is too big for just the two of us, and so far the Chapter hasn't been any help." Janie took a step forward, extending her arm to Kai. "Please, Kai. Let him go."

With hardened features and a glare that could kill, Kai flipped the stake into his belt and stepped away from Jerome.

"Why is Antony targeting teenagers?" Janie said.

"Do we have a deal?" Jerome persisted.

"I'm not making any deals until I know all of the details. Now tell me, why is he targeting teenagers?" Janie joined Kai.

"In order for Antony to Turn a human, he needs males with high levels of testosterone and endurance," he said. "Teenage boys have the most of both, especially the ones who have the endurance to play sports. That doesn't mean it will work every time. Some boys will just drop dead if their bodies aren't strong enough to Turn, but Antony figured out young male athletes are the strongest humans possible to survive the Turn."

Janie thought about the teenagers who had been attacked. Matt and Billy were wrestlers, and the boy who disappeared from his neighborhood had gone out to play basketball. All three guys were athletes. "What demonic component are they using?" Janie said.

"Lost souls. I've seen them. Antony had one in a glass container the night of that party you were at. That's some freaky shit." He grimaced.

"So you're saying in order for a human to be Turned into a Daychild, Antony needs an athletic teenage boy, a lost soul, and pure vampire venom," Kai said.

"You got it." Jerome's eyes fell on Janie. "Now it's your turn."

"What do you need from me?" she said.

"Antony has something of mine. I want it back and you're gonna get it for me."

"I'll get it for you." Kai inflated his chest as if to show Jerome that he'd be a better choice for the job.

"No, no, no—that's not gonna work. You see, that's no fun for me. I want to see her do it, and if she makes it out alive, I get what I need and so do you—we take out Antony, no more teenagers get jacked." Jerome set his dark gaze on Kai. "You see, my man, it's kind of a love thing. I killed Antony's girl last night, so he took mine. I figure, Miss Seeker gets my girl back, then you'll get your girl back. Everything works out."

"I'll do it," Janie said. She thought about the beautiful young Hispanic girl, Veronica, whom Jerome had killed. She remembered sensing anger and pain in Antony's voice, but she had no idea Veronica was Antony's girlfriend. "What is your girlfriend's name?"

"You don't have to do this. We can find another way without using the vamps." Kai placed his hand on the dip of her back and guided her to him. She inhaled the scent of clean sweat and lavender. She realized then that this was part of his human anatomy. That's why he smelled human and not like filth and decay. Wavy golden strands wisped over his furrowed brows. "You can't trust that he will keep his word, *if* you make it out alive."

"I forgot one thing," Jerome added, slicing through Kai's words. Janie rotated out of Kai's hold and set her gaze back on Jerome's cold black stare, seeing straight through his faux glam. "In the city, we vamps are a gang. We take sides. We don't see things neutrally," he snarled. "And her name is Tanya," he spat out.

Jerome switched his attention to Kai. Kai's nostrils flared and a feral growl reverberated through his chest. Janie had no doubt he wanted to tear the gang banger to pieces.

"If your girl doesn't get Tanya back, we'll choose a side, and it won't be yours. We'll offer up our venom without a fight. You're either with us or you're against us. What will it be?"

"With you," Janie said.

Kai protested.

Janie held up her hand. "I'll do it. I'll get Tanya back for you."

"She could already be dead," Kai said.

Jerome cracked his jaw. "She's not dead. I'd feel it. We're connected that way."

"Well, then, it's settled. We have a deal," Janie said.

"Good. I'll meet you back here at midnight. You have my girl and we have a deal." Jerome kissed two fingers and stuck them in the air, flashing a peace sign, and left.

Kai leaned into her.

She placed her hands on his chest. "You go back through the wall. I'm going in through the front. I need a glass of water and an aspirin. Suddenly I have a migraine headache."

"How will you get in? The door's locked." He looked at the house. The only room lit was Janie's.

Janie pointed. “Spare key, under the fake rock in the garden.”

Kai kicked at the ground, playing with the grass under his shoe. “Look, I’m going to go. Spending the night wasn’t the best idea. It probably breaks some of the friendship rules.”

Janie nodded. “Then I’ll see you after I get Tanya.”

“I’ll meet you outside the lair,” he corrected.

“You can’t. You have to stay far away, no matter what.” Kai didn’t speak. Janie spoke louder. “Do you hear me? No matter what. I’ll see you at midnight—here.”

Dark circles rimmed his eyes. He traced her skin with his finger, from the base of her neck to her cheek and curled a loose piece of her hair around his finger. He gently tucked it behind her ear. “Please be careful.”

“I’ll be better planned this time,” she assured him. His lush green stare stayed on her face.

“Maybe I should come by beforehand so we can strategize.”

“Kai—I’ll be fine. This isn’t the first time I’ve confronted a gang of them. I’ll admit, I didn’t do the best job planning my attack last night, but this time I’ll be prepared. I know what I’m walking into. Besides, we already took out a few of them.” She wasn’t used to having to explain herself to anyone but Abram. Even then, she made most of the Seeker decisions on her own.

Janie touched the scar on Kai’s chest. He closed his hand around hers. She let her eyelids fall and focused on his heartbeat under her palm. With her eyes closed and lost in the rhythm of his heartbeat, she felt his lips graze her forehead, her cheek and slide to the corner of her mouth.

She pulled back, a quiver in her voice. "I should go." She wanted to burst into tears, but had no idea why. She bit back the urge to release the floodgates. She'd save that for her pillow. She refused to let him see her weak. Besides, love got people killed. There wasn't any emotion worth risking the pain of loss. She knew that as long as she kept people at a distance, she couldn't get hurt. *It's not worth the risk.*

Kai's lips parted. "Good night, Janie." He seemed as unsure as she was about what had just happened.

The motorcycle roared to top volume. He turned back once to look at her and sped off, disappearing into the blackness. She didn't even care that he'd probably woken the entire neighborhood, even her mother. She was too angry with herself for letting herself fall.

CHAPTER 10

Janie woke to the sun filtering through her light curtains. Her comforter wrapped around her like a burrito. With her arms and legs pinned to her side, she figured she'd slept restlessly. She twisted out of the thick cotton material, lifted her body upright and stretched her arms over her head. The neon numbers on her clock caught her attention. She leapt from bed, realizing Matt would be there in a half hour. She remembered she'd told him noon would be a good time. Janie hadn't anticipated staying up until the crack of dawn talking with Kai and Jerome.

As the warm water ran over her head in the shower, she replayed the events of the evening. It turned out Kai was partly human. This explained his eyes, his heartbeat, his scars, his smell and most importantly, his soul. Janie squeezed her raspberry almond-scented shampoo into her hand and ran it through her hair, massaging her scalp with the soapy bubbles as if that would help process everything she'd just learned more quickly. *Unbelievable. Kai isn't a demon. He's part human. He's loveable, if I was capable of loving. At least my instincts weren't wrong.*

He'd been healed by a witch. The demon inside of him had expunged, leaving him both vampire and human. Albania had taken pity on a dying Daychild. She'd seen something special within him, brought back his humanity and taught him to live among human society again. Janie wondered how tortured he must be, living with the guilt of being a monster for so many years. The human scars were proof of the suffering he'd endured. No matter how many Daychildren he killed, nothing would fill the void created after years of living with the knowledge of the people he had murdered.

Janie wondered if Kai ever wished Albania would have left him to suffer and die. She shuddered at the thought. She'd lived without him for so long. Now that he was in her life, she didn't want to lose him. But she had to keep her feelings under control. *Friends, we are just friends.*

She turned off the warm water and wrapped her towel around her. *What have I done? Maybe Kai was right. But there was no other way. I had to make a deal with Jerome.*

She dried her hair with her towel, shaking her head in disbelief. *I've made a deal with the head vampire. Something I would have never considered before.* It was strictly forbidden within the Seeker Code of Conduct. Abram would be so disappointed in her, and the

Chapter, they would remove her Seeker status immediately. The thought of living a normal human life was tempting, but she knew her job wasn't finished.

She raked her brush through her hair, combing through the knots that had formed during a hard night's sleep. *What other choice do I have? I need Jerome's help.* She let out a frustrated breath.

And Kai. She'd refused his help. It annoyed her. Sometimes he treated her like a helpless girl. She'd survived without him for seven years. What made him think she needed him in order to do her job now? Emotions—they were getting too close, one reason she resisted getting close to people. She needed to distance herself from her feelings for Kai. They were interfering with her ability to do her job.

Janie slid a black lightweight sweater over her head and jumped into a pair of jeans. She hurried over to her dresser to apply her makeup. She set her mascara down and stared at herself in the mirror. "It's time," she breathed.

Isabelle read a book in the armchair with her legs propped up on the ottoman. Reading whisked her away to a world other than the one Isabelle knew existed. She sipped her tea, glancing up as Janie entered the room.

"Good afternoon. You decided to wake up today," Isabelle said.

"I was up late." Janie headed for the kitchen without looking at her mom. She wanted to avoid any of her mother's questioning. "I'm going to grab a bowl of cereal before Matt gets here."

"Matt?" Isabelle's reading glasses slid down her nose. She peered at Janie over the lenses.

"He called me last night. He has something to tell me in person." Janie rolled her eyes. "I'm nervous. What if he professes his 'fake' love?"

"You don't know that—and the love isn't fake." Isabelle seemed to take the remark personally. Her tone calmed. "Everything will be okay. There is no sense in getting yourself all upset over something you can't control."

Janie walked over to the coffee table to retrieve a magazine. "Your reaction isn't normal. You should be flipping out. This is awful."

"If it turns out you've Imprinted him, then we'll 'flip out,' but until then there's nothing to worry about." She pushed her glasses back up the bridge of her nose and continued to read.

Janie disappeared into the kitchen. Her stomach swirled with fluttering butterflies. Set to face a gang of Daychildren that evening, all she could think about was how she'd most likely Imprinted Matt. The tabloid magazine didn't distract her like she had hoped. She chuckled a few times, eyeing a few outfits Luke would undoubtedly wear. No other guy at school would dare step through the doors of Loch Raven High sporting any of these pieces. Luke always said he was the only guy in school who had any sense of fashion and the balls to pull it off.

The doorbell rang. Janie set her cereal bowl in the sink and glanced up at the wall clock—exactly noon. *Well, he's punctual.*

Taking a deep breath, she closed her magazine and headed into the living room to answer the door. Isabelle stood in the doorway, holding the door open.

"Hi Matt, I'm Mrs. Grey. It's nice to meet you," she said in an overexcited motherly tone.

"Good afternoon, Mrs. Grey. Is Janie here?"

"Yes." Isabelle gestured for Matt to come in. "Why don't you two hang out in the living room. I'll go out on the porch and read. I made some cookies, if you're interested." Janie rolled her eyes. She hoped Matt didn't get the impression they were made especially for him.

"Hi Janie," Matt said, stepping into the house. His moss-green sweater enhanced the green in his hazel eyes. She smiled. He always had that varsity jacket on.

Janie gave him a quick wave and slid her hands into her pockets. She looked past Matt. "Thanks, Mom." Isabelle winked and slipped out the door.

"Should we sit?" Janie said, wanting to avoid the awkward standing and staring scenario. "What did you need to talk to me about?"

"After you." He extended his arm for her to pass.

"You look good." She gave him the once-over. "You'd never know you were attacked—twice." Janie sat on the far end of the couch.

Matt bypassed the first cushion and chose the one next to her.

"Don't remind me." He focused on her mouth. "Your lip." He reached out, not quite close enough to touch her, but close enough to make her arch her back. "It looks painful."

"I'll be fine. It's healing." Instinctively, she touched the cut with her first two fingers. The salt from her skin stung the incision. She cringed.

Matt twirled his class ring around his finger. "I—I was wondering if you wanted to go to Homecoming with me."

Janie gasped. "What?"

"Do you want to go to Homecoming, with me?" He blushed. She felt bad about her outward display of shock, but his question came out of left field. Prepared for pretty much anything, even him saying he loved her, she coughed, trying to compose herself. *Homecoming, seriously?*

Janie ran her fingers through her hair. It was still damp underneath. She fumbled over how to answer. "I don't think you really mean that. Trust me. If I hadn't saved your life the other night, you wouldn't be asking me. You'd be asking Molly."

"The other night and Molly have nothing to do with me asking you." He moved closer to her, causing Janie to tense up even more. The arm of the sofa dug deeper into her back.

"You don't know what you're saying. I've Imprinted you. You like me because I saved your life." Matt stared at her with a look of incomprehension. "Matt, it can happen when someone like me saves a person's life. That person can feel drawn to the other, feeling as if they like them, when really they have just been Imprinted. What you are feeling is not real. It's an illusion."

"Why do you keep saying that?" He reached for the hand she rested on the cushion. She pulled back.

"Because it's true." She could tell by his unfazed expression that he didn't believe her.

He inched closer to her. "Let's just say you're wrong. Will you go with me to the dance?"

"No." She scooted to the edge of the cushion.

"Is it because you don't like me?" he pressed.

"No, I mean, I don't know," she stuttered.

Matt scanned the room and settled on the sofa table. Her rose was displayed in a small crystal vase. She hadn't realized her mother put it there. "The day you saved me, I smiled at you after class." He paused in thought. Janie's eyes widened; *he remembered.* "I liked you *before* you stopped that vampire thing from draining my blood."

Janie thought back to the day of the match, at Ava's locker between classes, before she had to rescue him from being killed by a Daychild that evening...

As Ava bent over to retrieve her book, she saw Matt Baker exiting the classroom behind her. Matt offered Janie a genuine smile. Ava stood up, blocking Janie's view of the star wrestler. Not that Janie cared. She had a job to do. That was it. Anything else just complicated things.

"I didn't smile back," Janie said, returning to the present. "It's not that I didn't want to—"

Matt waved it off, signaling that it was okay. "You don't have to explain yourself. Biology kind of sucks, with all the cheerleaders, and Molly. I didn't really expect to get a response from you."

She tried to explain. "Even if you did like me before that night, I don't think me saving your life helped the situation. You don't really feel the way you think you do about me."

"And how exactly do you know this, considering I've never told you how I feel?"

Janie realized he was right. He'd never actually told her how he felt. She just assumed. She wasn't the type jocks usually fell for. Maybe Isabelle was right. Janie had blown the whole situation out of proportion. Maybe she hadn't Imprinted him after all. "I feel like a fool. I shouldn't have assumed. I'm sorry." She met his hazel eyes.

A satisfied smile formed on his face. "So now that it's settled, will you go with me? I'd hate to have to keep asking you every day so that you'd get so annoyed with me that you'd say yes just to get me to shut up."

"You'd do that?" It was creepy and romantic at the same time.

"Do you really want to find out?"

"What about Molly? Aren't you going with her? She'll probably try to blow up the school with her aerosol hairspray when she finds out."

"Does that mean your answer is yes?" He leaned in. She could smell the plastic edging of his varsity jacket and his musky cologne.

"You didn't answer me. What about Molly? I really don't want to have to take down the cheerleaders."

"Janie?" He reached for her hand unexpectedly. She didn't have time to pull back. His hand was soft and warm around hers. She found herself comparing it to Kai's. Kai's hand felt rougher and more temperate.

She immediately pushed any thoughts of Kai from her head. It was finally clear now. She needed to end their friendship, or at least slow it down. She intended to tell him the next time she saw him. They were spending too much time together. *Feelings complicate things. Distance, that is the answer.*

Maybe going to the dance with Matt would help keep her mind occupied until she left. Give her an excuse to stop seeing Kai. "Yes, I'll go with you." Her tone contradicted her words. Matt didn't seem to notice.

"Sorry to spring it on you at the last minute. I hope you have time to find a dress and whatever else you need."

"I'm resourceful." Janie smiled.

Matt stood, lifting Janie to a standing position by her hand. "Then I'll see you tomorrow at school."

"I'll be there." She nodded awkwardly.

Matt brushed a sweet kiss across the back of her hand—but the sparks weren't there.

Janie placed her Algebra textbook and spiral notebook into her backpack. Her second time in Algebra II, and she still couldn't grasp it. Luckily, Ava had agreed to tutor her. She headed out the door. Clouds blanketed the sky, threatening more rain, maybe even sleet if the temperature kept dropping.

She stepped on to the driveway and smiled. The dull gray asphalt appeared shiny and black, covered by the earlier rain. It was nice to be able to drive her Honda again. Janie ran her fingers over the smooth metal of the car's hood and traced the fender with her eyes. Her car looked like new again. No large dent.

"It looks good. You wouldn't even know you hit a pole." Janie spun around. Kai leaned against the driver side door, dressed in his usual tee with dark jeans and black boots. She glared at him. He threw his hands out. "What, you told me to knock, but there isn't a door out here."

"You shouldn't be here." Janie shoved past him, holding her backpack securely over one shoulder. The smell of clean lavender hit her at once, making her heart race.

"Are you mad?" He turned to face her, stepping back from the car door. "Did I do something to upset you?"

She decided to confront him, to end the relationship right here and now. "No. I'm on my way out. Not everything is about you."

"Matt," Kai grunted. Like Matt was a virus that had infected her. It was all too much for her to handle.

"Not that it's any of your business, but I'm going to Ava's." Janie jerked open the car door and threw her backpack over to the passenger seat. "Matt already came by. Again, not that it is any of your business."

"Did he profess his love?" he said flippantly.

"You're an ass." She put one foot on the floor of the car and held the top of the door to steady herself.

Kai stepped forward. He sounded serious. "What did he want to ask you?"

Janie moved to get in the car, but something made her pause. Kai's look, it was so. . .determined. He *really* wanted to know. "He asked me to the Homecoming dance," she finally answered.

"He asked you to a dance?" Any seriousness flew from Kai's tone. He bent over into a laugh. His blond waves bounced around his head.

"I'm leaving." Janie plopped down into the driver's seat. Kai held the door open so she couldn't close it.

"What did you say to him?" He tried to give the appearance that her answer didn't bother him, but she could see the veins popping out of his skin; his blood raced violently within them.

"I said yes." Janie yanked on the door handle. "Now let go."

"You don't actually want to go with him." Although she knew he was anything but weak, he appeared frail. His strong, lean body slumped over the car door. Hard lines crumpled across his forehead and his scars seemed even more pronounced under the gray sky.

"Yes, I do." She made herself believe she spoke the truth even though every part of her screamed for someone else. *This is exactly why I shouldn't have let my feelings dictate anything.*

"What about us?" He let the door go, and defeated, he stepped back from the car. The grass crunched under his boots.

Janie sat silently in shock. She hadn't expected his question. "There *is* no us," she breathed, feeling just as defeated as he looked. She knew she was the only one to blame for causing both of them pain. She could have ended it the first night she met him.

Kai stood with his hands resting below his hips, thinking about something, maybe how to respond. "It's because of what I am. I shouldn't have told you. I should have let you think I was a monster." He looked out into the street. A group of kids wearing heavy jackets played basketball in the cul-de-sac.

Janie stepped out of the car. She stomped over to him, contemplating how to tell him how she felt. "What you are doesn't bother me. I just don't think we should be friends anymore. Ever since I met you, I've become sloppy, unfocused. I can't allow my feelings for you to interfere with my job."

His eyes left the ground and traced a perfect line up the front of her until they finally reached her eyes. "So you do have feelings for me?"

"That's not what I meant."

"You just said it." He stepped closer to her, with an intensity so powerful it drowned out the world. Nothing else existed—the bouncing basketball on the black top and the laughter of playing children disappeared. Kai's words flooded with raw emotion, a fresh wound that had been torn open.

"Then I said it wrong. Kai, I can't see you anymore." She pushed against his chest, but he didn't move. He grabbed both of her wrists and held her in place. His green eyes blazed with an impassioned craving to want and to be wanted.

"You are the only person I have felt comfortable enough with to talk about my past. You can't say you don't want to see me anymore. You're the only one who knows me."

"That's not my problem." She tried to turn away from him but he held her tightly in place.

"You're afraid," he said.

She laughed. "Afraid of what, you?"

"You're afraid of your feelings for me. You won't ever let anyone in. You think that if you run from your feelings you won't get hurt." She yanked on her wrists. He finally let go. She threw her fists into his chest. Again he just stood, still and hard like a statue.

"My mom loved my father and now he's dead. It's not worth it." She pivoted around to leave.

He shouted to her from behind. "What you're doing with Matt isn't right. You don't feel anything for him. He's safe."

"And you're not." She strode to her car. She wanted the conversation to be over. She didn't want to discuss Matt, Kai, or losing her father anymore. All the topics were too painful.

Kai materialized in front of her. Janie stumbled back, catching her heel on a lip of grass bordering the driveway. "You're safe with me." Kai wrapped his arms around her and guided her into his chest. For a moment she let herself have what she wanted. She let herself get lost in him. She dipped her head into his chest and let his heart beat loudly under her ear. "I know you feel it too," he breathed into her hair.

Janie raised her head. He stared down at her. She wanted so badly to tell him how she felt, but at what risk? He could leave, or even worse, die. She couldn't go through losing someone else she loved. She'd seen what her father's death had done to her mother. *Is it really worth it?*

"I can't. Please let me go," she whispered.

"Is that really what you want?" For the first time she felt his breath on her face. He was breathing.

She exhaled. "What do you want from me? A week ago I didn't even know you existed. Now you're always around and when you're not, you're all I think about. I wasn't supposed to meet you. I wanted to be alone." His strong arms anchored her to him.

"I don't get you." He lowered her back to arm's length. "You're so damn reckless, yet when it comes to me you proceed with caution. If it's not because of what I am, then what is it that makes you so careful with me? You don't react this way with Matt."

"I've really got to go. I have to study and get back in time to prepare for tonight. This isn't what I need right now. Please let me focus on tonight."

"If you still intend to go through with this, then at least let me help you prepare. Don't be so stubborn." He looked deep into her eyes. She felt as if they could pierce her soul.

"I'm not stubborn," she said.

"You're stubborn." He dipped his forehead into hers.

"Okay, maybe a little. I'll be back in a few hours. Why don't we prepare at your house? I don't need my mom finding out about *any* of this. She's already going to be unhappy when I tell her I'm going downtown after Abram suggested I lay low."

"I'll meet you here. We'll take your car to my house," he said. Janie slid her hand up his chest until her palm rested over his heart. He tightened at her touch. His words were sincere. "If it makes you more comfortable, I'll be satisfied just to have you as a friend, but don't walk away from me."

Janie drew invisible spirals on his chest. She couldn't imagine how lonely his life had been. What it would be like to have nobody to confide in or laugh with. She always had her mother and Abram, even though Abram hadn't been acting like himself lately. Something was bothering him about Kai; something more than what Kai was.

As hard as she tried, she couldn't be cruel to him. "I'm here," she said. He cupped her cheeks. A droplet of rain splashed on her face. She glanced up to the sky. Was it a sign from her father? In that moment, she surrendered. *Dad, I'll try. But your death broke Mom. I'm afraid.*

"Are you still with me?" Kai's white teeth sparkled through his smile.

Janie blinked, bringing herself back to the moment. "How will you know when I'm home?"

"I'll be around." He kissed the tip of her nose and removed his hands from her face. He walked away and disappeared around the side of her house.

CHAPTER 11

Janie drove up to her house. Kai appeared around the side of the garage. His hair and T-shirt were wet from the rain. Janie swallowed. The rain had molded the cotton to his chest. Janie quickly refocused her attention on a large oak tree in her front yard. Rain and Kai went well together. She didn't need the temptation.

Kai slid into the passenger seat. "Is something wrong?" he said. "Did you change your mind about letting me help you?"

Janie shook her head, still focusing on the thick wet bark of the old oak. No wonder her study session went so horribly. She and Ava had talked about everything but her exam. Unable to think about anything but Kai, Ava had acted as more of a therapist than a tutor.

"Then why won't you look at me?" He placed his hand on her thigh.

"I'm fine." She quivered. "Are you ready to prepare?"

He removed his hand. “I still think you should let me come with you tonight. You’re being ridiculous.”

“If Jerome found out, he might refuse to help us,” she said.

“And you’re sure we need the vamps to defeat Antony?” He ran his fingers through his wet hair, combing it out of his face. He looked down at his heavy jeans and T-shirt and grumbled, “I’m soaked.”

“You can run through walls. You should have waited inside.”

“Thanks for the tip.” He stretched his T-shirt away from his skin. It made a popping sound and adhered to his chest again. His wet clothing only distracted him for a moment. He let out a sigh. “Will you please consider revising the plan?”

“You heard Jerome. Even if we decide not to accept his help and refuse to get Tanya back for him, he’ll take Antony’s side. We don’t need the vamps readily handing their venom over to Antony.”

“I still don’t like it.”

“This isn’t your decision. It’s mine, so deal with it.” Janie threw the car in reverse. He moaned. “So help me, Kai,” she warned, “if you even attempt to go near that lair.”

“You’ll what?” He laughed. He grabbed the dashboard. “Cut the turn. You almost took out your mailbox.”

“I did not.” She placed the gear in drive. “No back seat driving. I don’t tell you how to drive your motorcycle.”

“Do you even know anything about motorcycles?”

Janie ignored him. She headed toward the main road and took the interstate exit. "I think it's time for you to tell me how you turn a disk into a Harley."

Kai retrieved the disk from his waist and flipped it between his fingers. "There's not much to tell. It was a present from Albania." He paused for Janie's reaction, but she sat silently with her eyes on the road. "I needed transportation, and she thought stealing a bike wasn't the greatest idea since I was newly 'reformed,' so she conjured up some spell and made me my own. I like my bike; it's compact."

"What about the helmet?" Janie changed lanes on the interstate. Kai sucked in a not-so-subtle breath. "I'm fine. That car wasn't even near me."

"Yeah," Kai said. "Anyway, Albania has this strange obsession with safety. She made me promise if anyone mortal rode with me, I'd have to make them wear a helmet. She originally created the one with flames." He tapped her leg. "You know, the one you left in the city?"

Janie had a flash memory of dropping the helmet after her head battered into a wooden door frame. "Yeah, I remember."

"I acquired the pink and the black one using my ability. It's easy to get things when you can run through walls." He smiled guiltily. "Albania wouldn't be too happy with me."

"So, Albania wants you to stay on the straight path and keep the mortals you ride with safe." Janie hesitated. "And how many mortals have you ridden with exactly?" He didn't answer, making her regret her question.

"One," he finally said.

"I take it that's me?"

Kai rolled his eyes and stared out the window, not playing along with Janie's attempt to elicit information.

"Well, Albania sounds like a good friend," she said.

"She is a good friend for some things. I don't feel as comfortable with her as I used to. We've been through a lot together, but she has her own life. It's not like it is with—" He pointed. "Take this exit. My street's a block away. I thought we'd park your car in front of my house and head to the park across the street. It's usually private, and we'll have space to move around. Besides, if we practice technique, my house is too cramped—I've seen you fight."

Janie smiled.

He hesitated and said, "I went back to the lair after I left your house this morning." He refused to look at her. Instead he watched a woman walk her dog along the sidewalk. "No one saw me, and I was able to get a good look at the layout."

Janie stopped scowling and focused back on the road. He turned to explain. "There is an alley that leads around back. If you go in through the back, you might be able to slip in easier. The key is to go unnoticed for as long as you can."

"Do you have any idea where they're holding Tanya?" She figured getting mad at him would be pointless. He only wanted her to make it out alive.

"My guess is the basement. She can't be near the light during the day. When you get inside, look for a set of steps that lead down to the basement. Make sure to tell Tanya that Jerome sent you, or you may end up having to stake her."

"Yeah, that would totally mess everything up." Kai shot her an agreeing look. "So, I'll go through the back alley, enter the home from the rear, find a set of basement steps and make sure to tell Tanya that Jerome sent me when I find her."

"Good. That's part of the plan."

"How do you suppose I get out once I find her? They aren't just going to let me take her willingly."

"That's the next part of the plan. . .you come out the same way you went in, kind of." Kai signaled for her to park. "As for getting back out quickly, we're going to work on that right now."

She parallel parked, noticing the park entrance across the street.

He smirked. "I'm going to teach you how to fight dirty."

Janie followed Kai to a large grassy area lined by trees. A few squirrels ran along the back of a park bench. A folded wet newspaper lay on the wooden seat next to a Styrofoam coffee cup filled with rain water.

"What's lesson one?" Janie unzipped her hoodie and threw it over the bench.

"Nice T-shirt." Kai laughed. "Buffy."

"I thought it was fitting. Ava got it for me as a joke."

Kai interlaced his fingers through hers. "Lessons one through ten are all the same—don't get killed." Kai stared past Janie into a row of thick trees lining the park. "She's going to help you with that."

Albania stepped between two trees. Janie stared at her for a few seconds and tightened her grip on Kai's hand. Albania always made her feel self-conscious. *No one, witch or not, should have such striking red hair and green eyes. Kai's eyes are beautiful, but Albania's green isn't even found on this planet.*

Janie knew Kai and Albania were just friends, but she moved close enough to Kai so their arms touched anyway. "I thought you were going to teach me how to play dirty," she whispered.

Kai squeezed her hand. "I am—we're going to give you an ability."

Her eyes shot up to his. "What kind of ability?"

"The only one I have to give." He acted entirely too composed. Janie, on the other hand, didn't feel as certain of the plan.

"I'm going to be able to run through walls!"

"Hopefully," Albania said, approaching. Her ankle-length skirt flowed around her feet in the breeze.

Janie turned to Albania. "I don't understand. That's Kai's ability. How can I get it?"

"I'm going to loan it to you." He brushed his fingers across her cheek with his free hand.

She shot him another annoyed look. "I understand that part. How?"

Albania greeted Kai with a kiss on both cheeks. "I've created a special concoction, and since Kai is willing, it should work."

"For how long?"

"I'm hoping you will keep it until you get safely back to your house with Tanya, where I'll be waiting for you," Kai said.

"But there's no way to know for sure," Albania interjected.

"My ability is an alternative for helping you find a way out, if needed. Make sure you can get back upstairs and then run through the wall. You'll be able to take Tanya with you if she's touching you."

"Like you do with me?" An elderly couple passed on a nearby walking path. Janie lowered her voice. "What if she's not in the basement? It won't be light outside. They won't need to keep her down there."

"They won't move her around. Tanya's too strong. They will want to keep her in one place, somewhere where no light can get in. They aren't going to keep her where she could escape." Kai shook his head. "The basement is just an educated guess. It's where I'd keep her."

"Are you both ready?" Albania removed Janie's hand from Kai's and held it, palm up. She traced the lines on Janie's palm with her finger. "Hmmm."

"Is something wrong?" Kai peered into Janie's open palm.

Albania ran her fingers over Janie's fingertips and gently closed her hand into a fist. "Janie's lines are strong. I don't know how long her body will accept your ability."

"All we can do is try." He noticed Albania's cautious expression and stepped closer to her. "Al, tell me what that means."

Albania offered a hesitant smile. "If it wears off while she's within a solid object, she could become trapped."

"Like in a wall?" Janie jerked her hand from Albania's grasp. Kai placed his arm around her waist.

She didn't have to ask her next question. Albania answered, "Yes, you will die."

Kai's arm tightened around Janie's waist. "We'll think of another plan. I can't risk your death."

Janie knocked his arm off her. "My death isn't yours to risk. If using your ability will help me get out of the lair, I'm going to use it."

"Stubborn—"

"Stubborn or not, it's me against a lair—I have a greater chance of being killed by them than getting stuck in a wall."

Kai turned his back on her to talk with Albania in private. Janie spoke loud enough for both of them to hear. "Albania, I would appreciate it if we could do this sooner than later. I'd like to practice, um, running through things."

Albania guided Kai to her side. "If you are still willing, I will do it." She laid a sympathetic hand on Kai's arm. "Janie has decided. Kai—ultimately, it's up to you."

After a moment of thought, he finally answered. "I'll do whatever Janie wants."

"Then it's settled." Janie interlocked her arm through Kai's. "I'll be fine. Like you said before—I need to play dirty to win."

He let out an annoyed breath.

Albania removed a small bottle, the size of a small cough medicine cup, from her skirt pocket. Red liquid filled the plastic container. "You and Janie will both need to drink from this bottle." She removed the lid and handed the bottle to Kai.

"Are you sure about this?" Kai held the bottle in front of Janie.

"I'm sure." She removed the bottle from his hand and took a swig. "Your turn."

"Stubborn," he repeated. He tilted his head back and threw the rest of the red liquid down his throat like a shot of tequila.

"Do you feel any different?" Albania said to Janie.

"Should I?" On instinct, Janie examined her body, half-expecting to physically change—sprout wings or grow flippers.

"Try to run through that tree." Kai glanced past her to the line of trees in the distance.

Janie scanned the empty park. No one would see her run smack into a tree or pass through it, however it panned out. She hoped for the second scenario. Besides, she was already recovering from a split lip and a black eye. A goose egg would be an unwanted addition to her list of injuries. Not to mention, she had Homecoming in less than a week—with Matt. *A goose egg, black eye, split lip and an evening gown. Perfect! Maybe Matt will refuse to take me if I look like I've been in a cage fight. Unlikely. My luck, I'll be healed by then.*

Janie ironed her pants with her sweaty palms. *I can do this.* "What do I do?"

Kai turned to her. “Remember, you have to run. Believe you can do it, and you will.”

“That’s it. That’s all the instructions you have. Should I close my eyes or something?”

“If you want.” Janie tried to focus on his touch. He seemed to believe in her. Besides, she never ran away from a challenge.

Albania stepped back to give Janie room. Kai stayed next to her. He held her hand so tightly. She had to wiggle her fingers free of his. “So I’ll run—straight for the tree.”

Kai nodded. He didn’t look as confident as she’d hoped.

“Here goes nothing.” Janie focused on the tall oak’s trunk. A large nodule poked out around eye level. *That‘s going to hurt if I hit it.* She sprinted forward. The crisp grass crunched under her boots and her heart pounded in her chest, each footfall slamming into her over and over again. She realized she was holding her breath and exhaled. Anticipating the impact of the tree trunk wasn’t helping her develop her confidence.

But then a calmness stoked through her—Kai wouldn’t let anything hurt her. He knew she could do it. *I can do it.*

Janie slammed into the tree trunk, but it didn’t hurt. She didn’t actually hit it; she passed right through. The molecules bounced her backward. She pushed forward, fighting hard against a forceful resistance, like running with a rubber band wrapped around her waist. “Kai—”

"I'm right here." His arms flew around her. "Are you okay?" He lifted her off the ground.

The coolness of his rain-soaked tee made her gasp. She ignored the dark cotton and let her body mold to his. His sweet smell filled her with a forbidden happiness. He placed her back on the ground and stroked her hair.

"I'm right where I should be," she said.

"You did it. I've got complete faith in you."

"I know." Janie glanced back at the tree she'd just run through. "That was kind of fun." She looked around. "Where's Albania? I want to thank her."

"She had to go." Kai twirled her ponytail. "I'll meet you at midnight."

They stared at each other, both hesitant to move. They were already so close. She could feel his breath on her mouth. He leaned in closer, so their lips almost touched. Then, he kissed her.

All rationale left her. She reached up and grabbed his neck, pulling him as close to her as she could. She twirled his blond waves around her fingers, pouring all of her fears and desires into him all at once. The intensity of his kiss felt forceful and hungry, like he tasted something delicious for the first time after starving for days.

His lips moved to the corner of her mouth and kissed her gently. He drew back. His words were hesitant, shaky, "Janie I—"

Janie placed her finger on his lips. "Just kiss me."

Janie arrived home around dinner time. She noticed Abram's Lexus parked in the driveway. She entered the living room, startled to see Abram sitting alone in silence. "Where's Mom?"

Abram eyed Janie from the armchair, still dressed in a suit, this one navy. He stroked his five o'clock shadow. Janie found this odd. Abram prided himself on being clean-shaven and polished. Janie didn't feel his behavior was related to the uprising of the Daychildren. She hadn't seen him look so emotionally exhausted since her father's death. Whatever the problem, it was personal.

"We need to talk." Abram raised his sullen blue eyes and peered at Janie over his glasses.

"Yes, we do. There's something going on with you. Please tell me what has you so upset. Is it Kai? Ever since he brought me home last week, you've been acting so strange." Janie took a seat on the sofa. She turned toward Abram. She wanted to rest her hand on his leg, offer him some sort of comfort, but his body language suggested he wanted to be left alone. "Kai really isn't like the rest of them. He is part human, like us."

Abram's head shot up. Hatred blazed from his glare, making the whites of his eyes appear red. Maybe they were red. He looked as if h hadn't slept in days. "He is *not* like us!"

Abram's sharp tone sent Janie back into the cushion.

Isabelle raced into the living room, clutching a dish rag in her fists. "What's going on? Janie, you're home."

Janie didn't speak, too afraid after Abram's outburst.

"Abram? Will someone please answer me?" Isabelle said.

Abram straightened his spine. The hard lines on his face and his crow's feet were more pronounced than ever. Janie could see the wheels spinning in his head. The day they told Janie about her father's death, he'd had the same expression, the same hesitancy to speak. *What could be so devastating?*

Her lungs constricted. She reached into her coat pocket and removed her inhaler just in case.

"It's about Kai." He spoke only slightly louder than a whisper.

"I already—" Janie prepared to argue. Abram raised his hand. She feared he would shout again. She bit her lip. When it came to Kai, holding back her feelings had become difficult.

"Go ahead, Abram. We're listening," Isabelle said.

Abram ran his thumb over the chair's arm, still deep in thought, searching for the right words. "As you know," he paused to swallow, "your father, Connor. . . ." Her father's name sounded like a rock lodged in his throat. Abram had to force it out. "Connor was a part of our world through association. He'd fallen in love with your mother." He glanced up at Isabelle. Her hands trembled. "And she, in return, fell in love with him. Shortly after they met, she stopped Seeking. She knew her lifestyle was too dangerous for him. They got married and she became pregnant with you, a future Seeker. This was a fact your father was unhappy with and expressed quite often." Abram rested his hand on Janie's knee. "He wanted to protect you from the monsters humans refused to acknowledge existed."

Janie spoke for the first time since Abram began. Her tongue was pasted to the roof of her mouth. "If he wasn't part of our world anymore, how did he die?" She couldn't believe it. It was the most Abram had ever spoken about her father's death.

Abram removed his hand from her leg. The anger returned. "Your father was downtown for a work conference. He'd left the steakhouse after a late corporate dinner to return home to you and your mother. Only he didn't make it home."

Janie retrieved a throw pillow off the center of the couch. She hugged it tightly.

"He was attacked by a Daychild, drained of all his blood. The police ruled it a homicide, gang activity, but we knew." He exhaled deeply and wearily. "I left the restaurant moments after Connor. When I arrived, it was too late. I tried to avenge his death, kill the monster that took him from you and Isabelle, but he was too fast. I've spent fifteen years searching for *him*, knowing one day we would cross paths again." The hate crawled back into his face. His face reddened as he involuntarily held his breath, denying himself air. "I will never forget those eyes. The eyes of your father's murderer—bright green."

Janie dropped the pillow. She fought to keep her hands from covering her ears. She knew what Abram was going to say next, but she refused to hear it. It couldn't be true. She'd finally put her guard down, tried to trust in someone other than her mother and Abram.

She'd finally found someone to love. It couldn't be. God couldn't be so cruel.

She slid the plastic inhaler into her mouth and squeezed.

Abram finished. "Kai killed your father."

CHAPTER 12

Janie threw the covers over her head. She'd fled to her bedroom so fast Abram didn't have a chance to finish. She didn't need to hear anymore. Kai killed her father, drained him of his blood and ripped him from her and her mother. Kai robbed her of a father and her mother of a husband. *Damn him!* For so many years she wanted to know what really happened. Now she didn't want to know. She wished she could push a rewind button and go back in time. *How do I move forward when the guy I love killed my father?*

Janie cringed. She could feel Kai's energy inside her. He swam through her bloodstream. Her flesh pricked to life—*his* life. He was a part of her now. She had gained his ability. She wanted so badly to rip it out of her. Knowing part of him lived within her made her ill. She threw her covers back and leapt from bed to the bathroom just in time. She vomited.

She stumbled back to bed and read the neon red numbers on her digital clock. It was late. She'd been in her room longer than she'd intended. At the moment, time didn't feel like it existed. As much as she wanted to lock herself in her room forever, she had to rescue Tanya.

Janie brushed her teeth, changed into another pair of dark jeans and a fitted smoke gray hoodie. She did her best to push all thoughts of Kai and her father out of her mind for the moment. She had a job to do—get Tanya and return her to Jerome so that he and his gang would help her take down Antony.

Janie parked her car along a side street close to the tourist-filled Power Plant area, but close enough to the hood that tourists wouldn't take their chances parking there. She remembered the look of horror that crossed a couple's face when they were attacked beside their car after a night of drinking. In the right place at the right time, Janie had saved them from a pair of savage Daychildren. She doubted the couple would ever park there again.

She strode toward the former law offices of *Bower, Reed & Associates*. The wind whipped strongly between the buildings. Janie hardly noticed the chill or that her hair swirled around her head like the funnel of a mini-tornado. She could have walked through the arctic and not felt the wet, frigid snow around her feet, or the icicles hanging dangerously close to her head. She felt numb to everything.

She cut through the alley and crouched behind a dumpster around the back of the house. One dim light sprinkled flecks of illumination over the room, casting the appearance of two large rectangular shadows. *Furniture, maybe.* Neither shadow appeared to move.

Brick steps led to a single back door with a tiny window. Janie peered through both first-floor windows. Still, nothing moved within the faint light. *It's now or never. It's not like I have anything to lose. I'm broken already*.

She tiptoed up the steps, her eyes set on the window to catch any ounce of movement. Nothing. She turned the knob slowly. It was locked. Normally, she'd kick it in. This time, she needed to be quiet. Not alert anyone to her presence.

She remembered once again that she had Kai's ability within her. Bile rose to the base of her throat. She ignored her nausea and backed off the steps to get a running start. She reached into the backpack she'd slung over her shoulder. It was filled with extra silver-plated knives and a few stakes, just in case.

Janie retrieved her Cherokee dagger from her boot and read the inscription…*U-le-tsu-ya-s-ti—brave.* The word gave her the courage to proceed.

Something vibrated, startling her. *My cell.* Janie drew in a deep breath and removed it from her pocket. *Matt.* She let it go to voice mail. A second later a text came through—*miss u.* She didn't reply. *Darn Imprint. Can life get any more complicated?*

Not allowing thoughts of Kai or Matt to creep into her mind, she focused on the task at hand. She jogged into a sprint and barreled into the door. A spring shoved her body backward like she'd run straight into a large balloon. She opened her eyes—to her surprise, she was still upright and standing in the small kitchen, backpack slung over one shoulder and dagger in hand.

She ducked behind a tall chair. It sat squarely in the middle of the room, not one other piece of furniture in sight, other than a wet bar near the back wall. She realized the chair had created the rectangular shadow she'd seen through the window. The refrigerator must have been the other large shadow. She cringed to think about its contents. She doubted it was filled with grapes and bottled water, like at Kai's.

As she stood to move, she kicked a red and white plastic cooler with the lid drawn open. She crouched back behind the chair and peered down into the box. A dark red, nearly frozen, human heart rested on top of the dry ice. *Ugh—that gives new meaning to the term "frozen dinner."*

Janie skirted the chair and ran over to the far wall, shaking the gory image of human organs and TV dinners out of her head. She smashed up against the wall and listened.

Voices echoed in the room adjacent to the kitchen. A room she knew well—the old law office, just through a narrow archway. She'd been in that room one too many times. Kai was there, too. Again, she pushed any thoughts of *him* out of her mind. *I have to focus.*

There were at least three of them in the main room. They spoke at the same time. She heard a slap and realized the woman had struck the man for speaking over her. *Apparently their manners were removed when their souls were.*

Janie crept down the hallway, searching for a door leading to the basement. Peeling paint curled from the walls. She brushed by a strip of paint. It crumbled against her shoulder and the pieces showered on to the ground. The paint chips crunched under her boots. Janie shrank back, afraid they'd heard her.

The woman snapped at the man again. Janie continued forward.

She spotted a door. Pitch blackness shone through a small crack. Janie slid her hand in the opening and slowly opened it. Wooden steps led down to what looked like a black hole. She stepped down on to the first step. The wood creaked. She froze. The arguing stopped.

A man said, "Did you hear that?"

"It's probably just the vampire. She could be awake," the woman answered.

"Should we check?" A different voice spoke, a boy, definitely younger than the other two.

"Antony said to leave her alone."

"Antony ain't here," the man said.

One of them, maybe the woman, stomped across the room. They continued to argue. Janie wiped the sweat off her forehead with the back of her hand. *It's hot as hell in here. At least now I know Tanya's down here.*

Carefully and slowly, she descended into the basement. She searched for any sign of Tanya. A splinter of wood sliced her finger. She retracted her hand from the wooden rail and placed her lips around the cut. She sucked away the blood, the metallic taste on her tongue. *Ouch!*

"Tanya," Janie whispered. She knew Tanya would hear her.

"Over here." Tanya's voice sounded weak. Janie wondered how they'd restrained her.

"My name is Janie. Jerome sent me to get you."

"The Seeker?" Tanya laughed. "Why would Jerome send you?"

"I guess he figured I was the best girl for the job." Janie stepped down on to the concrete floor. The smell of the basement made her nauseous—moldy cheese, stinky feet, feces, rotting meat and an outhouse rolled into one vile odor. Her boot adhered to something sticky. Unfortunately, she doubted it was gum. This was a time when gum under her shoe would have been a good thing. Her foot started to burn—Daychild blood. It had already begun to eat through the sole of her boot. *Tanya must have injured one.*

Ignoring the pain, Janie reached out in front of her. Her fingers brushed across a metal beam. Remembering her small flashlight, she slid it out of her pocket and clicked it on. "Where are you?" she said, waving the stream of light across the basement.

"You're close, honey. Step to the right and come straight back. The jerk has me chained to a pole." They had to be holding her with something other than silver. Silver burned their skin. They'd never be able to restrain her long enough to get the shackles on without injuring themselves in the process.

"Tanya, don't try anything when I free you. I have orders to return you to Jerome."

"Girl, if you get me out of here, I'll be indebted to you. I don't do filth. My mani-pedi is ruined. I'm a lady. Jerome keeps his Princess happy. . .and this—" Janie imagined Tanya scanning the room with a scowl stamped across her face. "This ain't happy."

Janie moved forward. Her foot squished like a wet galosh after a rain storm as she stepped down on to the concrete. She stepped lighter to lessen the burn. "Am I close?"

"Keep coming." Tanya grabbed Janie's arm. Janie spun out of Tanya's grasp, shining the flashlight directly into her eyes. Tanya whipped her head out of the direct light. The chain rattled, metal against metal. Tanya attempted to retrieve Janie's arm again. "How are you going to get these off me?" Tanya said. "And don't shine that damn light in my face again."

"Don't grab me again, or I'll leave you here to starve," Janie said. She hadn't thought about how to free Tanya from her restraints. Sure, she could move through objects using Kai's ability, but that wasn't going to free Tanya.

"I'm hungry and your Seeker blood sure smells good." Tanya made a sucking noise.

"Tanya," Janie warned.

"Just kidding, baby. Get me out of this dumpster and I'll owe you. Cross my beating heart."

"You don't have a beating heart." Janie jerked on the iron shackles.

"Details." Tanya tapped her high-heel pump on the floor. "Girl, now don't you think I've been trying that? Those chains don't budge." Tanya yanked at the iron bracelets, her long, dark hair spilling forward as she struggled to free herself.

Janie wedged her dagger into one of the links, attempting to pry the link open. Her jaw clenched and she thrust the dagger against the iron. "It's not working." Sweat rolled down her face. *Do they have the heat blasting?*

"Why don't you let me try?" Tanya said, pouting her lush red lips.

Janie relaxed her grip on the dagger. "You're not touching any weapons."

"Whatever," Tanya said.

Janie took a few steps back. The hilt of her dagger slid over her wet skin. She clutched it tighter. There had to be another way.

Abram's words echoed in her head. *Lesson five—resourcefulness. If you focus, you will always find the answer. You are gifted; special…there are no obstacles you can't overcome. Always remember…use the resources around you; anything can be used as a weapon.*

Dry ice—upstairs, in the kitchen. She'd seen something on Animal Planet about an alternative to hot-branding livestock—a freeze-branding iron using dry ice. *It could work—weaken the metal so it will crack.*

"I'll be right back." Janie scurried over to the bottom step using her flashlight and the faint light streaming down the steps to guide her to the exit. She skipped steps, landing quietly on the wood as she ascended. A step creaked. The three Daychildren stopped bickering for a moment. They resumed—another argument over what they'd heard. The woman said she'd heard a car outside. The man said it was Tanya. The boy didn't seem to have an opinion.

Janie scrambled into the kitchen and snatched the cooler off the floor. She raced down the hallway, back to the door and down the steps.

"What are you going to do with dry ice?" Tanya peered into the cooler. "And what is that red blob on top of it?"

"I think it's a human heart." Both girls grimaced. "Part of their diet."

"I love blood, but eating the heart, ugh—those half-breeds are nasty." Tanya yanked on the chain and twisted her wrists within the cuffs. Blood dripped on to the concrete from where the metal had filleted her skin open. "Can you hurry and do whatever you're going to do with that stuff?"

Janie nodded, barely listening to Tanya. She placed the flashlight back in her jeans pocket and focused on scooping out the dry ice. It seared her hot palms and smoke rose from her skin. She quickly spread it over each cuff.

Tanya didn't react to the cold. She couldn't feel it. "Now what are you going to do?"

"Attempt to break the cuffs. I'm hoping the iron will crack more easily now. The ice may make it weaker." Janie slid the dagger through the cuff and centered all her strength into the metal. With one quick upward jerk, the cuff cracked enough for Tanya to free her wrist.

Janie did the same with the other cuff. Tanya flicked her wrist and the other cuff split, fully freeing her. She massaged her wrists and examined her wounds. "Those hurt."

"We've got to get out of here." Janie grabbed Tanya's bicep and tugged her forward.

"How do you suppose we do that? He's home."

Janie and Tanya froze at the base of the steps. The sound of Antony's angry voice barreled through the upstairs office. He berated the three arguing imbeciles. "You idiots—who's watching the vamp?"

"She's still asleep," the woman said.

"How do you know? Did you check on her?" There was a large crack. "Don't make me plunge this through your skull." Antony stomped toward the basement door.

"I can take him," Tanya growled. She placed one red-soled Christian Louboutin pump on the bottom step. In the light, Janie caught a glimpse of Tanya's Rock & Republic jeans, dark with flashy rhinestones creating symmetrical swirling patterns over the back pockets.

"I'd be willing to bet he has the rest of his crew with him. We need to find a way out of here." Janie yanked Tanya behind the staircase and out of the light. "When they come down the steps and make their way over to your shackles, before they notice you're gone we'll shoot up the steps. Stay close to me and just keep running beside me. You have to be within reaching distance."

"For what? Why?" Tanya said.

"We'll be leaving through the wall."

"What?" Tanya chuckled. "No joke?"

"Just trust me. It will be faster than dealing with a locked door." Janie wiggled her foot around. She needed to remove her shoe. The demon blood had started eating away at her flesh.

"But I'm just as fast as they are. I don't need to run through walls, or whatever."

Janie spun Tanya around to face her. Tanya's bare arms were muscular but slim and toned. "I helped get you out of the restraints. Now you are going to help me get out of here, alive, and with you."

Tanya opened her arms, breaking Janie's grasp around her biceps. "You never did say why you agreed to do this."

Janie shrunk further under the staircase, taking Tanya with her. "Antony's coming. I'll fill you in later."

Heavy footfalls clomped down the wooden steps above their heads. A fine mist of wood showered them. Wood shavings coated Janie's arms. She raked her fingers through her hair, shaking out the particles. They watched four figures walk toward the empty shackles. Janie recognized Antony's plump, round body in the back of the group. She heard the commotion of Daychildren upstairs. On instinct, Janie's eyes shot up. *Who knows how many are up there?*

"Now," Janie said.

The two girls leapt to their feet, swung around the steps and hurtled the staircase. Tanya did as instructed. She stayed next to Janie, within arm's reach.

Antony's angry voice boomed through the basement. "Get them! They aren't leaving alive!"

They reached the top of the staircase. A set of fingers closed around Janie's ankle. She kicked back, but the boy only tightened his grasp. He grunted. As he squeezed, his fingernails dug deeper into her skin. Tanya stomped on his forearm with the heel of her pump. He dropped his hold. Janie stumbled forward off the top step, landing on the floor. She hit the ground for only a second. Tanya scooped her up and helped her to her feet.

Janie sprinted forward, Tanya still clinging to her arm. Angry Daychildren yelled obscenities behind them. Their voices grew closer with every step they took. She could pick out the words: *vamp, Seeker, they're getting away, rip out their insides*. The last comment made her tremble. She remembered the heart in the cooler of dry ice.

As they ran through the kitchen, Janie started to feel different, weak, like a fading source of electricity, a light bulb dimming. Kai's life force was leaving her. She didn't know how long she'd have her ability.

As she came closer to the brick wall, panic raked through her. Tanya's hand tightened around her bicep as if she also could feel the dread of running straight into the unmovable and completely solid brick structure. Tanya could heal fast, so hitting the wall would only sting for a little while if they didn't make it in time. *But what if we go through?* Janie wondered if Tanya would simply starve to death. *What about me? Will I die immediately or die of starvation? What happens to molecules when they become trapped within another solid object?* Chemistry wasn't her forte.

They reached the wall. Someone gripped the back of Janie's sweatshirt. The girls flew through the wall. They landed on all fours on the asphalt and stumbled upright. Tanya blinked, staring at the wall and Janie, the wall again and back at Janie. "D-did—Did we just go through the wall?"

Kai's ability faded, leaving Janie weak. She doubled over in pain. The ability had left her.

Tanya helped Janie stand. "We've got to get out of here, sugar."

Janie nodded and removed her corroded boot. She winced against the pain, and they took off up the alley.

CHAPTER 13

Tanya wrapped herself up in Jerome's bony arms. He looked hesitant to let her go again. "You held up your part of the deal, Seeker. You brought her back to me, in one piece." Tanya playfully tickled her red fingernails over his forearm and the dagger tattoo that ran up his bicep. He smiled, revealing a less gangster side of himself.

"Now will you help us?" Kai said. Janie guessed he felt her coldness. He stood closer to Jerome than her. She'd refused to look at him, even acknowledge his presence when they met in her back yard. It was too painful. This was business—she had to be near him for the moment. *But after tonight, it's over.*

She glanced at her dark house. With her mother working the night shift at the hospital, they were alone. She knew neither her mother nor Abram would approve of any of this. Janie refocused her attention on Jerome for his answer.

"A deal is a deal," he said. "You have the support of vamps. Whatever you need."

"We need to stop Antony from Turning any more high school students," Janie said. "Do you know what he plans to do next?"

"Word is he's planning something at Loch Raven High on Friday night. Some sort of mass Turning. Whoever survives the Turn, survives. Those who don't, don't." Jerome kissed the insides of Tanya's wrists, her raw skin almost completely healed. "Tavares wants to see numbers. Baltimore's down. It's Antony's way of stepping it up for the big man. And what better way to do it but on the Seeker's turf."

"Friday." Janie flipped through her mental calendar. She knew that date. *Something significant is happening this weekend: Matt, Homecoming.* "The Homecoming football game." She hobbled closer to Jerome. Kai reached out to help her, but she drew back and supported herself on her uninjured foot. "Antony's planning to Turn the whole football team at the Homecoming football game."

Kai stepped forward. "Now that we know, we'll stop him." He pulled his scythe out of his belt and rotated it by the tip of the blade and the bottom of the hilt. Janie knew he wasn't nervous because of Antony's plan. It was her. She radiated pure hatred; a hatred that could only develop when you love someone—the fine line between love and hate had been crossed. *When was he going to tell me he killed my father? Ever?*

"You okay?" Jerome addressed Janie. "You're kind of green, sick-looking. . .and angry."

Janie thought her sick feeling was from standing so close to Kai after what she'd learned, but she did feel nauseated. *Her foot—it really hurt.* Kai reached for her again. "I'm fine," she barked. He retracted his arm. Janie stared at Jerome, fighting the urge to wobble over and hit the ground. "Meet us with as many vamps as you have at Loch Raven High—six o'clock Friday night so we can plan." Jerome studied her expression. "Be prepared to fight."

Tanya whispered something in his ear. He deliberated and finally spoke, "Seeker, you've got it. We'll be there." Tanya winked. *Tanya said she'd be indebted to her for freeing her. She'd kept her word.*

Jerome switched his focus to Kai, waiting for him to slide the scythe back into his belt. "I heard something else. You're one powerful dude. Tavares made you. What's it like to go against your Maker?"

Kai didn't answer. Janie couldn't read his expression. One thing was apparent—whenever anyone spoke Tavares's name, Kai went silent.

Jerome didn't press. He flashed a peace sign, or a gang symbol; Janie couldn't tell. "I'm out." Jerome and Tanya disappeared.

"Let me see your foot." Kai slid his arm through hers, holding her upright.

"Don't touch me." She unhitched her arm and stumbled to the ground. *Lesson two, the most important—don't let them see your weaknesses.* Unfortunately for her, he was her weakness. She wouldn't let him see her broken heart. How crushed she felt after letting herself become vulnerable. *Never again.*

"Did I do something to upset you?" He knelt down beside her. Her heart tightened. He looked so worried. The bright green of his irises had washed to gray. Usually so cocky and strong, he appeared worn and feeble.

She made herself look at him, confront him head-on. "I think you know what you did." She pulled her knees into her chest and curled into a ball. Her foot throbbed. Her sock had been eaten away, exposing her raw skin. At this point she wasn't sure what hurt worse, her foot or her heart.

"We need to clean your foot. If you don't get the demon blood off, it's only going to get worse." He bracleted her ankle and tugged. She extended her leg, letting him draw her foot closer to him. Not that she had much of a choice. He was too fast. He examined the bottom of her foot. "It's not too bad. Let's get you inside."

Before she could protest, he flipped her into a cradle-hold and sprinted forward. They landed in the kitchen. Janie glanced back at the hideous ivy wallpaper. They'd gone through the wall. She felt sweet breath on her face. Her focus slid back to Kai. She appraised his beautiful features—high cheekbones, angular jaw line, and the lush blond lashes encasing his striking green eyes. He was gorgeous; a monster, but still gorgeous. She wanted to tangle her fingers in his waves and pull him into her. *He killed my father. He can't be trusted. How can I love someone like that? What's wrong with me?*

Kai turned on the faucet and tested the water. "Here, it's warm. Put your foot under. I'll hold you."

She placed her foot under the stream of water. He used small, light strokes to massage the blood from her open wounds. She closed her eyes, imagining them on a warm white sandy beach, splashing around in calm crystal waves. She lay on her back while Kai massaged her feet. She seemed to float weightlessly. He twirled her around and guided her forward and back.

The water shut off and the image faded. She opened her eyes. They weren't on the beach. They were in her ugly kitchen, and the facts remained the same—they could never be together.

Kai handed her a towel.

After drying off her foot, she hobbled into the living room and flopped onto the sofa.

"I would have carried you," Kai said. He rounded the corner and smirked, exposing an adorable dimple. He wore a solid orange T-shirt and jeans. He looked good in orange.

"You need to leave." She tried to make her words sound harsh. Maybe then he would go. He was stubborn—like her. She doubted it.

As she suspected, he didn't listen. He chose a seat on the neighboring sofa cushion, not close enough to invade her space, but still close enough to be next to her. Clean lavender floated through the air around him. "I'm not going anywhere until you tell me why you're so angry with me."

The veins in her forehead throbbed. She could explode, like a cherry red tomato squeezed so tightly it burst. "Did you recognize Abram? Is that why he looked as if he could kill you on the spot? Is that why you left so quickly?" She trembled. His rough hands cradled hers. She ripped them from his grasp.

Kai swallowed. "I need you to be more specific." She could tell by his shaky voice that he didn't need specifics. He already knew.

"You're going to make me say it." She glared at him. "Coward."

Kai pressed his fingertips into his forehead. "Okay." He moved closer. She held him back with her hand. "I recognized Abram. He was there *that* night."

"What night?" Janie felt as if she could rip him to pieces. All of the anger, pain and questions she'd grown up with rushed back to her consciousness like a crashing tidal wave.

His words were softer. "Janie—you know what I'm talking about."

"Say it!"

"Janie—" He put his hands out, but this time he didn't touch her. It was a signal to calm her. It only made her more irate.

"Just say it!"

Kai let out a breath. "The night I killed your father."

Janie crumpled. The flood she'd been holding in came pouring out. Kai didn't attempt to comfort her. She'd probably kill him.

Kai continued. His voice quivered, but he did his best to speak calmly, not wanting to upset her any more than he already had. "I recognized Abram. I suspected the man I killed could have been your father, but I wasn't sure. It's been years." He swallowed, a seizure of pain apparent in his forlorn features. He stood and circled the coffee table. He scooped her father's picture off the side table and stared at it. "Then I saw this picture and knew for sure." He was silent again. "His face haunts me every night in my dreams. Not a day goes by that I don't regret—" He couldn't finish. It didn't matter. She didn't want to hear him say it again—*killing your father.*

Janie wiped her tears with her sleeve. She wouldn't show him any more weakness or how much she still loved him despite the circumstance. "Abram said something that's been bothering me."

Kai didn't speak. He waited, gently placing the frame back on the table.

She continued. "You weren't a monster when you killed him. You were part human. I trusted you, thought you were different, but you're no different. I actually thought that I—" She stopped. She refused to use those words to describe him, ever.

Kai collapsed in front of her. His knees thudded on the hardwood floor. "I am different. Albania returned my soul and my humanity. The only demonic quality I possess is my ability."

She glanced over at her father's picture, the handsome, blond-haired, blue-eyed Caucasian who had fallen for her Cherokee mother, a Seeker. She inhaled and exhaled slowly, turning her head to address Kai once again. "Abram said he would never forget your green eyes. True Daychildren have black eyes. Albania had already healed you, restored your humanity. . .or so she thought. You had both of us fooled." Her voice fell to a whisper. She closed her eyes, once again envisioning them on the beach. A slight smile crossed her face.

Returning to his gaze, Janie said, “Have you ever felt anything human?” *Felt anything for me?*

Janie’s words sliced through Kai. He’d been laid open, wounds exposed for all to see. Never had he felt so vulnerable, even when he was one hundred percent human. Never had he felt so guilty and broken. The only person he truly loved hated him. She had every reason to hate him for what he’d done. He hated himself for it. He’d live in his own prison for the rest of his life. “I never felt as human as I do when I’m with you.” She had to believe him. She hadn’t turned away from him. Maybe there was a chance he could make this right.

“You’re a monster,” she said. The words were like daggers stabbing him over and over again, like someone held him down and smeared salt into his bleeding incisions. The lungs he didn’t need tightened.

Kai cried out in defense. “Abram almost killed me. I wish he had. I’m so sorry. I didn’t mean to hurt you.”

He tried to look away, but she held his gaze. “But why? If you say you had a soul, how could you kill him?”

“It was my first night as what I am today. I only knew how to be a Daychild—I had an ingrained instinct to kill, granted to me by the most powerful vampire. His power is almost impossible to deny.”

“Tavares,” Janie said.

Kai nodded and clutched her legs. He had to make her see the truth, understand the inner turmoil he’d endured. “I left Albania’s. I was so confused. And the pain. . .the guilt of all those years of killing. . .what I'd done." He didn't know whether to continue or how much she knew. *It can't be any worse. No matter what I say, she already hates me.* "Your father was in the wrong place at the wrong time. I tried to stop, but when I did, he was already dead. I'd drained him of too much blood."

"And Abram?" Her words were hard, emotionless. *He'd really lost her.*

"He was a strong fighter, and I was broken." Kai held up his arms, exposing the human scars. "He injured me, left me scars to always remember him by, but I got away." He glanced at the three lines streaking down his forearm. "My humanity was so fresh. I healed like a human, not a vampire." He placed his hand over his heart. "The only other human scar is here." He breathed out, he'd forgotten. "And here." He pointed to his knee. "I fell off my bike when I was ten."

Janie's features softened. "I can't begin to understand how troubled your life has been, the tortures you've gone through, but we are talking about my father." She looked away. "I can't forgive you."

He redirected her with his finger under her chin. "I understand. I will never forgive myself. Words can't express how truly sorry I am."

All emotion left her voice. "It's a lot to process. Let's just get through Friday. We have bigger things to worry about than us." He knew she'd put up a wall. He wouldn't get through to her now.

He clutched her jeans. It was only Sunday. She expected him to get through Friday without her. Going from love to loneliness was worse than not knowing love at all. At least then he didn't know what he was missing. Now that he'd found her, he refused to let her go. "Please give us a chance. I'll spend eternity making it up to you, showing you how sorry I am."

"Why do you care?" She seemed defeated. "Humans—we are expendable to your kind. What makes me any different?"

"Humans. . .my kind—have you not heard a word I've said to you?" Sometimes the things she said infuriated him. "I'm not like them. I'm more like you than you choose to believe. We have the same purpose—rid the streets of them." His voice deepened to a growl. "Don't ever call me one of *them* again. I'm not one of them."

"So you felt, for me. Can *you* feel?"

His palms traveled up her thighs and settled around her lower back. He slid her forward. She wrapped her legs around his waist and locked her ankles. He knelt on the floor, clutching her at arm's length. Kai knew if it weren't for his grasp she would fall. He'd never let her go. His eyes stung. They were wild, filled with passion—he could feel it. Any emotion he'd ever felt pierced straight through her, to the depths of her soul. He finally spoke, "I can feel."

She breathed heavily. Her eyes swirled with fear and yearning, like he was a forbidden fruit she wanted and hated at the same time. "What do you feel?" she exhaled.

Kai drew her into him, placing his lips on the smooth skin at the base of her neck. "You're beautiful." He traced a perfect line up to her chin with the tip of his nose. He breathed heavily on her neck. Tiny goose bumps formed along her skin. "You're smart." His lips found one corner of her mouth, and slid over to her lips. "You're strong." He lost himself in her soft, warm kiss. "Janie—"

"Yes." She combed her fingers through his hair, causing his body to spasm, creating a sensation he'd never felt before—ever.

"I feel," he said. *More than you will ever know.*

CHAPTER 14

Janie opened her locker and a bouquet of red roses sprung out at her. She jumped and quickly slammed the door to hold them in. She let her heart settle back into her chest. It was like snakes springing out of a can—unexpected.

"You don't like red?" Matt said. He walked up behind her.

She spun around to face him. He smiled. "I do. I just didn't expect anything to fly out of my locker when I opened it. How did you get in, anyway?"

"Your locker?" His brows rose. "It's easy. They aren't secure." Matt reached around her and pounded his fist into the metal door. It flung open. Flowers showered the floor. "Sorry, I'll get those." He knelt down.

She joined him. "Thanks."

"Did you get my text?" He handed her the seven or so flowers he plucked off the floor and stood up.

She rose to her feet and placed the flowers back in the locker. "Um, no." Then she remembered—*miss u.* "Oh yeah, I did. . .I was really busy last night. I didn't have time to respond."

"It's okay." He interlaced his fingers through hers. She stiffened. "I'll walk you to class."

"You don't have to." She wiggled her fingers free of his.

"Janie—we're going to the same class." He reached for her hand again. She grabbed a book out of her locker to avoid his touch. "So we're still on for Homecoming?"

"Homecoming?" Luke said. He swaggered up beside them wearing a fashionable black leather coat over a white tee. He looked chic, like a model out of a fifties fashion magazine. "You're going. . .together?"

"Don't look so surprised, Luke," Janie snapped.

"I—I'm not." Luke looked at Matt in confusion. "I thought you were going with Molly. That's all she talked about last period. She's already picked out a couture gown. She had a pic. It's totally red carpet."

Janie glared at him. "I'm just sayin'." He fluttered his hand. "Never mind. You'll look gorgeous, too." He hesitated, studying her jeans and hoodie. "We'll find something for you to wear."

Ava joined them. She stood arm-in-arm with Luke. "I thought I told you Matt asked Janie to the dance. It must have slipped my mind."

"Have you asked anyone yet?" Matt asked Luke.

He went catatonic. "Luke—" Janie waved her hand in front of his face.

Luke blinked. "Sorry—I was just picturing the cheerleaders roasting you like a pig. Molly's going to freak." He placed his hand on his waist. "And no, I haven't." Luke glanced down at Ava. A look of uncertainty flashed across his face.

"Uh—I'll probably just study that night," Ava said.

"You're coming with us. We'll go as a group," Janie said. *Please, please, please say you will.*

"But it's not like a couple thing, 'cause that would be weird." Ava's eyes shot up to Luke again. "Right?"

"Right." Sweat beaded across Luke's forehead.

The bell rang. "We'd better get to class," Matt suggested. He grabbed Janie's hand before she had time to dodge him, too busy watching Luke and Ava's weird reactions to each other.

"Luke—later bro," Matt extended his free hand for a fist bump. Luke glanced down at his own hand, made a fist and tapped Matt's. Luke turned around and shook the pain off.

Matt winked at Ava. She started to blush.

Janie slid into her car after school. She'd finally shaken Matt. The Imprinting thing was getting way out of hand. He was always there. She couldn't wait to get home, where she could be free. It's not like she didn't like him. He was cute, popular and courteous, but those crazy I-want-to-see-you-every-second and I-can't-live-my-life-without-you feelings weren't there. *Not like with Kai.* Matt was a safer choice. Could she even move forward with Kai after everything she'd learned?

She started the car, trying to think about how to tell Abram about Friday's somewhat-put-together plan. As her mentor and "boss," he had to know—it was against Seeker rules to go rogue. She could make her own decisions, but Abram had to be informed of her actions at all times. She planned to Seek that evening. She'd use that time to think of the best way to tell him.

Janie decided it was best to Seek far from Antony's lair. She didn't want to interfere with Friday night. The vampire community had agreed to help defeat Antony. She couldn't let anything get in the way of that plan.

She straddled the border of Baltimore City, next to Towson. Even though it was a Monday, the college students were out. They sported wrist bands indicating they could get all the keg beer they wanted at a local bar. A group of girls giggled. The bouncer accepted their fake IDs and waved them in. Janie envied their carefree attitudes. They went through a "normal" sequence of life—one round of high school. She realized that by this time, had she been allowed to go straight through school, she'd be very close to graduating from college.

All day, she hadn't heard from or seen Kai. He usually let himself into her room or snuck up on her while she Seeked. She wondered if he still "felt" for her. She wasn't easy to be with, and he had his own reasons to be distant.

Her cell vibrated in her pocket. *Abram.*

"Hi, what's up?" she answered, hesitant after their last conversation.

"Where are you?" He sounded angry. She didn't like this side of him.

"I'm in the city, outside Towson." Janie chuckled. "It's five dollars drink-all-the-beer-you-want night at the local bar."

Abram grunted. He didn't seem amused. "You need to come home. We have to talk. The Chapter met this morning."

Janie shrunk back into a childlike stance on the sidewalk. Abram was not only angry, he was disappointed—in her.

Instead of going straight home, she found herself at Kai's, standing on his porch. The porch light lit a small area around her. Janie willed herself to ring the doorbell. She wanted so badly to speak with him: to see his green eyes, watch his wavy blond hair fall into his face when he became angry or defensive, trace his imperfect human scars with her finger. She wanted him to hold her. She could taste the scent of lavender on her tongue just thinking about his kiss.

She pulled her hand back. There was a reason he hadn't come around. *Not tonight. I'll give him time.*

Janie left the porch and descended down the concrete steps toward her car.

"Janie—what are you doing here?"

She whirled around. "You're home?"

Kai smirked. "That's usually where I am on a Monday night." He stepped out on the porch, shirtless and exposing every scar. Sweat rolled down his chest. "I was training for Friday."

"I'll let you get back to that." Janie turned to leave.

"Did you need something?" Kai's words were careful, distant. She felt like they were back at the beginning of their relationship, when they didn't know where the other stood. It was awkward.

"No. I—" Janie looked past him, through the door, and noticed three boxes stacked just inside the doorway. "What's going on?" Her lungs tightened. She rustled around in her pocket for her inhaler.

Kai followed Janie's gaze. "Oh, those." He cleared his throat. "I'm packing."

"For what?" She stepped back, tripping off the step.

He stepped out the door. He seemed hesitant to speak. "After Friday. . .I'm leaving. I thought I'd go to Tucson. Check on my family. I haven't decided whether to approach them. I guess I'll decide when the time comes."

Janie stood, silent.

"It's better this way—for you," Kai continued.

"Don't presume to know what's best for me." Janie started for her car. She couldn't even look at him.

He appeared in front of her in the street. "I killed your father. You've already made it clear you will never forgive me." He sighed. "I can live with never forgiving myself. It's a torture I've readily accepted, but the thought of you hating me. . .that kills me."

She brushed his hair out of his eyes. "I could never hate you."

"For now, but as time goes on—" His voice cracked. "You could start to resent me. I can't take that chance, for either of us."

Janie took a puff of her inhaler, partly to control her asthma and partly to stop her from blurting out something she'd regret. *How dare you tell me what's best for me or how I will feel in the future? It's not your call.* "Will you come back?"

"I don't know." He cradled her face in his hands. The sweat from his chest had dried in the cool air. He kissed her.

She spoke with his lips on hers. "Please don't leave me."

Her phone vibrated. She pulled back from Kai. He dropped his hands from her face. A text from Abram—*where r u?*

"I have to go."

"Matt?"

"No, worse—Abram. He found something out today. He wants to talk. He's angry." She started toward her car. Kai placed his hand on her arm. She stopped.

"Do you want me to come with you?" He looked right through her. It stung.

"I don't think that's a good idea, considering your history with each other." She examined the scars on his forearm, the scars Abram had created.

"You're right." He let go and stepped up on the curb. "Call me if you need me."

She nodded and left.

Abram removed the tea kettle from the stove and poured boiling water into a mug. He didn't say anything to her at first.

"Isn't it a little late for tea?" Janie said. "I guess Mom's working an extra night shift."

Abram nodded. "It's going to be a long night." He dropped a sugar cube into the water; the tea bag hung over the side of the mug. He motioned her to the table. "Why don't we sit?"

He pulled a chair out for her and chose the seat next to her.

For a moment Abram collected his thoughts. He stirred his tea with a spoon. His tired, blue eyes met hers. "You know I think of you like a daughter. I'd do anything for you." She nodded. "Today, I lied for you."

"Why? For what?" Abram cut her off with a raised hand.

"The Chapter knows about last night. They were afraid you'd gone rogue. I told them I knew you rescued the vampire and that I supported you."

"I was just doing my Seeker duties, protecting the innocent."

"Janie—you rescued a vampire. They aren't innocent."

"They are trying to be, kind of innocent, in a way. They aren't like the Daychildren. As I told you before, they're evolving, trying to blend in with human society. They don't want to be considered monsters. They don't have to kill to feed. There are plenty of humans who will give them blood willingly."

"It is not our job to protect vampires. We are Seekers. We protect humans."

Janie's blood pressure rose. "That is the way of the Chapter. It is ancient and outdated. Vampires aren't the main threat any more. Daychildren are the new demonic breed humans should fear. I didn't rescue Tanya because of—"

Abram laughed tightly. "Tanya. You're on a first-name basis with the night children." He sighed and raised a disappointed brow.

"That's not the point."

"It is the point. You can't go making friends with the vampire community. You are a Seeker."

"You're not talking about Tanya, or any of the others; you're talking about Kai. He has nothing to do with what happened last night. In fact, he was against it."

"For once I agree with *him.*" His words were spoken out of disgust. "You shouldn't have rescued a vampire."

"I didn't have a choice. If I didn't help Jerome—"

"Jerome—I can't listen to this any more." He dismissed her with a wave.

"Yes, the head vamp in Baltimore, Jerome." She took hold of his wrist, forcing him to listen to her. "He said he would help me take out the Baltimore gang of Daychildren. Their leader, Antony, is planning to Turn the Loch Raven football players on Friday night in an effort to please Tavares, to up his numbers." She unintentionally tightened her grip. "Has the Chapter even spoken to other Chapters? This is happening in cities other than Baltimore. Antony just happens to be in *my* city."

"That still doesn't explain why you helped Tanya."

"Jerome promised me we would have their support Friday night. He said the vampires would align with me. . .and Kai. He said they would help us stop Antony."

"And you trust a vampire?" His eyes tightened. When he was a Seeker, they killed vampires; they didn't trust them. *Lesson one—don't trust the undead.*

Janie threw her hands in the air. "What other choice do I have? It's just me and a whole gang of multiplying Daychildren."

"I wish you would have come to me. You always come to me. What made it different this time?" His voice cracked. He coated his throat with tea.

"Kai—you couldn't accept him. Even when you saw how much he meant to me." She touched his arm. "Now I know why. I understand. He killed Dad. I don't blame you. You witnessed it first-hand. You fought Kai and he got away."

He spoke softer, lowering the intensity of their conversation. "How do you feel about him now that you know?"

"I love him. It's not something I can just turn off. Of course I'm upset and hurt. I feel betrayed, but that doesn't change what's in my heart. I love him."

"I can't support your relationship." Although calmer, she could see his disappointment.

"You don't have to. He's leaving Friday, after the game. He has to live with Dad's death every day. Dad's face haunts him in his sleep. He's not the same person he was that night. He's changed."

Abram appeared to ignore her defense. "That's what's best, him leaving." He didn't seem overly joyous, either. This led her to believe he didn't fully believe his own words. Maybe he had heard some of her argument. She knew he cared more about her feelings than Seeker etiquette.

"As for the Chapter," he continued, "I won't tell them that you've aligned with the vampire community, but I will have to warn other Chapters about Tavares's plans."

"Thank you. That's all I ask." Janie rose and kissed the lines on his forehead. "If that's all, good night."

CHAPTER 15

Kai lay across Janie's bed, waiting. He switched from his back to his side, and back again, finally settling on his side. She'd been talking with Abram for a while. He was tempted to listen in on their conversation again, but he didn't. He'd heard enough. Instead, he waited. He noticed a book on her nightstand and scooped it up. *Twilight.* He laughed, shaking his head. *A Seeker who loves vampire stories.*

He heard footsteps outside her bedroom door. He put the book back in its place and flipped on to his back. The door opened. Janie entered as she usually did, not surprised to find him in her room.

The front door shut and locked. Seconds later, Abram's car started up and he left.

"You okay?" Kai said.

"Yup." Janie took a seat next to him on the bed. "I didn't expect to see you again tonight, although I'm getting used to you being in my room." She fell silent. "It's not gonna be the same after you leave."

"I was worried about you." He sat up and slid next to her. Her feet dangled over the edge of the bed. His touched the floor. "Did it go okay?"

"Yes, he supports me." Her voice was low, sad.

"He supports you in aligning with the vampires, but he sounded happy that I was leaving town." He regretted his words. Every time he thought about leaving her, a little more of him chipped away. *She'll never trust me. I don't have a choice.*

"I'm not so sure of that. He knows the pain it will cause me." Kai didn't say anything. He'd already rationalized his decision. There was no point in arguing. She would never be able to forgive him for taking her father away from her and her mother.

Kai turned to face her. "You know we have no idea how Antony intends to execute his plan. We can't just have an all-out brawl at your high school."

She jumped off the bed. "You're right. We need a plan. Are you tired?" One moment she acted sullen and defeated. The next, she could be pumped up like she'd been injected with steroids. He knew her well. Aggression helped mask her pain.

"Why?" He recognized the reckless look in her eyes.

"We need to go back to the lair." She left the bed and slipped on her boots.

"So that you can get yourself killed." He confronted her. "No." She'd just gone there last night. He refused to take the chance.

"I'll be with you." She batted her brown eyes. Her long black lashes melted away any common sense. *I'd do anything for you.*

"Don't try to butter me up," he said. "You know damn well you can take care of yourself." He shook his head, staring at the ground. Stubborn—a quality he loved about her. "Fine. Let's go see what we can find out."

They crouched behind the dumpster she'd hidden behind the night before. The same small light created rectangular shadows, what Janie now knew reflected a refrigerator and a lonely chair. Their arms touched. She could smell him, taste him. Her heart raced. It was all she could do not to grab him and kiss him. She couldn't. *He doesn't think I can ever trust him again. He is wrong.*

"I hear Antony near the front of the building. He's angry," Kai said.

"As usual." Janie focused back on the old law firm. "Can you hear what he's saying?"

"No." He exhaled. "I don't know why I'm going to suggest this."

"What?" she said.

"We need to go inside. Did you say the kitchen was in the back? I'll be able to hear them better in there." A police car whizzed by the alley, siren blaring. "It's too loud out here."

"Through the wall?" she said, standing to align herself with Kai.

He smiled. “You read my mind. Run with me. Just make sure you hold on tight.” Kai wrapped his arm around her waist. “Ready?”

“Ready.” His muscles constricted across her back.

They sprinted toward the stone building. She gripped his hand that encircled her and they leapt through the wall, landing on the kitchen floor. He coiled her into him to steady her.

She covered her nose with the sleeve of her coat. “I’ll never get used to the smell.”

Kai tugged her behind the wet bar. “Someone’s coming.”

Antony and the spiky-haired girl Janie remembered entered the kitchen.

“Did you get what we need?” Antony said.

“We did,” she answered. “We have enough souls to Turn the whole team.” She laughed, her voice squeaky and resonating in an abnormally high pitch. “The demon world isn’t lacking in supply.”

“Good. How about the vampire venom?” Antony paced the floor.

“It’s being taken care of as we speak. Jerome won’t know what hit him.” The girl spit on the floor. “Serves them right.”

“Jerome sent a Seeker to my home. He will pay,” Antony said.

The girl laughed, though it sounded more like a snort and a screech.

“He chose to align with the Seeker. He will soon know how much of a mistake that was.”

The girl's brows rose. "So, we're still going to move up the timeline. You don't want to wait till Friday?"

"No—" Antony said. "We'll do it at practice, tomorrow."

Kai mouthed *Shit*, his stare still planted on Antony and the spiky-haired girl. Janie figured his sudden stiffness had to do with Antony's plan to move up the attack. But it was something else entirely. *What's wrong?*

"I smell Seeker. She's here." Antony darted in their direction. At the same time Kai hurled her into the air, grasping her arm and running for the wall.

Antony grabbed hold of her ponytail and yanked her out of Kai's grip. She landed back on the kitchen floor. "You aren't gettin' away this time."

Janie searched for Kai. He was already through the wall. Antony spun her on to her back and straddled her. His fat body crushed her pelvis into the floor. She swore she heard her bones crack. He flattened her ear against the hardwood floor, exposing her neck. "I'll suck the life outta you."

Janie arched and walked her fingers across her lower back until she found the hilt of her dagger. She slipped it out of her waistband and popped her knee, catching Antony in the groin. He groaned and grabbed himself, releasing her. She rolled out from under him and jumped into a fighting stance. Her blade reflected the light of a faint overhead brass chandelier.

"Janie—" Kai stood next to her again. He'd come back through the wall for her. "Let's go."

"But I can take him," she said. The room flooded with Daychildren.

"You'll have to get through them first." Kai twirled her around. "Another time." He shot back through the wall with her in his gasp.

Outside, Janie stormed up the sidewalk. Kai kept pace. "Where are you going?"

"To warn Jerome. You heard Antony. He's going to attack the vamps tonight and Turn the football players tomorrow at practice." She dodged a group of guys who had just exited a dive bar. They were clearly drunk and taking up the entire sidewalk. They exhaled into the cold air, sending the smell of beer and cigarettes her way.

"Hey, babe," one said to Janie. "Nice ass."

Kai growled and lunged at the guy. The guy put his hands up. "She's yours, got it."

"What time's practice?" Kai said, ignoring the drunks.

"Why?" Janie turned down an alley. She stalked forward. "Where's Jerome? There aren't any vampires out."

"Daylight." Kai sped in front of her, blocking her path.

She smacked into his chest and stopped in her tracks. "Crap—" she realized, "practice is right after school—three o'clock. The vamps can't help us. They'll be asleep. And if they aren't, they'll burst into flames."

"Albania," Kai said.

"Will she help?"

"I can try."

"You go find Albania. I'll find Jerome." Janie pushed past him.

He held her in place. "Meet me at your car. No longer than thirty minutes or I'll come looking for you." He gave her a quick kiss. "Be careful."

She touched her lips. "You too."

Kai paced the floor. He thought he had more days with Janie. The timeline had been moved up, so now he had only one night left with her. He stared at a floral painting at the end of the hallway. *Come on, Albania. Answer. You've got to be here.*

The door swung open. Kai breathed a sigh of relief. "You're here."

Albania was dressed in a long black silk nightgown. It skimmed the floor, sweeping over her hot pink toenails. Her red hair framed her petite face. "What is it? Is it Janie?"

"Janie's fine. Can I come in?"

"Sure." She motioned for him to pass. Albania kissed his cheek and wove her fingers through his. She led him over to the couch. "Please sit with me." She still held his hand. "Did it work? Was Janie able to rescue Tanya before your gift wore off?"

"She did. Thanks to you." He smiled. Her presence calmed him. His first instinct had always been to react, but Albania had taught him to think first. He had to keep a level head in order to make the wisest decisions. *Lavender.* Bathing in lavender had been Albania's idea, something about it being a soothing herb. She once admitted she liked the smell on him. "I need your help again."

"Anything." She squeezed his hand.

"Can you create a spell that will make the night children walk in the daylight?"

She gasped, taken by surprise. "Why would you want to do that?"

"It would only be temporary, only for a few hours."

"Kai, I can't do that. I swore to use my gifts for good. I'll never do anything for vampires."

"This isn't for them. It's for Janie, me and a whole team of high school football players."

"Now I'm really confused." Albania scooted closer to Kai. She removed her hands from his and traced a line around his face, eyeing him adoringly. "When I found you, I was drawn to you. You lay dying, a silver blade so close to your brain that death wasn't immediate, but would be slow and painful. I felt for you. I've always hated vampires, but with you. . .you were different somehow. I felt as though I loved you even then, before I even knew you." She placed one finger on his lips. "Tavares knew you were different. He tried to kill you before you could reach your full potential. You were such a disappointment to him. The first Daychild created, yet you showed signs of a conscience. How would his new race of vampires succeed, grow and flourish, if the first one he created showed signs of weakness?" She kissed his lips. "But you are anything but weak. That's why I love you."

"Then trust that I'm only asking this of you because it will save many human lives. Trust in what we have meant to each other, what we still mean to each other, and help me."

Albania stared deeply into his eyes as if reading something written behind them. "You're leaving?"

"You know me well." He looked away. Airplane lights flickered outside her apartment's expansive window.

"You and Janie will miss each other."

He tried to hold back his emotions, but tears stung his eyes. "She knows what I did."

"Abram told her?" Albania said. Kai nodded and returned to her worried gaze. Albania closed her eyes. She breathed deeply, taking in everything around her within a state of meditation. "I don't feel anger when I think of Janie. Only love. She loves you. She'll move past this. She's human. You have to give her time to heal."

Kai's words came out with a forced edge. "Are you certain of this? Certain enough not to destroy Janie's life? She's never wanted love. She runs from it. What I did suffocated her ability to let someone in, to let someone love her. She's grown up empty, afraid if she needed anyone too much she would lose them." He breathed. "Love isn't worth the risk to her."

"And you love her?" Albania's head dipped forward. "You never loved me like that. It was never me. I knew it." Kai tried to speak. She lifted her gaze and covered his lips with her fingertips. "Don't. You don't need to explain. I'll help you."

"Thank you."

Albania pushed her wide, bony shoulders back. He could always count on her to set her own feelings aside and focus on what needed to be done. "I can only grant a few of them access to the sun. Choose the ones you want and have them meet me in the harbor right before sunrise. I'll find them. They will be given the ability to walk in the sunlight for only one day. After the sun goes down, they will return to the night."

"You have possibly just saved the lives of many." Kai kissed both of her cheeks and stood. "You're not just a witch, you're a guardian angel." He hustled over to the door. "I need to meet Janie." He reached for the doorknob and glanced back. Albania sat, legs crossed under the silk, watching him. "I do love you. I always have and I always will. I'm alive because of you. I can love because of you."

"Janie," she whispered.

He nodded and left.

Thanks to one of his gang members, Janie finally found Jerome with Tanya at the Dead Solitarian, otherwise known as the "vampire graveyard," located within the human graveyard, only their bodies weren't buried. When vampires died, their bodies vanished, much like Daychildren. So, instead of burying bodies, they lay tombstones of remembrance.

Jerome stood over a cluster of at least twenty new headstones. They were well polished and glossy under the moon's shine. One read—*Bubba Jones, may he finally have a cheesesteak to go with the blood—go Philly.*

"Am I too late?" Janie waited for Jerome to finish his prayer. He kissed his gold cross and directed his attention to the sky. *Do vamps pray? She knew their aversion to crosses was a myth, but praying? Whatever.*

"Seeker," was all he said.

"Hey, girl." Tanya draped herself over Jerome's shoulder.

"I'm sorry about your gang. How many?"

"Twenty-three." Jerome cleared his throat. "They drained their venom and staked them."

"Antony wants to strike the high school tomorrow."

"I heard." He didn't look at her.

"Are you still going to help stop him?"

"No," he said. Anger rose in Janie's chest. He'd promised. Now that things had changed, he couldn't just go back on his promise.

Jerome continued. "I'm going to *kill* him."

"Tonight?" *That would solve everything. They wouldn't even have to worry about the football players or the sunlight issue.*

"No, unfortunately." Jerome caressed his cross with two fingers. He still hadn't made eye contact with her. "They just moved their lair. They knew we'd retaliate, so they vanished. I have my gang searching the city. It's probably useless. Antony won't hide where he knows we can find him."

"They will be at football practice tomorrow afternoon. That's where they plan to Turn the team."

"Seeker, in case you've forgotten, we are vamps; we don't do daylight. It'll have to be another time for us."

Janie skirted a tombstone, stepping closer to Jerome and Tanya with determination in her tone. "How many vamps do you need to defeat Antony and his crew?"

"They've got about twenty, so five of us should do, with you and Kai. They ambushed us tonight. That's the only reason they were able to do what they did." He kissed Tanya. "Why? It doesn't matter—we can't go in the sunlight."

"I just spoke with Kai. He has a friend who can arrange things so that you *can* go out in the daylight." For the first time, Jerome *really* looked at her. Janie held up her hand before he could speak. "Only for tomorrow. Pick five vamps from your gang, including you, and meet her at the harbor before sunrise."

"The harbor's a big place."

"She'll find you," Janie said. "Kai was right. Meeting on school grounds was a bad idea. Meet me at my house—two-thirty. We'll go together. I'm not exactly sure how Antony plans to execute his plan, but I'm pretty sure he doesn't care about exposure." She shot Jerome a serious look. "*We* are going to minimize the exposure—got it." She brushed a chunk of loose dirt from a freshly buried tombstone to expose the inscription—*Brotherhood.* "If the Chapter finds out I've allowed Daychildren and vampires to invade my high school. . .well, let's just say I'll be screwed. Luckily, most of the students will be leaving by three. Only the jocks, a few teachers and maybe students in after-school clubs will be left."

"Then it's done. We'll meet this friend of Kai's and be at your house." Jerome knelt down in front of another grave. He bowed his head.

"See you later, sugar." Tanya fluttered her red fingernails and knelt down beside him.

CHAPTER 16

Janie cornered a stone building. Kai was standing with his back against her car, his arms crossed in front of him. The car seemed to be holding up all his weight. Janie stopped to stare at him for a moment. He was beautiful, even with all his flaws. She realized she loved him because of his imperfections. She also realized she had forgiven him the moment she learned he'd killed her father.

She crossed the road.

"Hey." He didn't look up from the ground.

"It's done. The vamps are in." She snuggled up next to his ribs. He draped his arm around her. "Thanks for calling. That's great. . .about Albania."

"Yeah," he said softly.

"What's wrong? Other than the usual Daychild issues and," she paused, "other things."

"I'm just thinking about my conversation with Albania."

"Is she okay?"

"She's fine. She brought up something I've never told you before."

"What—that she loves you?"

Kai coughed, or choked, kind of a combination of both. "No—I mean yes, but that's not what I meant."

"It's okay. It's obvious the way she feels about you. The way she looks at you. I noticed the first day I met her." Janie bit her cheek. She tasted blood. Maybe their relationship affected her more than she had realized. "Do you feel the same? I mean—do you love her, too?"

"I love her. Not the way she'd like me to, but I love her as a very dear friend—the person who saved my life at one time and taught me how to live again. It's not like how I feel about you. She knows that." He caressed Janie's face with his free hand.

"What were you going to tell me?" She leaned into his touch.

"You already know Tavares was my Maker. I was the first Daychild he created. He had high hopes for me." He laughed. "I guess I wasn't living up to his expectations. I started to develop a conscience." His mood deepened. "I became depressed in a way. I was a killer, but afterwards, after I killed, I felt physically sick." Kai dropped his arm and leaned farther back against the car. Janie was afraid the metal door frame might crack. "He was ashamed of me. He didn't want to start a race of cowards, so he tried to kill me. Albania found me with a silver dagger through my skull. I was moments from death."

"So that's why you react the way you do when you hear his name. He was your Maker and he tried to kill you."

Kai tilted his head back. He stared at the star-filled sky. "He treated me as a son, in his own screwed-up way, and I let him down."

Janie couldn't believe he was saying this. The logic was so twisted. She grabbed his hand. "You can't feel ashamed. He's in the wrong. He's creating a demonic species that can't even begin to coexist with humans. They're killers. Even the vampires can't stand them. You are right and *he* is wrong."

He brought his gaze down to hers. "I know. It's just another one of my many issues. I'm broken. You deserve better."

She bit her tongue. *Could he really believe this?* "Kai Sterdam—don't you ever say that again. From a very young age, I set my life on a course of loneliness. I thought it was better to run from love and be alone then to take a chance. *Love gets you killed.* That's what I always told myself. I was wrong."

"Albania told me to stay. That you'd forgiven me." He angled his body to face her and slid his arms over her shoulders. He pinned her between himself and her car, exactly where she wanted to be.

"Albania was wrong. I've already forgiven you," she said. He kissed her.

Janie did her best to make it through her morning classes. She found herself staring at the clock for most of the morning, making the time creep by even slower.

After school she'd be meeting Jerome and the other vampires he picked to help them stop Antony. She glanced out the cafeteria window. Only a few puffy clouds lined the sky. *If Albania's spell doesn't work, Jerome and his crew are going to be toast.*

Kai would also be there. It might be the last time she would see him. She still hoped he'd change his mind. Before he came along, she couldn't imagine doing anything but her job. Now, things had changed; her priorities had changed. One thing stayed true—love complicated things. The question remained, though—was it worth it? *Definitely.*

Ava and Luke approached her cafeteria table. They'd chosen to eat on campus. Janie felt a need to stay close to school with everything about to take place after classes ended.

Luke cast a smile Ava's way. His eyes were blue again—colored contacts, no glasses. As they walked, their arms brushed together. Ava giggled nervously and her face shaded to scarlet.

She'd been so wrapped up with Kai and everything else going on, she hadn't noticed that her two best friends were actually flirting with each other.

"What's up, you two? You're looking awfully giddy today." Janie took a bite out of her apple, regarding both of them suspiciously.

"What do you mean?" Luke pulled out Ava's chair. She thanked him with a smile.

Janie made a circular motion with her hand. "I mean all of this. The giggling, blushing and *pulling* out the chair." She paused. "Come to think of it, yesterday, when Matt asked you about Homecoming, you were acting weird then, too. Is there something you need to tell me?"

"It's nothing." Luke looked away. "I forgot a napkin. Do you need anything?" he asked Ava.

Janie breathed in. "No Pippy comments today. Does she need anything? Come on, you're not fooling anyone. You like each other." She took another bite of her apple. "You are so going to the dance with us because you like each other." Janie finished chewing. "It's kind of weird, but I'll go with it, if you're happy."

"Believe what you want," Luke said. He pivoted and sauntered toward the kitchen, one hand on his hip. *He can't be into Ava; she's a girl.*

Janie became serious and leaned in closer to Ava. "I've got to talk to you before Luke gets back."

Ava put her un-eaten sandwich down. "What's up? Did you and Kai, or Matt, or—" She waved her hand around hesitantly, not sure which guy to mention, "—break up or something?"

"For the record, like I told you. . .I Imprinted Matt, so we are not really 'together.'"

"So he wants to be with you, but you're just not that into him."

"I guess." Janie rolled her eyes. She didn't know for sure. This Imprinting thing was new to her. "Isn't that a movie?"

"A good one, but I think it's the other way around—*He's Just Not That Into You.*" Ava popped open her can of soda. "And Kai?"

"I'm into him, and I think he feels the same." Janie's heart hurt. "Anyway, it doesn't matter. After today he'll be gone."

"What? Why?"

"I'll tell you about that later. I really do have something serious to talk to you about before Luke gets back." Janie searched for Luke. He'd stopped at a table full of guys, not jocks or brainers, but somewhere in between. *Like Luke.* "I need you and Luke to leave right after school today. Don't hang out in the parking lot, just go straight home."

"Are you going to give me a reason why?"

"Remember when I told you about Antony and his crew of Daychildren the day you helped me study for my Algebra exam?" Ava nodded. "They're planning to Turn the football team today at practice."

Ava's mouth dropped open. "How are you going to stop them?"

"The vamps have agreed to help us. We don't really have a plan since we don't know how Antony intends to carry out the mass Turning." Luke approached. Janie shoved the apple in her mouth. "Just make sure you're gone," she said through a mouthful of chewed fruit.

Ava switched to covert agent. She often did this when they were discussing "secretive" Seeker stuff. "Affirmative."

"What's affirmative?" Luke sat, neatly laying his napkin over his lap.

"It's girl stuff," Ava said.

Janie stood. "I'd love to stay and chat, but I've got to go." Her eyes shot over their heads. They traced her gaze. “Oh, no. Matt’s here. I’ve managed to avoid him for most of the day.”

“Oh—come—on, he’s cute. Have you ever seen eyes like that. . .and the hair? Who wouldn’t give to have that hair?” Luke fluttered his lashes. *Seriously, girls? No way!*

“Leave her alone. She has her reasons.” Ava tapped him on the leg. Her hand rested there longer than Janie felt comfortable. *They can’t be together. It’s practically incestuous.*

“Kai,” Luke said. “He’s pretty hot, too. The motorcycle thing is bitchin’.”

“Bitchin’?” Janie and Ava said.

“I’ll tell him you said that.” Janie smiled.

Luke glared at her and turned a deep shade of tomato red. Janie laughed. “I’ll see you later.” She whispered in Ava’s ear. “Remember what I said.”

Ava saluted.

She had to do it. She’d avoided him all day. He stood next to his locker getting ready for his next class. His varsity jacket hid part of his *very nice* butt. *Focus.* All she had to do was tell him to leave school on time. She’d feel horrible if anything happened to him. He’d already been attacked twice and Imprinted. *Here we go.* She continued forward.

Janie greeted Matt at his locker. “Hey.”

“Hey.” Matt turned, dropping his books. He bent over and picked them up. After righting himself, he said, “Are you avoiding me? I’ve hardly seen you today.”

"Nope, I've just been kind of busy." She noticed Molly over his shoulder, standing with a pack of cheerleaders, smacking her gum and shooting Janie looks that could kill. *I don't have time for her. Ignore her.*

"Are we still on for Saturday?" Matt looked so excited, it broke her heart. *What had she done to him?*

"Do you still want to go?" *It was worth a try.*

"I do. . .I just wanted to make sure it's still cool with you and all." He placed his hand on hers.

"It's cool." *Kai is leaving. I can go with Matt as a friend. There is nothing wrong with that.*

"Do you want to do something after school?" He moved closer to her.

"That's kind of what I wanted to talk to you about." She stepped back against the locker.

"Go ahead." He waited.

"Do you remember the undead things that attacked you, twice?"

His face went blank. "The ones who turned Billy into a zombie thing?"

"Yes, them, but they aren't zombies. . .never mind." Janie drew in a deep breath. "What I'm trying to say is, they are planning to do something here at school this afternoon. I'd like it if you left right after school. You've already been attacked more than anyone should be in a lifetime."

"What are you going to do? Come with me." He reached for her as if grabbing her physically would convince her to flee with him.

She pulled back. "I can't. I'm the Seeker. It's up to me to stop them."

"But you could get hurt." He moved closer again. She could smell his cologne—spices and musk.

"I've got help."

"Who Kai, Albania?" A hint of jealousy in his tone.

"Among others, yes." She didn't feel she had to explain herself. She only wanted to warn him, not explain her relationships or the reasons for her actions.

"You like him—Kai."

"I'm not going to lie to you. I do," she finally said. *Maybe he'll drop it now.*

"He'll never feel about you like I do."

"You're probably right." *You've been Imprinted, he hasn't.*

"Promise you'll be safe. Use those tiny Bruce Lee moves." His demeanor turned playful again.

"I will." She smiled. He was a good guy. "So then you're leaving, right after school."

"Stop worrying." He grabbed a book from his locker and closed the door. "I've seen you kick vampire-zombie ass. You'll do great."

Thanks for the support. "Well, then." She tapped him on the shoulder.

He roped her into a one-armed hug. "Be safe."

She held him for a moment. It hurt not knowing if she didn't make it through the fight she'd never see Matt again. She stepped out of his embrace. "I'll see you tomorrow."

CHAPTER 17

Janie accelerated into her driveway and parked behind Abram's Lexus. *Crap. What's Mom doing home? And Abram. This isn't good.*

She entered the living room. Kai stood in the doorway to the kitchen. His hand rested on the wall. He looked pale and somehow thinner. She couldn't read his face; he looked somewhere between ready to fight, worried and exhausted. Deep circles ringed his eyes, making the green appear duller. The only brightness around him were the white highlights streaking through his sandy hair from the sun pouring in through the kitchen window behind him.

She sprinted into his arms. He tightened his hold around her. With one large breath, she took every inch of him in. *If only we could stay like this forever.*

"Janie," Abram spoke behind her. His heavy footfalls shook the hardwood floor. *Is he wearing boots?*

She turned, still holding onto Kai. She stared at Abram with wide eyes. "Where's your suit?" Abram wore an old Duke sweatshirt and camouflage khakis, Army grade. He paired the get-up with Doc Martins. His thick belt was equipped with at least four silver daggers, including one under his pant leg, strapped to his ankle. She hadn't seen him dressed like a Seeker since he had trained her. Even then, he never walked around layered in weapons and camo. *He looks tough.*

"Your boyfriend paid us a visit today. He's worried about you." Abram stepped closer to Janie, his eyes locked on Kai. "He told us what will be happening after school."

"Us?" Janie looked past Abram. Isabelle entered the room, dressed in a black sweatshirt and camo pants. She'd never seen her mom and Abram look so matchy-matchy. Silver daggers were placed strategically around Isabelle's belt. Janie blinked, surprised at how tough her mother looked—a side of her she'd never seen before.

"Kai thought it was best if we knew," Isabelle said. She focused on Janie's arms around Kai. Pain filled her eyes, like the distant longing for Janie's father. But this longing was stronger, deeper, like when the wound was fresh. Even after she'd "healed," Isabelle never acted the same. *What's going on?*

"We've decided to help. The more of us, the better our chances." Abram still hadn't taken his eyes off Kai. They weren't as hate-filled as before, but they were anything but accepting. Janie knew the only reason he hadn't attempted to kill Kai was because of her. He'd spent years searching for the Daychild with green eyes.

She'd gotten some of her stubbornness from Abram. He had to hate the resistance of not killing Kai.

"You're going to fight?" Janie broke from Kai's hold and turned to face Abram and Isabelle. Kai's arms folded around her waist. She trembled at his breath on her hair.

"Don't be so shocked. We're not that old. We have done this before." Abram shot Isabelle a hesitant look.

"There's a catch. Isn't there?" Janie stiffened. Her pulse started to race. "Abram, tell me why you keep looking at her!" She turned to her mother. "What's going on?"

Isabelle tried to calm Janie. "Honey, we are Seekers and we're family. We want to help you. It's our duty. Those are the only reasons we want to fight alongside you." Isabelle's words didn't reassure Janie.

"Abram," Janie said. She enlaced her fingers through Kai's. He held her tighter. His chest no longer rose and fell against her back, and she could no longer feel his breath on her hair. *Is he breathing? Something's very wrong.*

Abram didn't speak for seconds. He was doing it again, looking for the right words, darting his eyes back and forth to her mother. As he thought, Abram formed a steeple with his hands. The tip of his fingers rested against his mouth. "I've told Kai I'd stop hunting him." He cleared his throat. "He's obviously been an asset to you. He's proven his loyalty on multiple occasions. And for that I've promised not to kill him for what he did to your father."

But—I know there's a "but" coming. Janie could hardly focus on Abram's words. There was a catch; she knew it. She realized she was holding her breath, too. Trying to breathe became too difficult. It felt as if walls were caving in on her. Everything came crashing down around her. *But why?*

Abram brought his gaze from Kai down to Janie. "This afternoon Kai informed us that he intended to stay and deviate from his original plan to leave. Naturally, your mother and I don't agree. We have decided he isn't a positive presence in your life. What you had was temporary. It is time he moved on." Abram cleared his throat. Janie couldn't move or breathe. Shock absorbed her entire being. "We've also discussed our feelings with Kai, and he has agreed to leave after we defeat Antony this afternoon. In return, I will respect his honorable action and spare his life."

Janie shoved Kai's hand off her waist. "Spare his life. What is this, the Medieval Times?" *Has everyone seriously gone mad? And Kai—did he really agree to this?*

She knew Kai might be leaving, but this felt like a betrayal—her parents and her boyfriend plotting her fate, deciding what was best for her? It wasn't their decision to make! She was almost eighteen, in a sense. That infuriated her as well. Next year she'd be much younger than Kai, again. She wanted it all to stop. She wanted to live. She wanted to love. It wasn't fair.

"How dare you?" Janie stepped away from Kai and walked to the center of the room, able to see everyone, able to look into each of their back-stabbing eyes. "This is my life and I'm getting sick of everyone deciding what's best for me."

"Janie—" Kai attempted to move toward her.

She extended her hand to stop him. "Shut up." Tears rolled down her face. "I've already told you I've forgiven you. What else do I have to do to convince you of that? I *don't* blame you for my father's death. I know what you were then and who you are now. You aren't the same. You're not that monster. You've shown me how to love and be loved. I haven't been this happy since I can remember. Since my father pushed me on the swing or took me for walks in my little red wagon." Janie wiped the tears from her face. "If you don't love me—"

"But I—" Kai said.

"Let me finish." For the moment, Janie forgot Isabelle and Abram were in the room. It was only her and Kai. It was always only her and Kai. It had taken her a while to realize this, but now she knew, for sure. "If you don't love me, then feel free to leave. I won't make you stay." He tried to speak again. She cut him off. "But if you do—*stop* being a coward. You say I run from happiness? Well, so do you. Right now—" She pointed to the ground. "Right now, I'm confronting my fears head on. So you have flaws—we all do. You carry a lifetime of guilt with you—let it go. You're not the same guy." Her voice fell to a whisper. "I love you for your beauty and your scars—the scars that run down your forearm and cross your chest, and the scars that weigh on your conscience and tug on your human heart. I love you because you're you."

Sobbing erupted from behind her, making Janie remember her mother's presence.

"She's right," Isabelle said, sniffling. She spoke to Kai. "We were wrong. This isn't our decision. We can't dictate who Janie loves."

"Isabelle—" Abram took her hand. "What are you saying? We already discussed this. Kai leaving, it's what's best."

"Best for who—you? You can't bring Connor back." Isabelle held his gaze. "No, Abram, you decided this was for the best. I listened and I don't agree. I know what it's like to love someone I'm told I shouldn't, but you can't help who you fall in love with. I was a Seeker and Connor was an innocent. Life with me was too dangerous for him, but nothing could keep us apart. You know that first hand." Abram's usually confident stature sank. Janie knew it had something more to do with her mother, her father and Abram's history than she understood.

Isabelle joined Janie. She cupped her face. "I never told you how I met your father. It is time that I did." She let out a deep, shaky breath and began. "I was responsible for the Houston district. It had just rained. It was evening. I had just finished running errands for my mother. She needed supplies for a protection ritual against U`tlûñ'ta." Janie remembered the Cherokee legend her Gran used to tell her about the shape-shifter who ate human livers.

Isabelle stared past everyone, reliving the night she met Connor all over again. It was as if the movie of her life was playing on the wall behind them. "As I was leaving the Native American store, I saw him—Connor Grey. I remember the first time I saw him like it was yesterday. He was tall and strong with blond hair and eyes the color of a cloudless blue sky. Janie, your father was so handsome." She gripped Janie's face tighter. "But no matter his mortal strength, he was no match for the vampire preying on him. I had to do something."

"You saved Dad?" Janie gasped. Now she knew why her mom reacted the way she did when she told her about Matt. It all made sense now...

"How do I stop it?" Janie returned to her mother's warm brown eyes, hoping desperately for an antidote.

Isabelle frowned. "You can't. He'll love you forever, or at least until he can find someone else to settle for, unless you fall in love with him, too."

"You Imprinted Dad and fell in love with him." Janie broke away from Isabelle's grasp. She couldn't handle this—*Kai leaving, Abram insisting he go, her father being Imprinted, her mother never telling her.*

Kai wrapped his strong arms around her from behind. "I'm sorry to interrupt. I know all of this must be very overwhelming, but Jerome and the others are out back. We should go before they change their minds."

Janie didn't move. "And after—will you still be here?"

"We'll talk later." He kissed the back of her head. "Now's not the time." *Is it ever?*

Jerome and Tanya stood at the far end of the yard. They brought three other vampires with them: a large guy with an afro, a tall thin girl with platinum hair and too much eye makeup, and an average-height bald guy wearing a Baltimore Ravens jersey. Tanya wore a black pair of designer jeans and heels. Her top slid loosely off one shoulder. It matched her cherry-red lipstick.

Three had on shades, including Jerome. The other two squinted. Janie was relieved to see they hadn't burst into flames. She guessed getting used to the sun after years of avoiding it wasn't easy.

Abram wore a look of shock. "Are those vampires? H—How are they outside, in the daytime, in the sunlight?"

"I have friends," Kai said.

"Abram—did you know about this?" Isabelle swayed in place. The color drained from her face. "They're vampires. We don't fight with vampires. We fight against them."

Abram steadied her. "I spoke with Janie last night. It's okay. Times seem to be changing." He rested his hand on her shoulder. "I'll explain later. They are here to help. They have also suffered at the hands of Antony and his crew."

Jerome stepped forward. "I've got to tell you, Seeker, this sunlight thing is okay. But it's hard to see, too darn bright. I'll stick with the moon and stars."

"Thank you for helping us. You kept your word."

Jerome acknowledged Janie's appreciation with a nod. He crossed his arms over his chest and cleared his throat. "So, how are we doin' this?" Janie wasn't sure if he was tired, but his voice sounded weaker than usual, more vulnerable. She wondered how long he had spent at the graveyard. She remembered one of the tombstones read *Brotherhood.* He cared for his gang. Though he was a vampire, he mourned the loss of his brothers and sisters. Antony didn't share the same quality. He was a demon—pure evil.

Abram stepped forward to address the group. "I'll take the lead. I've been doing this the longest. How are we for weapons?"

Janie slung her backpack over her shoulder. "We have silver blades."

The vamp in the jersey lifted his shirt, flashing an assortment of blades encased in leather and shoved in the waist of his low-riding jeans.

"The football players should be in the locker room changing before practice. Janie and Kai—stand outside the locker room door. If you hear anything, go in," Abram said. "Jerome—you and your gang will take cover under the bleachers next to the field where they practice." Jerome nodded. "Isabelle and I will patrol the parking lot and inside the school. Remember, we need to take down Antony as inconspicuously as possible. It's going to be hard enough to explain this to the Chapter. We can't wage an all-out war in public."

"If we take down Antony first, his crew should be useless," Janie said.

"Not necessarily. When one leader dies, another takes his place. They're young. They will scrap like children for the position," Jerome said.

"But they'll be distracted fighting among themselves. We can use this to our advantage," Abram said. "Jerome, how many are we dealing with? How outnumbered are we going to be?"

"They've got at least twenty. We're going to be outnumbered, but we're better fighters. Most Daychildren are babies." Jerome looked at Kai. "They can't fight like you. . .whatever you are. You were the first, created by the king. With age comes wisdom."

Janie checked her watch. "It's time to go. Practice starts in twenty minutes."

CHAPTER 18

Janie and Kai stood outside the locker room, located in the basement of the school, along with the weight room and a few mechanical rooms. The football players laughed behind the door. Lockers slammed shut as they retrieved their gear and discussed plays.

One conversation perked her ears. It sounded like Scott Turner, the quarterback. “Did you hear, man? Molly’s not going to Homecoming with Matt. She’s free game.”

A player Janie didn’t recognize answered. “No joke. They broke up?”

“I guess. I heard it’s ‘cause he’s into Janie Grey,” Scott said.

“Huh. . .isn’t that something?” Both guys laughed. “Go for it, dude.”

They sounded so innocent in an annoying frat boy kind of way. They had no idea what hunted them or how their lives were going to change if Antony wasn't stopped. Some of the players wouldn't survive the Turn, maybe even Scott, and the ones who did survive would become demonic immortals, a fate worse than death.

Kai caught the tail end of the conversation. "Antony's not in there. I don't hear anything unusual, other than an irritating bunch of jocks."

"Not everyone can be as cool as you." Janie ran her finger down Kai's chest.

"True." He smiled. One brow rose. "You're the topic of conversation. I guess that means you're still going to that dance with Matt."

"I have to. I told him I'd go with him. We're just going as friends. Besides, Ava and Luke are going with us." His bemused expression didn't change. "I'm serious; friends, that's it," she assured him.

"For you, but I guarantee he feels differently." Kai's features hardened. He changed the subject. "I wish Antony would hurry up and show his face. Those boys stink."

"Like sweat?"

"Among other things," he said.

Janie didn't ask, too busy focusing on another familiar voice in the locker room. "What's up?" Kai moved closer to her. He rested his hand on her arm, causing her heartbeat to accelerate. The pounding of her heartbeat in her ears blocked her ability to hear Matt's discussion. When Kai touched her, nothing else seemed to exist.

"Matt is in there. I told him to go home." Janie's hands balled into fists. "Why don't guys ever listen? Can you hear what he's saying?"

"He's warning someone to leave practice. That something bad's going to happen." Kai paused to listen. "The other kid doesn't believe him. He told him to go home."

"Did Matt say anything about vampires or zombies?"

"Zombies?" Kai eyed her quizzically.

"Never mind," she said. "Did he say anything about what's about to happen?"

"No. Not that anyone would believe him. He already sounds like a nut job."

"I've got to get him out of here." Janie reached for the door handle. Kai grabbed her arm.

"It's not your job to save his life." He dropped her arm. "He's like a cat. . .he has too many lives."

"You don't mean that."

Kai let out a frustrated breath. "What are you going to do? You can't just walk into the boys' locker room."

"But you can." She realized.

Kai stepped backward. "I'm not going in there. You don't think I'll stick out like a sore thumb? I'm not a member of the football team, and I don't exactly look like a jock." He opened his arms. His scythe hung at his waist.

Janie ran her eyes over Kai. His hair was longer than most of the jocks, and he was definitely prettier. His arms were exposed in his white tee. Lines raced down his forearm. His jeans appeared dirty, even though she knew they weren't. Janie could smell their clean lavender scent. Kai's black boots looked like they'd been chewed on by a teething puppy. She could tell he'd tried to clean them, but Daychild blood had eaten through the leather.

Janie had an idea. "You're fast. You can retrieve Matt before anyone sees you. You don't even need to use the door."

Kai grunted. "I'm only doing this for you. He doesn't mean anything to me. . .he's in love with my girlfriend."

"You're jealous."

He shrugged.

"You're leaving. . .does it really matter?" she said under her breath.

"Not right now, Janie!"

Always the same reaction—*not right now.* This infuriated her. "When is it ever a good time to discuss anything? You are continually shutting me out. Maybe you should let me know when you're ready to talk—"

"Janie—" Kai interrupted. He pulled her into him and kissed her hard, releasing all of his pain, guilt, fear, regret and. . .love. "Please," he said. "It's harder for me. You're the only person I've opened up to." His forehead lowered to hers. He fisted her hair, holding her tightly against him. She didn't attempt to move. She wanted to grab him and pour every bit of herself into him right there.

She didn't. He was right. It wasn't the time. She wondered if the time would ever come.

He breathed heavily on her face. "I want to discuss this, discuss us. I'm trying to focus on what's about to happen. If we don't focus, you could get killed. That, I couldn't live with." He half-smiled, making her heart melt like warm butter. "Right now I have to get your Imprint." Kai released her and disappeared through the wall.

He returned within seconds. Matt clung to his arm like a koala bear. "What the hell?" Matt's eyes bulged. "Did we just go through the wall?"

"What do you think?" Kai shook Matt off his arm.

"I think, but that's impossible—" Matt stopped speaking halfway through his thought. "I take that back. Nothing's impossible anymore."

"Wow, Janie, you got yourself a dim bulb. I guess it's true what they say about jocks," Kai quipped.

"I don't like you." Matt forced his shoulders back and stepped up to Kai.

Kai didn't back down. "That makes two of us."

"Kai—cut it out." Janie wedged herself between them and threw her hands out, pressing against both of their chests. "Matt—what are you doing here? I told you I had it covered. You're supposed to be at home."

"I was worried about you." His eyes were warm and sincere.

"You—" Kai laughed. "*You* were worried about *her*. You aren't the brightest. She's a Seeker. She can take care of herself. She doesn't need you." He stepped away from them. "You shouldn't even be here. There is *nothing* you can do. You're weak."

"Why, because she has you?" Matt took hold of Janie's hand and twisted her into his side.

Awkward. Janie removed her hand from his. "Seriously, do we have to do this—now? Antony could already be here for all we know." She directed Kai. "Get ready to fight." Kai nodded. She turned to face Matt. "Go home."

"But—"

"I'll call you later."

"It's too late. He stays." Kai extended his scythe.

"Why—" Janie readied herself in a fighting stance. Then, she felt them through her Seeker sense. "They're here."

Antony rounded the corner with a crew of Daychildren following behind. There were at least ten or twelve of them, many Janie recognized. Others were obviously newbies. The newbies were eager to begin the fight. Drool dripped from their fangs and their black eyes flickered uncontrollably from Janie, to Kai, to Matt and back again. The only impulse they knew was to kill violently, and eat.

"What can I do?" Matt said.

"Stand behind us and shut up," Kai said.

Janie looked deep into Matt's hazel eyes, willing him to follow her directions for once. "Go through the locker room and exit at the field. There is a group of five vampires under the bleachers. Find them and tell them Antony's here. Direct them this way. Make sure you tell them you're with us."

"I'd do anything for you." Matt kissed her cheek and disappeared through the locker room door.

Kai rolled his eyes. "You do realize you've just sent your Imprint to confront the head vampire." A hint of satisfied humor rang through his tone.

"He'll be fine. Jerome wants Antony, not Matt." She punched Kai's arm. "And stop calling him that."

He winked at her. "You ready?"

"Yup." She removed her dagger from her boot. As Antony approached she gripped the hilt tighter, preparing to retrieve the other from her waist at any moment.

Antony let out an annoyed laugh. "I can't say I'm surprised to see you two. You've been a thorn in my side lately." He stared at Janie. "Seeker, you've got balls, coming up in my house like that. Tanya wasn't your concern. You've pushed me too far." He stopped walking and held up his hand. His followers stopped behind him. Janie recognized the girl with spiky hair at his side. Antony addressed the group, his eyes still planted on Janie. "She's mine." He smirked. "Your death won't be pretty. I'm going to cut out your organs and have them for dinner."

Janie stepped out from behind Kai. "I'm looking forward to seeing you try."

"Touch her and I'll make you beg me to send you to hell." Kai made a circular motion with his blade.

"I knew it." Antony fell into a belly laugh. "Wow—I never thought I'd see this day. No wonder Tavares tried to kill you. You're a pathetic excuse for a Daychild. The first to be created and the first to fall in love with a human. . .and the Seeker at that." He spat on the floor. "You're a disgrace to your kind."

"I think you're jealous. My girl is right next to me. Yours was sent to hell and you weren't strong enough to stop it. You're an inferior leader. You've proven that time and time again. Tavares doesn't care about you. It's all about his cause." Kai cracked his knuckles. "Let's get this over with."

"Caleb, Michaela, Sera, Jorge. . .get to the field. Start the process," Antony said.

"I've got this—go," Kai said to Janie. She hesitated, but did as he instructed.

Janie flung the locker room door open. The smell of sweat and testosterone smacked her in the face. She covered her nose and proceeded forward. If she could handle the rotten smell of Daychildren, she could certainly handle a football team—*maybe, BO was a uniquely nasty smell.* Clothes were strewn everywhere, lying over long wooden benches that lined the wall-length rows of metal lockers. Extra helmets and shoulder pads cluttered the lockers. She stumbled over a jock strap. *This sucks.*

"Janie?" Scott said as she passed the urinals. *That was embarrassing.*

She ignored him and kept her focus on getting to the field. Daychildren were faster than she was. She exited the locker room and sprinted to the track that looped the field. She called Abram on the way. He answered on the first ring. "They're going to the field." She spotted the girl with spiky hair, who Antony referred to as Michaela, at the far end of the track and hung up.

Janie didn't see the others. She slid the dagger back into her boot, not wanting to attract any more attention than she already had. The football players were too wrapped up in practice to notice her, but she didn't want to take any chances. She circled the track, keeping her eyes peeled for the other three.

She thought of Kai. He was up against at least ten. She knew Kai could fight, but she hoped Matt had been successful in finding Jerome. Kai could use the vampire gang's help. She scanned the underside of the bleachers and didn't see Jerome. That was a good sign.

As Janie reached the end of the bleachers, something slid across the track behind her. Blindsided by a punch to her jaw, Janie kicked out in the direction of the punch and made contact with one of them—another girl, Sera. She grabbed Janie's leg and dragged her under the bleachers, where the other two guys waited.

Janie twisted her leg, freeing herself from Sera's hold and jumped to a fighting stance with her dagger in hand. The one Antony referred to as Jorge lunged at Janie. She ducked and caught him in the stomach with her fist. He stumbled back, but came at her again. She whirled into a round house kick. Her foot landed on the side of his face. He fell into the last one—Caleb.

The impact didn't faze Caleb. He steadied himself, protecting the two bottles in his grip. She assumed one bottle held the vampire venom, and the other held the lost souls. If she could destroy both bottles, Antony wouldn't be able to carry out his plan.

Something hard and flat struck Janie in the back of the head. The object sent her flying forward. She landed on her hands and knees. The loose asphalt dug into her palms. She closed her hands into fists, and her fingers stuck to the thick red liquid. Her knuckles bled from clutching her blade. Pain raked through her head. She tried to touch the wound, but one of them shoved her to the ground with his foot.

"Finish her. She's down. What are you waiting for?" Sera said. She moved closer to Janie, displaying a large two by four.

"We can't. You heard Antony. He wants her for himself," Jorge said.

While they argued, Janie tightened the wet grip she had on her dagger. She took Sera's legs out from under her with a sweeping kick to her ankles. Sera landed on the concrete next to her. Janie flipped onto her feet and plunged the dagger into Sera's skull.

Horrified and visibly pissed about Sera's death, Jorge came at Janie with his arms extended. *Crap, that must have been his girlfriend.* He barreled forward, straight for Janie's throat. She quickly stepped to the side. Jorge's forehead smacked the descending bleacher. He bounced back, unfazed. Janie launched her dagger through the air. It struck Jorge between the eyes. *Perfect, right through the skull.*

Caleb set the bottles down and came at her from behind. He wrapped his arm around her neck and squeezed. "Don't try anything, Seeker, or I'll snap your pencil neck."

"I'm not going to let you get away with this." Janie wiggled around, but she couldn't free herself from his hold. His decaying stench burned her nose and his smell fried her lungs. She tried not to breathe in too deeply.

"What can I do?" Matt appeared under the bleachers holding something long and skinny in his hands.

CHAPTER 19

Kai had already taken out three of Antony's men, with about seven or so to go. He paused to take a breath and assess his injuries. He glanced down at his chest, where his tee had been sliced down the front. His once worn-in jeans were now full of fraying holes. Dried green blood coated his left leg.

He touched a gash just above his forehead. It had already started to heal. A petite girl sprung at him and sliced a silver dagger across his bicep. He cursed and assessed the depth of the incision—only a flesh wound.

The girl's eyes widened. "Red, why is your blood red? You're one of us."

Kai grunted. "Hardly."

"Wait!" Antony said. The older Daychild stood at attention. The newbies fought to gain their composure. One twitched against the wall. The task of going in for the kill and stopping mid-fight tortured the new ones.

Kai took the opportunity to behead the petite girl with his scythe.

"So, it's true." Antony glared at Kai. "Tavares was right. You aren't one of us any more. Your blood runs red like a filthy human, or vampire."

"Filthy—look who's talking." Kai pulled a rag from his back pocket and wiped the blood from his scythe. Antony stiffened. "What's wrong, big dude? You jealous? Tavares didn't make you. You'll never be stronger than me. I was his favorite," Kai said.

"Maybe then, but now you're just a disappointment. A child who grew up to be a source of regret."

Kai laughed. "But you, you're pure evil. You'll follow him because that's all you know. You're his pawn. Do you really think you can earn his respect? He doesn't know how to do anything but hate."

Antony focused on the crisscross scar over Kai's heart, exposed from where his shirt had been ripped. "A human heart." He let out a humored puff of air. "How sweet!" His voice switched back to anger. "You're weak, part human. Is there even any demon left in you?"

Kai released his fangs.

"Oooh—" Antony shook. "So you're still part vamp. Big deal. They've also proven to be inferior."

"What'd you say?" Jerome stepped out of the locker room, displaying a hard look of rage. His chains dangled around his neck. He strutted down the hallway toward Antony.

At first Antony didn't appear surprised to see Jerome. "I should've known you'd join the Seeker. You get even more pathetic every day, or should I say—

night." Antony glanced past Jerome, at the four vampires following behind him. "H—How are you here? It's daytime. You should be a pile of ashes."

"There are perks to knowing the Seeker." Jerome smiled, exposing his gold-plated fangs. "Killing you will be the biggest perk. But I'm enjoying the sun."

"You aren't going to make it out of here alive." Antony raised his chin. "We've got plans and they don't include you."

"Whatever. Let's kick this off." Jerome fronted Antony.

Antony ran his hand through his wiry hair and raised his hand, stopping the vamp's advancement. "Hold up, Jerome." He smirked, suggesting superiority. "What does it mean when the king of vamps creates a new kind? Could it be that he's not happy with his own kind?"

"He's a turncoat," Jerome spat.

Antony shook his head. "It means he's ashamed of vampires. Your kind is useless. You've adapted to human standards, no longer living like vamps should."

"And how exactly is that?" Jerome appeared bored.

The vein in Antony's forehead protruded, his eyes black and cold. Hatred seeped from his pours. "Humans are food, that's it. Drain them of their blood and leave their corpses to rot."

"And where is the vamp you call king? Where's Tavares—huh?" Jerome said. "He was dethroned, in case you didn't hear. He isn't the vampire king anymore. If he's your king, where is he now?" He put his hands out and looked around as if Tavares would suddenly appear.

"He doesn't deal with matters like you. He sends in the big dogs."

Jerome laughed. "Big dogs—like you? Are we done yet? I've got a score to settle. You're just wastin' my time." The vampires dispersed.

"Oh, we're done. Let's go, vamp." Antony made a "come on" motion with his fingers and signaled for his crew to resume fighting.

"Remember—Antony's mine!" Jerome said.

The vampires and Daychildren collided. Fangs tore into flesh. Green and red blood sprayed everywhere. Antony gave orders to a set of twins. They were young and fit, maybe teenagers. Both had black hair neatly slicked back into a ponytail. They soon slipped out the way they'd come.

Jerome flew over the massacre and landed on Antony, throwing him into the wall. Drywall and splintered wood crashed down around them, clouding Kai's view of the feuding gang leaders. Kai took the opportunity to slip in between the crowd. He passed Tanya, draining the blood of a Daychild. His body hit the floor and she shoved her blade into his skull. Kai shot her a congratulatory smirk.

Kai strode down the hallway with caution, tracking the twins' stench. They were ahead of him, but not by much. As he advanced, the smell became stronger. Kai found himself thinking about Janie. He wondered if she had been able to stop the mass Turning. Hordes of wild newbies wearing football uniforms hadn't swarmed the school, so the Turn hadn't occurred yet.

Kai exited through a double metal door. He stepped down on to a path that led to the track and field. The sound of a nearby scuffle fractured his focus. Kai peered around the side of the building. The twins had someone pinned to the ground. *Janie.* He sprinted forward and grabbed one by his shirt, flinging him backward. The other twin moved out of Kai's reach before he could do the same with him.

Abram's cold blue eyes stared at Kai in disbelief. Anger still resonated within them, but a different type of anger lingered.

Both brothers ran off. They didn't care about Kai or Abram. Abram had been nothing more than a roadblock. They had a job to do.

"Why did you do it?" Abram refused Kai's hand and pushed himself upright.

"Do what? They were about to kill you." He extended his hand again. Abram ignored Kai's gesture and rose to his feet.

Abram brushed the dirt from his pants. "It would make your life easier. You could be with Janie without fearing your death at my hands."

"I don't fear you." Kai wiped the blood from the cut along his arm with his T-shirt. He stared at the ground for a moment. He hadn't done anything for Abram. Everything had been for Janie. He lifted his eyes to meet Abram's. "I made the decision to leave because at the time I thought it was best for Janie."

"And now?"

Kai didn't know the answer Abram wanted. He didn't care. "I haven't decided."

"You really do love her." Abram shook his head. "How—it goes against everything we've learned. You aren't supposed to be capable of loving a human."

"There was a time Janie felt the same," Kai said. "She'd learned the same lessons you learned. The same lessons you taught her. Janie and I weren't always as close as we are now. The first time we met, she wanted to kill me."

A satisfied smile crossed Abram's face. "That's my girl. How did you convince her otherwise?"

"It took awhile to gain her trust. She finally realized I wanted to help her. That I had no interest in killing her."

"And you fell in love with her," Abram said. It didn't seem to be an accusation. Something else lay under his tone—an understanding.

"Only by accident. It wasn't my intention. We're so different. She's innocent and I'm, well," his mouth twitched, "not."

Abram let down his guard, surprising Kai. "Isn't that always how it happens? We never fall in love with the right person. They're either too different or already hold a place in someone else's heart." Abram sighed. "You don't even know how you feel until it's too late to do anything about it."

There was a longing in Abram's words, a painful dip in his usually hard brow. Kai had the feeling Abram was referring to someone other than Janie.

Abram cleared his throat, pushing back any pain that had slipped out. “Anyway, I just want you to know that everything I’ve said or done has been for Janie. She’s like a daughter to me. I love her and her mo—” His words broke. He stared at the ground for a moment. “I love Janie very much. I don’t want to see her hurt in any way.”

“I feel the same.” Kai extended his hand.

Abram hesitated and shook Kai’s hand. He looked Kai directly in the eyes, as a father would regard his daughter’s boyfriend. “You’ve proven to be different. Treat her well.”

“I’d lay down my life for her.” Kai almost laughed at the sound of himself speaking those words. Not long ago, self-survival ruled his actions. He’d hunted Daychildren as a penance for his crimes, but to care more about someone other than himself was non-existent.

“I know you would.” Abram patted Kai on the back. It had a double meaning—acceptance and warning. “I *will* be watching you. . .whatever you decide to do, stay or go.”

Kai nodded. He understood. A moment of loyalty couldn’t cancel out over a decade of hatred. He’d be patient with Abram. “Let’s go find Janie and stop the Turn.” Kai stopped and turned back to Abram. “Where’s Isabelle?”

“I left her in the parking lot. There are still a few students and teachers lingering. She didn’t want them to get hurt.” He started forward again. Kai kept pace.

Relieved and furious to see Matt, Janie focused on the long object in his hand. *What is he doing? He's going to get himself killed. And what is he holding?* "Is that a jousting lance?"

He smiled. "Pretty cool, huh? I found it in the theater room. I think it's real." He hushed his tone. "Oh, and I did what you asked. It's taken care of."

Janie breathed out. Caleb could still hear him. "Thanks." *Hopefully Jerome and his gang are helping Kai.*

Matt's smile straightened. He glared at Caleb. "How do I kill him?" He shuffled forward, jabbing the lance at Caleb.

"You're going to kill me with that?" Caleb erupted into laughter.

Janie directed her eyes to the bottles behind them in an attempt to signal Matt. He gave her a confused look. "Smash them," she said.

Matt focused on the bottles and nodded.

Caleb tightened his grip on Janie's throat. "Shut up! There will be no more talking out of you. If you so much as squeak, it will be the last noise you make."

"Why haven't you killed me yet?" she said. "What are you waiting for?"

Matt inched forward. "Janie, do you think that's the best thing to say right now? He does have his arm over your windpipe."

"Listen to your boyfriend. Shut up." Caleb squeezed her throat harder. Janie gasped for air.

"Just do it already." Janie thrust her head backward, smashing into his nose. She winced. The pain of her earlier injury shot down her skull. Green blood oozed down his face and on to the back of her bare neck, causing her skin to burn. Her flesh sizzled. The burned stench stung her nose.

Caleb readjusted his arm around her throat. "You're just trying to piss me off. It's not going to work. I'll kill you when we're ready."

"You will not!" Matt sprinted forward with the lance pointing outward.

Caleb's grip loosened. Janie spun out of his hold. The lance pierced through his stomach and exited out his back.

"Nice job." Janie shot Matt an approving look and lunged for the bottles. Caleb whirled around, knocking Janie to the ground with the part of the lance that protruded from his back. She fell inches from the bottles.

With one quick forward jerk, Caleb ripped the lance from his torso, not as wounded as Janie would have liked.

"I guess that's not how you kill them." Matt bent over and retrieved a second lance. "Luckily, the theater had two. I'll aim for the head next time."

The twins appeared under the bleachers. They wore muscle shirts, exposing their large arms. At first they ignored Janie and Matt. "Caleb, where are the bottles? You were supposed to keep them on you at all times."

Caleb glanced down at Janie. "The Seeker got in the way. It's okay. They're right here." He bent down to retrieve them. Confusion flashed across his face. "Yo, Quinn, they were right there, man."

"Looking for these?" Janie held up both bottles and smashed them against the asphalt. The glass shattered into pieces. Vampire venom flooded the ground. Balls of screaming white lights—the lost souls—bounced in the air like large molecules with nowhere to go.

"You idiot." Quinn struck Caleb with his fist. "Antony told you not to put those down."

The other twin grabbed Janie by her hair and yanked her to her knees. "Miss Seeker, Antony has plans for you."

"Let her go." Matt jabbed at the twin with the lance.

Quinn ripped the lance out of Matt's hands and struck him over the head with it, knocking him unconscious. "Nate, let's go. It's time to continue with the plan."

"You can't," Janie said. "I've released the souls and you don't have any more venom. You're finished." Quinn backhanded her. Janie spit blood.

"Quinn, where are we going?" Nate said anxiously. "We can't Turn her without Antony."

Quinn appeared to be the more level-headed twin. "Last I saw, Antony was fighting Jerome inside."

"Where's Michaela?" Nate twitched, showing Janie how much he feared Antony.

Quinn took charge. "I'll find her and tell her to meet us inside. Get the Seeker there—now." Quinn passed Janie off to Nate with a firm grip on her hair. She'd already been cracked over the head by a two-by-four, it stung too badly to resist. Every tug made her more nauseated.

"What about him?" Nate pointed to Matt. Janie thought she saw Matt's eyes flutter. The twins didn't notice. "Can we eat him?"

"Leave him. We don't have time. He's useless to us." Quinn kicked the broken glass and cursed under his breath.

"He could be an athlete. We could use him." Nate sized him up. "Look at his varsity jacket."

Quinn became enraged. "Not now! We'll come back for him. Our priority is the Seeker." Quinn grabbed Caleb by the shirt and lifted him to eye level. "No more screw-ups. Go with Nate and get the Seeker to Antony." He shoved him backward.

A puddle formed at the base of Caleb's pants.

CHAPTER 20

Kai and Abram found Matt crouched under the bleachers. He held his lance between his knees. His hand was pressed firmly against a gash in his head. Blood seeped through his fingers. Kai felt bad for him—for a fraction of a second.

Kai tapped Matt on the head. His head shot up. He fumbled backward, pointing the lance at Kai.

"You look terrible," Kai said. "And what are you holding?"

"Back off, Kai." Matt rose to an unsteady stance.

"Touchy. I was only stating the obvious." Kai's words were brisk. "Janie told you to go home. You didn't listen." He plucked the lance from Matt's hand. "And you think this is going to stop them. As I said before, you're a dim bulb." He threw the lance to the ground. It splintered in two.

"You can't have her," Matt said.

"What did you say?" Kai's stepped inches from Matt. The demon who used to live inside him wanted to rip the boy apart. Then he realized it was the human inside of him. The demon no longer existed. Humans had evil thoughts, too. The difference was, they didn't usually act on them. Kai wouldn't either. He still didn't like Matt. Matt complicated things, but Janie seemed to care about him.

Matt pushed forward. "You heard me. You can't have her, Kai. She'll always be connected to me through this Imprint thing. You'll never be rid of me. You will never truly have her for yourself, and that kills you."

Kai lunged at Matt, causing Matt to stumble back. Matt's reaction made Kai smile. It showed weakness, and right now he needed to see Matt's inferiority to hide the truth—Matt was right.

"The Imprint doesn't apply if you don't exist." Kai cornered Matt beneath the bleachers.

"Hold on, both of you," Abram said. "Neither of you have her, trust me. Janie's too independent to *need* either of you." Abram grabbed Kai's bicep to restrain him. Kai jerked his arm out of Abram's grasp. "Now, both of you, grow up. We need to find Janie. Last I heard, she was heading to the field."

"We didn't see her, and we just walked half the track," Kai said. He paced, refusing to look at Matt. Abram was right; fighting didn't help find Janie.

"She was just here. They took her," Matt said.

"Took her where?" Kai clutched the collar of Matt's jacket and lifted him off the ground. "Tell me." He shook Matt.

"Put him down. You're not even giving the boy a chance to speak," Abram said.

"Fine." Kai lowered him, but didn't let go. "Where is she?"

"I don't know exactly where she is. Now get off my collar." Matt swatted at Kai.

"Useless." Kai released Matt and pounded his fist into a bleacher. The metal bench concaved under his hand.

Matt fixed his collar, his jacket soaked with blood from his head wound. "Give me a chance to talk." Matt pointed to the broken bottles. "Janie smashed the bottles. Whatever was inside of them is gone."

"The vampire venom and lost souls." Kai examined the puddle on the ground. He dabbed his finger in the venom and smeared the liquid between his fingers. He smelled it to make sure. *It's vampire venom.* "Without the venom or lost souls, Antony loses."

"The twins didn't seem happy about it," Matt said.

Abrams eyes shot up from the puddle of vampire venom. "The twins who attacked me were here?" He stepped between them to speak to Matt. "What did they say?"

"They thought I was unconscious. One of the twins, Quinn, said something about moving forward with the plan and needing Antony's supply to 'Turn' Janie."

"We've got to find her. Antony must still be alive, or they think he is. If so, Antony has more venom. While I was inside, Antony and his crew killed at least one of Jerome's vampires. Antony's in possession of pure venom." Kai brushed past Matt and Abram. "We don't have much time."

"Wait—Kai, you said he needed a lost soul. Where is he going to get one?" Abram said.

"He'll take a soul from a human. There are plenty around to choose from."

"And the testosterone, Janie's a female."

"A very strong female. She's got more endurance and strength than any of those football players." He pointed to the field. The quarterback launched a spiral down the field. Kai turned back to Matt. "You've got to think. Did Quinn or his brother say anything about where they took her?"

"Quinn was going to find some girl named Michaela," he said quickly. "He told his brother, Nate, and this other one, Caleb, to take her inside."

"Let's start in the basement and work our way up," Kai said. He removed a smaller blade from his belt.

"Should I grab Isabelle?" Abram said.

"No, if Antony is searching for another lost soul, we'll need her patrolling the parking lot." Kai started forward. "Abram, are you coming?"

"What about me?" Matt said.

"Go home." Kai pointed in the direction of the parking lot. "You're going to end up getting Janie killed."

Kai found Jerome where he'd seen him last—lying beneath a crumbled wall outside the locker room. Kai slid his blade back into his belt and knelt down beside him. Jerome's tattooed arm draped over his chest, resting under a wooden stake.

Jerome strained to open his eyes. He struggled to speak. "Dude, you're okay."

Kai tried to act as if there wasn't a stake pressing up against Jerome's heart. Close enough to cause a slow death, but not close enough to kill him instantaneously. "You look good, man."

Jerome coughed. Blood seeped from the corner of his mouth. "Tanya?"

Kai shook his head. "I don't know. I'm sorry." He gripped Jerome's hand. "Last time I saw her, she was kicking some Daychild's ass."

"That's my girl." He tried to smile. "How about Janie?"

"I don't know." Kai inspected Jerome's wound. All the memories he'd been running from came racing back. He fell forward. His knees smacked against the linoleum floor. Watching Jerome die so painfully, in such a similar way, made it feel like it was happening all over again. . .Tavares stood over him, ready to plunge the dagger into his skull...

"Kai—I thought you were the one. I was so proud the day I created you. I had such high hopes for my prodigy. What a disappointment." Tavares gripped Kai's throat and slowly lowered him to the ground. "How—how did you develop a conscience? It's impossible. . .you're soulless."

Kai tried to speak, but Tavares had crushed his windpipe. Kai stared into Tavares's cold red eyes. Unlike Kai's human complexion, left over from his demon days, Tavares was a true vampire, very pale. His platinum hair blended with his skin, giving him the appearance of an albino.

"What, nothing to say?" Tavares made a sound somewhere between a laugh and an echo of pity. "I thought you'd put up more of a fight. Love has weakened you." He lifted his silver dagger. "Her death will be less painful than yours. . .I promise." His voice grew louder. "You just had to have her. Well, now you will both pay for wronging me." Tavares plunged the dagger into Kai's skull at just the right position to cause a slow, torturous death. Kai's last image before everything faded to black was of—her.

"Hey, you with me?" Jerome choked.

"Yeah, man. I'm here." Kai blinked back to the present moment. "It'll be over soon. I've been where you are." Kai lifted the cross around Jerome's neck and placed it in Jerome's hand.

"Tavares did this to you and look at you now. You're tougher than ever." Jerome coughed. His white tank soaked with red. "There's hope for me."

"You'll be good, bro." Kai tightened his grip around Jerome's hand. "You don't go down easily. You're a leader. You should be proud."

"Antony got away. I think my crew is dead." His voice cracked. "Tanya?"

"You did well," Kai said. "We couldn't have done it without you. Janie stopped them. We've accomplished what we came to do. Don't worry about Antony. I'll make sure he doesn't make it out of here alive."

"Take care of yourself." Jerome squeezed his hand. His grip weakened as time passed. "You're alright, Kai

Sterdam. I like you. Whatever you are—vampire, human, demon."

Kai did the only thing he knew would ease the pain. He shoved the wooden stake further into Jerome's heart. He swore he heard Jerome say "thank you" right before his body combusted into ashes and vanished.

"That's the craziest thing I've ever seen. And I've been doing this for years." Abram stood over Kai. "Vampires *are* evolving. I've been wrong about a lot of things." Abram extended his hand to Kai. "Let me help you up, my friend."

Kai accepted Abram's hand. "It'll be an honor to kick Antony's ass with you."

"So Tavares did the same thing to you?" Abram shook his head. "From what Janie told me, Jerome killed Antony's girl. That was reason enough for him to punish Jerome, I guess. What did you do to make Tavares want to punish you like that?"

Kai placed his hand on his heart. "My past. Janie is my future."

Abram motioned for Kai to lead the way. "I understand."

CHAPTER 21

Janie came to, chained to some sort of loud machine. Sweat rolled down her face. The temperature had risen. *Where am I?* She noticed an open door directly in front of her. The sign on the door said *Boiler Room.* As far as she could see, she was alone. She tugged on the iron cuffs, but they didn't budge. Outside the door she heard someone talking, maybe Antony. Things were foggy. She couldn't reach the back of her aching head, and her neck burned from Caleb's blood. Thinking back, head-butting Caleb wasn't the brightest idea. But it felt good at the time.

"Are we good?" She recognized the squeaky high-pitched voice—the girl with the spiky hair, Michaela. The room flooded with the sounds of enormous washing machines and idling car engines. Janie had to strain to hear their conversation over the machines.

The next voice boomed, drowning out the whooshing. "The boy will do," Antony said. "I need a soul. Throw him in with the Seeker. I'll kill him after I inject the venom. I want the soul to be as fresh as possible before it's transferred."

"Take whatever you want from me, just don't hurt her." Janie tensed. *Matt.*

"You're making the ultimate sacrifice," Antony said. "We'll remove your soul and give it to the Seeker, but she won't need it for long. Two souls can't inhabit the same body. Both souls will eventually die. Then the process will begin." His voice sped in excitement. "When the extra-strong dose of vampire venom is injected directly into her bloodstream, the transformation will begin. And when the souls depart, she will be close to the Turn."

"You need her strength to finish," Matt said. Janie cringed, surprised by how much he knew.

"This one's been paying attention," Michaela said.

"There's no doubt she'll survive. I'll be the only leader with a Seeker. This has worked out better than I could've planned."

Matt appeared in the doorway, his hands bound with rope and his varsity jacket missing a sleeve. Red stains decorated the varsity lettering. A gash started from his forehead and ended somewhere behind his hairline. Dried blood crusted around his eyes like flaking dried paint.

Michaela guided him into the room and tied him to another loud machine. Her large hoop earrings grazed her shoulders as she secured the knots.

"Turn me," Matt said. "I'm an athlete. I can handle it. Let Janie go."

"Shut up." Michaela slapped him. He fell to the side, still suspended by the rope. Michaela left the room and slammed the door behind her.

"Matt, are you okay?" Janie tried to get to him. The cuffs wouldn't budge.

"I'm fine. I hate her." He fell silent. "Janie—" He sounded exhausted. "I don't think they're zombies."

"No, Matt, they're not." She expelled an exhausted chuckle.

"Sorry." His voice came out low and defeated. "I did what Kai told me. I guess I wasn't fast enough. They caught me before I even hit the parking lot."

"Kai—you saw Kai." Hope and relief rose within her. "He's okay?" She did her best not to shout.

"They went looking for you."

"They?" She tried to sit up straighter. The cuffs jerked her back.

"Kai and Abram."

"Together?" *Something had to have happened. Abram would rather kill Kai then work directly with him.*

"Is that a problem?" Matt squirmed within the rope. He cursed under his breath.

"I guess not," she said. "I didn't think they got along." *Maybe this means he'll stay.*

"I told them Nate and Caleb were bringing you inside. They planned to start looking for you in the basement." Matt scanned the room. "Where are we, anyway?"

"The Boiler Room. I think we're in the basement."

"Good, then they'll find us before they take my soul and turn you into one of them."

"I can't wait that long." The wheels in Janie's head started spinning. She had to think of something.

"What are you going to do?"

"Get out of here. Seeker training lesson five—resourcefulness."

"Seeker what?" He shook his head. "Never mind; let me know what I can do." He didn't sound confident.

Janie scanned the room for an object she could use to get the cuffs off her wrists. *Where's dry ice when you need it?* Nate and Caleb had taken all her blades. *Think, Janie.*

The doorknob turned and stopped. Fear consumed Janie. She'd rather die then turn into the monster she'd been trained to hunt. *That's it.* She wouldn't let Antony win. If she died, he couldn't use her as a weapon. It wasn't the resourcefulness she originally thought about, but she didn't have much other choice.

She decided not to tell Matt about her plan. He most likely wouldn't agree. Janie noticed loose rope hanging next to him. She wasn't that far from him in the small room. Antony would enter soon. She had to act fast.

"Hey, Matt, throw me that rope."

"Why?" he said. She gave him a look.

"You're the Seeker," he said. "I'll try." He slid his bound hands across the floor. When he hit the rope's resistance, he extended his fingers until he reached the excess rope. "Got it."

"Now throw it to me. You've only got one shot, so make it a good one."

"Pressure—okay, here goes nothing." He flung the rope forward with a flick of his wrist. It landed next to her.

"Nicely done." Janie inverted her feet and clutched the rope between the heels of her boots. She pulled her knees into her chest, bringing the rope closer to her cuffed hands. She drew in a deep breath and reached out as far as she could to grab the rope. The metal cuff sliced into her flesh. Blood dripped from her wrists.

"What are you going to do now?" Matt's face turned green at the sight of her blood.

"I'm sorry to leave you. I don't know of any other way. I'm too dangerous to be Turned. With me under Antony's control, he would be unstoppable. They aren't interested in you. Kai will be here soon. He'll save you. Otherwise, I wouldn't leave you. Antony will be too preoccupied with me to touch you before Kai gets here."

"Janie—what are you saying?" Matt scrambled into a semi-seated position.

"I'm so sorry for everything. . .the attacks, the Imprint, and all of this."

"Janie—no, you aren't, you can't," he said desperately.

"The Imprint should go away when I'm gone." She blinked. A tear rolled down her cheek. "You won't feel this way anymore. It will be better for you."

Matt tugged on the rope in an attempt to free himself or pull it from Janie's grip. "Don't tell me what will be better for me," he said. "Do you know how many people love you? Kai, your mom, Abram, Ava, Luke. You can't do this to them. . .or me."

"I don't have any other choice. It's better if I'm dead than a killer." She smiled faintly. In dying, she'd save so many. She could make that sacrifice. It was her job. In everything she'd learned recently about herself and the people around her, she always knew one thing. . .she was a good Seeker. No matter what, she'd get the job done. "Goodbye, Matt." She looped the rope around her neck.

Abram strode next to Kai through the concrete hallway in the basement, daggers in hand and ready for anything.

Kai pushed Abram into an open door.

"What's wrong?" Abram aligned himself with Kai along the wall.

"I hear footsteps." Kai listened out the doorway. "There are two sets of them. Get ready." Kai held his arm up. Abram raised his chin, ready to spring on cue. "Now—" They leapt out of the room, daggers drawn.

Kai sprinted up the wall and catapulted into the air. On his descent, he jabbed the dagger into the woman's skull. She slumped over, dropping the girl in her arms to the linoleum floor.

"Dang, Kai—that hurt." Tanya yanked the dagger from her skull. "If you were trying to kill me, you missed my heart by a mile." She shook her head. "Watch where you're plunging that thing next time."

Kai fell to the floor. *Janie.* He scooped her up into his arms and clutched her to him. "Tanya—what happened to her?" He placed his ear to her chest. Her breathing was shallow and weak.

"I don't know. I found her and that boy," she pointed to Matt, "tied up like this."

"She tried to strangle herself with a rope," Matt said. "I tried to stop her, but I couldn't reach her."

Kai glared at him. "Why are you *still* here? I told you you were going to get her killed." Kai traced the red line around her neck with his finger. *You have to be okay. Wake up!*

"I tried to leave! They caught me and threw me in the boiler room with Janie. She was chained to something. Antony was about to inject her with vampire venom and use my soul to Turn her."

"But why would she do this?" Kai stared at the red line. He couldn't lose her. Abram was right. You don't know what you can't live without until it's gone. *Stay with me please.*

Matt continued. Hyperventilating, he said, "She said it was the only way to keep people safe. With her gone, she wouldn't be a threat."

Kai appraised Janie's beautiful face. "You would rather die than become a monster. A Daychild with a Seeker's skills and strength would be deadly, and you knew that." Kai kissed her forehead. "Your dagger says it all. . .*U-le-tsu-ya-s-ti.* You're so brave, stubborn and reckless, but brave."

"There they are, get 'em!" Antony said.

Antony and the remaining Daychildren appeared at the end of the hallway.

Abram placed his hand on Kai's shoulder. "Give her to me. You are the only one who can defeat Antony."

Kai kissed Janie one more time. "You'll be okay. You have to be." He slid her limp body over to Abram. "Move her back to safety." Abram nodded.

Kai ripped his scythe from Tanya's hands and blew through Michaela, Caleb and the twins in a direct route to Antony. He entered and exited their bodies faster than they could process what had happened.

He did a flying side kick into Antony's stomach, sending him to the ground. He whirled around and sent the blade whizzing toward Antony. Antony held up his arm to block his head. The blade severed his arm. It rolled to the ground beside him. Green blood squirted from the stump. Antony shrieked.

"This is for Jerome!" Tanya decapitated one of the twins. In one continuous motion, she swept her arms in a circle. Caleb brandished Janie's dagger, ready to strike Tanya, but she was too fast—the blade severed his neck. "Rot in Hell, both of you." Caleb's gooey flesh disintegrated. Janie's favorite dagger clattered to the ground.

The remaining twin stared in horror. He turned to Antony for direction.

"Quinn—I command you to kill that vampire-human freak."

Quinn stared down at Antony with anxious pity. He didn't speak at first, weighing his options. "You're reign is over, Antony. Baltimore is my territory now." He retreated, disappearing down the hallway and out the door.

Kai held the blade to Antony's throat. Blood seeped from the incision the tip made. "It looks like your crew isn't as loyal as you thought."

"What are you waiting for? Just do it. Kill me." Antony glanced off to the side, refusing to look at Kai in the shame of defeat.

"Kai—"

Kai spun around. *Janie.*

Abram helped her to her feet. Matt hurried over and slid Janie's arm around his neck. Her chest jerked in uneven convulsions as she fought to breathe. Her beautiful brown eyes were fixed on his. Kai found it hard to look away and sighed. He thought he'd lost her.

"End this. Kill him," she rasped. Kai placed his hand over his heart. She smiled faintly.

Kai turned, glaring down over Anthony, the blade still wedged in his throat. "I will show you more mercy than you showed Jerome and Tavares showed me. It is proof that I was never like you." Kai flipped the blade up and shoved it into Antony's skull. A moment later, Antony joined his crew in Hell.

CHAPTER 22

Janie scanned the gym, lit up with rope lights and a mess of gaudy decorations. Every portion of the gym was covered in some sort of paper catastrophe: streamers, posters, confetti. Life-size cutouts of movie stars supported the "Hollywood" theme. How had she allowed Matt to take her to the Homecoming dance? Kai left. She had no excuse not to go.

The music changed to a slow song. Matt slipped his deep charcoal suit jacket over his teal dress shirt. He took Janie's hand and smiled warmly. "One last dance before we leave."

Janie followed his lead to the dance floor. He wrapped his arms around her waist. She rested her hands on his arms. "Thanks for taking me. You're a good guy, Matthew Baker."

"You're not too bad yourself, Janie Grey." He kissed her lightly on the forehead.

Janie noticed Luke and Ava pressed up against each other on the dance floor a few couples away. So much had changed in just a matter of weeks. Luke and Ava together—who knew? And she was at Homecoming, with Matt Baker. . .and in love with Kai. The biggest shocker of all—*I'm in love.*

"Matt, I'm really sorry for everything. Almost getting you killed on multiple occasions and Imprinting you." Janie wondered if this was how it had been with her mother and father. *Did my mother really fall in love with my father the first time she saw him, or did she fall in love with him after the Imprint? Maybe my mother doesn't even know the answer anymore.*

"I don't regret anything." Excitement filled his eyes. "Besides, I got to shove a lance through Caleb's stomach. I know better now. Next time I'll go for the head and make sure to use a silver blade."

Janie eyed him. "Let's hope there isn't a next time."

"Come on, we're friends. I don't think I can avoid it." He held her tighter. "Now seriously, no more talking. I have only two minutes left to hold you." Janie relaxed and did her best to enjoy the last song of the night, but her mind wandered somewhere else. . .always somewhere else. . .with Kai.

They exited the gym. Janie smoothed her clingy strapless black dress. After many arguments with Albania, she'd finally chosen a strapless number that fell a few inches above her knees. *At least it was black.* She looked down at her aching feet—red high heels. Another one of Albania's suggestions. Janie longed for her boots. They didn't smash her toes or raise her heels so high that the arches of her feet felt as if they were going to crack in half. She intended to pry them off and never put them on again once she got home.

"Did you have an okay time?" Matt held the door open for Janie.

She stepped outside and offered him a thankful smile. "Surprisingly, I had a good time, minus these heels. How about you two?" Janie glanced at Ava and Luke. They weren't quite holding hands, but they were close enough so their hands brushed together as they walked.

"Some of the attire was totally off-putting, but other than that, they played some decent tunes," Luke said. He adjusted the collar of his suit jacket. "I still think there should have been a crown for best-dressed. This tie was imported from Italy." Luke nudged Janie. "Senior Homecoming Queen. I'm proud of you, J." He glanced over to Matt. "Sorry, dude, it's not like we didn't see your crown coming."

Matt shrugged, not seeming to care in the least about the title of "Senior Homecoming King." He already held the crown of Junior Prom King.

Ava doubled over, laughing. "I thought Molly was going to have a canary on the dance floor. She probably wrote her acceptance speech in elementary school. I guess she'll never get to give it." Ava's nose crinkled and her voice deepened. "Serves her right. She's rude and selfish and. . .I don't like her."

"We've got to work on the insults." Luke wrapped his arm around her shoulders. "Try catty, pestiferous and odious."

"I don't even know what those words mean," she said flatly.

"Now that's the Luke and Ava I'm used to." Janie wobbled over to Ava. She focused on not tripping over her own heels. "When can I take this sash and crown off? The crown is digging into my head." Janie tugged at the rhinestone monstrosity. "Ava, how many bobby pins did you use?"

"You've got a lot of hair." Ava flipped her hand in the air. "Stop—you look beautiful."

"So do you." Ava wore a rusty-orange tank dress that showed off her pale, freckle-covered legs.

"I've got to tell you I'm surprised. I wasn't sure how I was going to feel about the whole you and Luke thing. Hell, I didn't even think he was into girls." Janie smiled. "You make a cute couple, though. It's nice to watch Luke dote on you. How many times did you send him for punch?"

"We aren't really a couple. I'm not sure how he feels. We're just really close friends. I don't know if anything more will ever happen." Ava shrugged. "I'm hoping." Ava directed her eyes out into to the parking lot. She gasped. "Kai's here."

"What?" Janie followed her gaze. A chill shot up her spine. She realized the temperature had dropped into the thirties and she was wearing barely any clothing. It didn't matter. Her focus stayed on one thing. . .Kai. He stood at the far end of the parking lot propped up against his bike, dressed in well-fitted jeans, long sleeves and his half-eaten boots. His hair was a deeper blond in the dark. The subtle waves fell flawlessly around his face. He looked just as he always did—perfect.

Janie nodded in his direction, her eyes still fixed on him, afraid to look away, that somehow he might be gone. *Ava sees him, so he can't be a mirage.* "I don't really know where we stand either."

"Is he still planning to leave?" Ava tripped over the curb. Janie caught her.

"I'm not sure. We haven't really spoken much since we took down Antony. He's been kind of distant. I've given him time to sort through things. Not wanting to push him and all."

"It looks like he's ready to talk now. He hasn't taken his eyes off you."

Janie's nerves returned. She had no idea if Kai had decided stay. He left right after he killed Antony. Abram assured him she would be fine. As hard as it was to see him go, she had to believe he'd come back to her. And he had, just like he'd promised. Her heart skipped multiple beats. *He's back…but for how long?*

"J, I'll see you later." Ava waved to Kai. She turned to Janie and mouthed, "Call me."

Luke and Matt walked a few steps behind. Janie glanced back. Ava pushed her forward. "Just go," she said. "I'll tell Matt you'll call him later. Kai's waiting."

Janie smiled uncertainly at Matt. He caught her gesture, focusing on Kai. After a hesitant moment, Matt returned her smile, indicating he understood, for now.

The twenty or so foot walk from Matt's car to Kai's motorcycle felt like an eternity. So many questions circled Janie's mind. *Where did you go? Are you staying?*

Do you still want to be with me? She made a mental note not to blurt them out all at once.

Within reaching distance, his smell surrounded her. She hung back and rested her hand on the seat of his motorcycle. He appraised her and smiled. "You look, amazing." His eyes settled on her legs. "Wow, you need to bring those out more often."

"Thanks." She fussed around with the crown until it finally pulled free of her hair. "I agreed to the dress and the shoes, but I did *not* agree to this." She flashed the crown. "I'm not Homecoming Queen material. I don't see how girls actually wear these."

"You're perfect." Kai removed the crown from her hand and placed it on the back of his bike.

Janie glanced back at school. "Do you know that I've been in high school for almost eight years and I've never been to one dance?" She watched a group of students exit the building dressed in formal attire. A guy she recognized as a junior twirled his date into him and kissed her. The couple seemed to be in their own little euphoric world. For the first time in a long time, Janie felt *normal.* She didn't have to watch from the sidelines. *I played the game and I survived, no matter what happens next.*

Her gaze returned to Kai. "I'm glad I had the experience." She brushed her hand across his. "How have you been?"

"I've missed you." He stared at her for a long, suffering moment. "I'm sorry it took me so long to find my way back."

"I wasn't sure if you were ever coming back." She swallowed the hard lump in her throat.

He touched her cheek. "I promised you I would." His words were soft, lightly stroking through her and making her pulse accelerate.

"Where did you go?" She stepped closer to him. His hand slid down her arm, tickled over her wrist and settled in her hand. At his touch, she wanted to feel his lips on hers, to hold him forever. She composed herself. *I don't even know how he feels now.*

"I went to Tucson," he said. His eyes didn't leave hers.

"To see your parents?" She hesitated.

He drew in a deep breath. "They seem happy," he said. "They moved. I guess they didn't need a big house anymore, since I was gone." Pain filled his voice. He cleared his throat to force his feelings down. "It was better that I didn't approach them. I'm not what I was when I disappeared. How would I explain my looks? I haven't aged a day. I still look eighteen. And they. . .they look, well, older."

"Are you glad you went?" She attempted to comfort him with a sympathetic smile.

"I don't have to wonder anymore."

Janie tightened her grip on his hand. "When did you get back?"

"Last night."

Her eyes widened. *Why didn't you come over? I've been waiting for you. Every day and every night I sit and wait. Every time I enter my bedroom part of me dies when you're not there.*

She held her emotions together. He'd just visited the life he'd been ripped from as a teenager, a life he could never have back. She knew seeing his parents again must have been excruciating. She couldn't imagine. *Dad—what I'd give to see you again.* As hard as she tried to conceal her emotions, her eyes flooded with tears. She blinked in an attempt to stop the tears from forming. It didn't work.

He drew her hand closer to him, appearing concerned. "Janie?"

"I don't mean to cry. I don't want to make this any harder on you." Tears spilled over her lashes. "Just hearing about you seeing your parents for the first time in so many years. . .I miss my Dad."

"It's my fault he's not here." He dropped her hand and threw his leg over his bike. "Your friends are still here. Go with them. I'm not good for you."

Janie gripped his leg to physically restrain him from leaving. She knew it would never be possible to stop him if he really wanted to go. She didn't care. She'd lost him once. She refused to let him go again. "It's no one's fault. It happened. It was tragic, but it happened. Please. . .I've already lost one person I love. I can't do it again."

Kai stared forward. "How can you still want me? I've only added heartache and complication to your life. Janie—I killed your father. I don't expect you to get past that."

"Look at me. Look into my eyes." He turned to face her. Wet streaks lined his cheeks. "You made me feel again." He didn't speak. *Am I even getting through to you?* "Do you hear me? I feel again. I am no longer numb. You aren't allowed to carry any more guilt for his death. Do you understand me? No more guilt. He's gone and I will miss him every day, but you're still here and I refuse to let you go." She pushed him. He blinked. Another tear trickled down his cheek.

"Why won't you talk to me? Are you leaving?" She waited. His forehead crumpled. He looked away again. "Damn you." She breathed out. Her heart felt as if it had been ripped from her body. "Do what you have to do. I'll say this once and then I'm leaving. You'll never have to see me again. I'll never be a source of your guilt again. You can live without having to look at me every day." Out of breath, she said, "For what it's worth, I. . .I love you."

She turned to run away, but her legs didn't budge. She pried her feet from the ground and left him sitting on his bike, speechless. *Is that all I meant to him?*

Janie let her tears fall to the pavement. She raised her head to make sure her friends were still there to drive her home, but she didn't see them—Kai blocked her view. She stumbled to a halt. He snatched her up, embracing her tighter than he'd ever done before. "Without you, I don't want to live."

She drew back from him. "Do you mean it? Don't say it if you don't mean it."

"More than I've ever meant anything." He combed her hair back and held her head tightly within his grasp. "I love you."

She choked out the question she had to know the answer to in order to move forward. "Are you leaving?"

His eyes traced every line on her face. She could feel his breath on her lips as he took her in. "My heart is here, with you. If you'll still have me?"

Janie laughed and cried at the same time. Relief washed over her, along with an unequivocal need to be close to him. "Can we please get out of here?" She peeled her high heels off. "Now."

"Where do you want to go?"

"I'm yours tonight and every night, forever." She rose up on her tiptoes, her hands clutching his shirt in her fists. "Your house," she said softly.

Kai flipped her up into his arms and placed her on the back of his bike. He removed the helmet from the back and handed it to her. "This is going to be a quick ride."

"Whatever gets us there fastest!" She ran her hands up his chest, stretching to get her arms around his neck. He bent forward and kissed her. She grasped his collar and lowered him down onto the bike.

"Let's go." Without another word he spun around, straddled the bike and booted the kickstand. Janie wrapped her arms around his waist and held him tightly. The bike lurched forward.

In the morning, Janie ran her bare legs up and down his satin sheets, his arms still wrapped around her. She smiled and tightened her arm over his.

"You're awake," Kai said. Goose bumps formed along her skin.

She rotated to face him. "How long have you been awake?"

"Awhile." He brushed a kiss over her nose. "I've been thinking."

She examined his morning look. His perfectly disheveled mess of wavy golds and whites fanned out around his dark pillow. She plucked the tangled ribbons of white highlights out with her eyes. "What are you thinking about?"

"We're good for each other." He kissed her forehead and flipped onto his back. He stared at the ceiling, exposing his crisscrossed scar. Janie traced it with her fingers, waiting for him to finish. "Neither of us was looking for love. Actually, we both tried to stay as far from it as possible, and look what happened."

Janie rested her head on his chest. "You just had to come into the alley that night. Otherwise, who knows, we may have never met. We would have stayed lonely, miserable fools forever."

He held up his hand. "You're forgetting. You tried to run me over with your car. You initiated our encounter."

She weaved her fingers through his. "Really? You didn't have any interest in me. You only wanted my kill."

He laughed. "Who, Mr. Muscles and the newbie?" He became more serious. "I noticed you before that evening. I have a confession to make." She eyed him interestedly. "I followed you home that first night, after you ran into the pole." He rolled onto his side to face her. "It wasn't a coincidence that we met in the alley."

"Let me guess. You followed me there, too?"

"I was curious, intrigued by you. And you were so damn frustrating in the alley, and the night in the parking garage, and pretty much every night after that."

"You weren't exactly a bowl of cherries yourself. You almost let me ride the bus home with a poisonous demon splint in my head." On instinct she touched her head.

He placed his hand over hers. "I wouldn't have really let you go." He paused. "It didn't matter. I knew you would stay."

"Oh, really, Mister Confident." She pushed him backward.

He wrapped his arms around her. "I'm a catch, a dysfunctional mess, but a catch."

"That makes two of us. . .well, the dysfunctional part." She gladly accepted his embrace. "So what's next, I mean, with Tavares?"

"He'll continue his quest to create a new type of vampire. You stopped him from succeeding in Baltimore. You did your job."

"And Jerome, what's going to happen to his gang?"

"I heard Tanya took over as head vamp."

Janie mused. "That should be good. I like her." Janie thought about the last time she saw Tanya. If it weren't for her, she'd be dead. "By the way, thanks for getting my dagger back for me after Tanya beheaded Caleb."

He smiled. "I know how important it is to you."

She stared at the blank TV on the wall. "You know, I'm leaving in less than a year. I don't know what city they'll put me in next. I don't want to lose you."

He directed her chin over to meet his stare. "Janie—you aren't going to lose me. We'll work it out. And don't completely write off Baltimore yet. Quinn has taken charge of Antony's crew. Baltimore still needs you. Tanya's going to need you." He skimmed her lips with his. "I will always need you."

"Baltimore needs us," Janie said.

"Us—" Kai rolled her onto him and kissed her.

ABOUT THE AUTHOR

Taryn Browning graduated with a BS in Education from Towson University and went on to earn a MS in Reading from Hood College. She lives in Virginia with her husband, two young sons and their dog. When she's not writing, she enjoys reading, spending time with friends and family, dancing, music, movies, and the beach. Visit her at www.tarynbrowning.com, on twitter and facebook.

Made in the USA
Charleston, SC
01 October 2011